Tomatoes Free for the Asking

Previous books by Kent Otto Stever:

Growing Up on the Mississippi (2013)
Kinder, Gentler Ways (2014)

Tomatoes Free for the Asking

A Minnesota Boyhood

Kent Otto Stever

North Star Press of St. Cloud, Inc.
St. Cloud, Minnesota

ISBN: 978-0-87839-795-2

First edition: May 2015

Printed in the United States of America

Published by
North Star Press of St. Cloud, Inc.
P.O. Box 451
St. Cloud, MN 56302

northstarpress.com

Table of Contents

Author's Note

"Tomatoes Free for the Asking" is a quaint term remembered from the 1800s, yet heard in another era of which I was a part. It was a simple expression that may have been written on a piece of cardboard set alongside a pile of tomatoes near someone's garden or on the front porch. It was an invitation to take as you wish, with the expectation of acknowledgement—a simple courtesy to honor the offer.

Little tidbits of courtesy such as this remind me of days when kids shared a tin cup at the water pump, when we helped a neighbor out with a car stuck in a snow bank or in moments of just being alone with the stars and our thoughts. We were free to wander with our friends. Throughout the days were lessons of freedom and responsibility to carry us into another time and an uncertain future.

These are lessons that sustained and guided me as I practiced them with new generations. Some of those lessons are contained herein, in stories and topics that made up part of life for me. I simply wish to share them—with the intention to preserve concepts, histories and remembrances. I present them for consideration, wishing to see how they play out to others, after a lifetime of finding my own understanding.

You are invited to share some of the fun, with researched and continuing histories. There are ten pieces of local, small-town history to center the reader, with twice as many small stories surrounding. My youthful reflections return, as well as some philosophical meanderings and the application of learned values. Response to the format by those reading and attending earlier book events has been well received and understandable. Juxtaposition and surprise await and entertain.

A chapter of personal memoir centers the book. I reflect upon remembrance and experiences not as a set of picture postcards that we study one at a time; the view is more like that of the machine in the penny arcade of the visiting carnival. We would insert a penny and turn the hand crank to see a series of pictures zip by our squinted eyes resting in a goggle-like, metallic frame to create a "moving picture" that left us with a theme and an experience—and one less penny.

As we go through our lives we seem to use up a handful of pennies as we view the scenes of our lives. We take away a series of emotional segments upon which we build our lives. I sit here today as a compilation of those scenes and vignettes and mixed hues. The challenge of articulating the themes into a series of lessons on how to live life is immense.

To extract one picture is to not see the whole. In the book by Richard Bach about *Jonathan Livingston Seagull* comes the line, "He who flies highest sees furthest." It's a theme for me that suggests an approach to problem solving, to decision-making and to life in general. We need to step back and view the realities of the moment in the larger context. We need to run our mental pictures through the aged penny machine to see the whole and grasp the concept.

Hopefully, I flew higher for you

Chapter One

Lessons of Writing: A Life of Blending and Sending

I print and stack stories.

As with an aging athlete's suit size, my stacks just keep spreading. As they grow, my small home office begins to be overwhelmed. I just don't have the space. My wife frequently suggests that I clean out the small room—or take over a larger room in the house. I nibble at the edges and toss a few pages, but don't feel the spirit. The piles continue to grow.

I have recently done an accounting of stories created over the years. In putting together a simple database, I find that I have surpassed one hundred and fifty stories of various lengths and subjects. Some are hometown. Some are juvenile-oriented. Some are adult reflections on experiences and philosophy. Others are memoir-based.

For nearly thirty years, I have tagged together this assortment of stories and unfinished writings. They have bounced from an Apple II to a first Mac to today's newest iMac and Mac Air. With each upgrade of computer, I have carried a disk (now a chip) over to the new computer. And here they all exist—little stories and a few small books.

The author's home office. (Photo courtesy of the author.)

I have worked hard on *Ollie GoFast*. He's now about twenty thousand words long. I don't know yet where he's going. I have work to do everyday on memoirs. In those pages, it feels good to blend little stories of youth with work reflections and remembrances. Stories keep coming and flowing. I'm looking at Ireland, at "Sloppy Joes," at a follow-up to "Suzy's Apples" and boathouses—all at the same time. A couple of leadership and effective-living books have evolved as well—but like *Ollie*, they're still in process.

I have fun creating all of them. Sometimes one intersects with another. I pull a part of one and put it into another. I watch the finest of writers do this. They develop a new theme, pull pieces from their various publications—and end up with a new book. To do so, they must have developed some order in their writer's storage system. For me, I open a file and wonder where to find one story or another. Thank goodness there's a "Find" button on my computer.

On Palm Sunday I blended a bit, taking the occasion of the day to greet family and wish everyone an early Happy Easter. I enclosed for each my story of the "Middle Room"—a remembrance of the day of our mother's death, which happened to coincide by date that year with Palm Sunday. It was a tender moment for me to share the story and say a prayer on that day. Hopefully, I brought a sense of a grandmother unknown to our kids—and a reminder to my remaining brother and sister of "from whence we came."

Most of my stories have a message. They are personal, in a fashion. I initially printed a few of them and created a small book as a Christmas gift for my wife and each of our four kids. My hope was that it would increase the chances of the stories being preserved if I made a hard copy of some.

Left as a computer file, history, stories, and philosophy could all easily vanish at the press of a "Delete" button. I have since done three more printings and placed over sixty stories in their hands. It is my hope that there will be value in reclamation for those who follow. Possibly one day a great-grandson or great-granddaughter will discover some tattered pages and renew the words for a new generation.

As I blend stories, so too do I break them apart. Recent suggestions by a daughter of a lead to follow caused me to separate one story into three. As I do with this story, I add a few words, change a few lines and let it sit until another opening. Eventually the theme emerges.

I began writing on my own and am yet today the lonely writer. In the 1970s, following a suggestion from a source, I attempted to write with my left hand to draw out the other side of my brain—to see what evolved. During quiet, singular lunch hours in summer days of the '70s, I snuck off to the quiet of the faculty lounge of the high school I served with a small bag of Fritos, a cup of coffee and more writing with left hand or right. Keeping my pencil to the paper without lifting (another writing tip), I continued to write to see what it might bring.

I looked for a class and found one in night school. The instructor told me where to send items, but I had nothing yet to send. I was looking for creative impetus, but didn't find it. Over the years, I asked a teacher or two at my work in the high school for review of my writings to gain a tip or two. But I still looked for someone with real, live creative juices who might take my hand and walk me down the road. Forty years later, I haven't yet made that connection, although inspired a time or two.

My stories have been completed as hobby, as interest, as history, and as learned life lessons. My first "real" publication was with Turtle River Press—"a publication of creative energy." "A Budding Writer" appeared in the shopping-bag-colored pages, and I was thrilled. At the same time, I achieved a modicum of success and support from children and family with research and printing of four separate family histories, wherein small stories were integrated into pages of genealogy.

Several years later, my children received from me that first "book" for Christmas, entitled *A Boy's Adventures*. The attractive, handmade book weaved together a dozen short stories into a delightful physical product. With a couple of boys skilled in page setup and graphic alignment, the support of Mike, the high school print shop teacher, and some quality equipment and paper, we created a publication suitable for the shelves of Barnes & Noble. After school hours and in my garage, I punched and stitched and pasted together about twenty-five copies that have since been distributed to friends and family—with kind reviews.

Reaction from my kids is mixed—from initial high interest to quiet placement in their files. They mean well. But their lives are busy. Intended for grandchildren, the pages have yet to be cracked by those hands holding iPods, smart phones, video games and hockey sticks. Nevertheless, the physical printing of family histories and multiples of additional stories since given are now on at least four sets of shelves. Thinking optimistically, they cannot purposefully be tossed in four separate households. My attempt has been to have them in a place of residence beyond my singular computer file.

With relatively positive feedback from a friendly few, I have set out to send the stories to others. Unaware of the challenges of getting published, I pursued story distribution and found that one is easily ignored. Hand-written letters to editors or stories sent off electronically with either a query letter or sample story drew limited response. I sent one story to a girl's magazine, another to a publisher of young adult stories, other topics to self-help publishers and books to book publishers.

My professor emeritus friend and I discussed the story receivers' absence of common courtesy. A simple acknowledgement of receipt of a story or book would be nice. A note of acceptance or rejection would be even better. But they are the gatekeepers. A recent response from a milk marketing organization told me they didn't know where a "freelance" writer would send his material (the story of a recent visit to a major Wisconsin dairy farm.) In the opinion of the director, all their writing is to be done by "staff."

My successes have come from local and regional magazines and from a hometown newspaper. A very skilled editor of a statewide magazine has used and likes my stuff. Designs by his volunteer graphic artist made my stories come alive. The hometown pieces on page one of the hometown paper have been historical and fun. It feels good to have those stories now a part of history of the community–with more to come.

I broke into the big time with a story recently published in *Chicken Soup*. I thought I had found the formula. A dozen more stories to *Chicken Soup* yielded no response, however. The challenge is to persevere.

As I share my stories, I ask questions of myself:

Should a writer challenge life?
Does one's writing have the possibility to influence?
Is my writing meaningful and/or profound?
What value do I add to the life of the reader?
How does one break down the barriers?
Do I write for others–or for myself?

Assuming the positive, I've concluded that it's all right for me to create and disperse. I will continue to "blend and send." Thanks to you, three books have thus far been the result.

Author event at a Rochester Barnes & Noble. (Photo courtesy of the author.)

Strolling Down the Sidewalk: An In-Town Journey

A sidewalk is a path along the side of a road.

It may accommodate moderate changes in grade and is normally separated from the vehicular section by a curb (British English: kerb). In some places, the same term may also be used for a paved path, trail or footpath that is not next to a road, for example, a path through a park.

There is evidence that sidewalks were built in ancient times. It was claimed that the Greek city of Corinth was paved by the fourth century, and that the Romans were particularly prolific sidewalk builders—called semitas.

However, by the Middle Ages, narrow roads had reverted to being simultaneously used by pedestrians and wagons, without any formal separation between the two. Early attempts at ensuring the adequate maintenance of sidewalks were often made, such as the 1623 Act for Colchester, although they were generally not very effective.

Following the Great Fire of London in 1666, attempts were slowly made to bring some order to the sprawling city. In 1671, "Certain Orders, Rules and Directions Touching the Paving and Cleansing the Streets, Lanes and Common Passages within the City of London" were formulated, calling for all streets to be adequately paved with cobblestones for pedestrian use.

We didn't have cobblestones.

In my neighborhood of the 1950s, we boys pushed one another down the concrete sidewalk in a wagon. Taking turns at pushing or pulling, we went from house to house in our quest to gain scrap newspapers, rags and metal to be hauled away free. We sometimes helped the lady of the house straighten out the garage or old shed at the same time to earn a few additional nickels.

Once loaded from our irregular route of neighbors, our newly gained largesse and teetering load was carefully headed toward Sam Weisman's Junk

Yard on Second Street. Sam or one of his sons (Sam, Herman, or Sol) would weigh the separate categories of goods on the Fairbanks-Morse scale with all of its well-used, semi-shiny brass weight balances.

He would then calculate with pencil on his notepad the value per pound times the number of pounds of each. The big step was when he reached into the center pocket of his bib-fronted overalls for his long coin purse, from which he would extract the exact coin value. Most often, our return for effort was less than one dollar. But then, a nickel bought a Coke or a Popsicle, so our needs weren't too high. Comic books, baseball cards and penny candy weren't so much, either.

The sidewalks of Winona began with Mr. S.W. Morgan's placement of stone in front of his soon-to-be–well-known jewelry store in the Morgan Block of Third Street. "An ordinance relating to streets, alleys and sidewalks" was passed by the City Council in 1857, which read, in part, "No person shall throw or deposit any dirty water, dirt, filth, straw or other rubbish in any street, sidewalk or alley in the City." The penalty was "one dollar for each and every offence." As good measure, the City Council also proposed an ordinance "for licensing and regulating Billiard Tables and Nine and Ten-Pin Alleys."

The ladies of Winona objected that sidewalks weren't sufficiently provided to keep their long dresses clean. They tired of walking in the mud. In the "Sidewalk Agitation" of 1877, "We, the ladies of Winona, do most earnestly desire that sidewalks may be given to us."

The mayor responded: "No! The ladies must wear shorter skirts."

Wooden sidewalks, 1900. (Photo courtesy of VanierCollege.qc.ca.)

It was suggested by the ladies, "Gentlemen support billiard parlors and drinking saloons," but, "they keep this great convenience from us." The owners of the grand Choate's Department Store must have heard their plea, for by 1898, they had installed the finest, hardy "Winona Stone" as a front walk to their edifice at Center and Third streets.

By 1900, there was a "Sweeping Order," wherein the City Council "ordered two miles of these walks" in twelve-, eight- and six-foot widths. The cost to the lot owner was an average of twenty-five cents per lineal foot. Thus, the sixty-foot lot owners paid a grand total of fifteen dollars—a major cost of the times for their paved brick sidewalk.

Being on Grand Street, midway between the lake and bluffs on one end and the Mississippi River on the other end, we had but to choose which way to turn from home as we hit the sidewalk. It all depended upon the day. One day we would gather rags. The next we could head down the separate brick and concrete sidewalks and cross the lake bridge to hike and camp out in the hills.

Our best days were in summer. We scooted back and forth to the playground and to frolic on foot or bicycle. Every block was surrounded by concrete walkways imprinted with the name of the cement contractor(s). Homes with cement driveways ramping down to the asphalt street allowed us a smooth move of our bicycle onto or off of the sidewalk.

The late afternoon paper route took my big-basketed old Schwinn and me across the sidewalks of *Republican-Herald* Route Forty-two, where I knew every crack in the concrete and every one of my one hundred customers in the nine-square-block area. Saturday mornings were filled with household chores, like doing the wash or cleaning—or collecting for my paper route. Sam closed his shop at noon on Saturday, anyhow.

School days were out of the question for wagons and bikes, of course. We put away the wagon and followed the signed cement squares, punctuated with an occasional sixty-foot brick walkway, to the back or side door of the school. We never entered the main entrance. We also never took our bikes. Why was that?

By fall, any income we gained happened after school by working in someone's garden or raking lawns. By winter, our wagon had been put in the shed as we negotiated over snow piles. A sled was available, but almost useless in pulling loads—save for the firewood we slid from the backyard woodpile to the back porch. Early in the cold days of winter we shoveled snow before school. Getting out at three o'clock from school found most of the sidewalks already shoveled.

The snow police were out there in 1962, when they traveled the streets of Winona to note that seven thousand homes had shoveled walks, with only eleven having not done so. The violators of the clean sidewalk ordinance were sent a letter of delinquency. The standard had been in force for over fifty years. In 1908, 1913 and 1922, Chief of Police Schoening or his successor resolved to "give due notice that the ordinance will be strictly enforced." "Mr. B.A. Man" was said to walk the sidewalks of Winona in 1894 noting violators, especially those with unshoveled lots on the way to Madison School or the Normal School (now Winona State University). He was apparently a dedicated and lone vigilante who supported the city standard.

The really big problem facing the citizenry with the addition of sidewalks was "the wheels." "Stenographers and teachers and clerks who find it impossible to ride the miles of sandy or muddy streets" used those darn bicycles, estimated at twenty-five hundred in Winona in 1898. The city crews tried to accommodate the riders by sprinkling Broadway with water to keep down the dust, but often created muddy conditions instead.

The City Council of 1889 proposed banning bicycles from the sidewalks, finding from objectors "that prohibiting bicycles on sidewalks would practically prohibit their use altogether, on account of the sandy streets." The ordinance was passed nevertheless, with penalties for violations ranging from five to fifty dollars. Alderman Hodgins inquired if the bicyclists would be "willing to use bells and lights" to forewarn pedestrians.

The sidewalk cycling issue continued for all the years. In 1898, "Any day can be seen groups of persons journeying on the sidewalks, driven therefrom in terror and alarm by some 'scorcher' on a wheel. The Lord only knows where, or who, he intends to strike."

By 1926, miles of new concrete sidewalks were being installed in Winona. When the "nine miles of walks" were completed, the built-up part of the city had been supplied with sidewalks. Coinciding with concrete walkways was the paving of streets with bricks, and later, asphalt. By 1948, the city job of sidewalk construction was complete—with last sidewalks ordered in undeveloped areas.

In junior high days we continued to walk the streets. We had lost the wagon. Alone or in small groups, we walked back and forth to junior high to get there early. As official school patrol members, a few of us stayed late on Broadway corners to guard the sidewalks and the children. Farm kids got on their school buses, but the rest of us walked back and forth to the Central Junior High School from the west or east end. Some "outliers" of Goodview and the far reaches of the city were issued Winona Transit bus passes.

The school was indeed central in the town, being only a block off Main Street. There were no buses for in-town kids, so there was a lot of "hoofing it" across the concrete. Occasional brick sidewalks of the past century caused interruptions to our otherwise smooth roller skating path. Bricks added a challenge and an historic flavor to travels of our hometown, settled more than one hundred years before.

We rode our bikes all around town, but generally kept them off the sidewalks, save to put down the kickstand outside Deilke's Grocery as we stopped for a cold eight-cent, twelve-ounce Pepsi. In the 1930s, people (including my wife's grandfather) were still being ticketed for riding on the sidewalk. The fine was two dollars or a day in jail.

In senior high school days the sidewalks were still there, as were the city buses on their Main Line and Lake Line routes across town. But by then we had our fifteen-year-old driver's licenses—gained without driver training. Through a rigid state examiner's ride starting at the old Armory on Johnson Street, we were sufficiently challenged by rules of the road, downtown traffic, use of the floor clutch and shifter for shifting and stopping—and the examiner's stern demeanor. How could we even begin to pass the exam? Where did they get those guys, anyhow?

Cars began to take us on another journey. When not driving, we occasionally were "Standing on the Corner" outside Howie's Varsity Inn on Fourth and Johnson to watch the girls go by. Dean Martin offered in a song of the times:

Standing on the corner
Watching all the girls go by
Standing on the corner
Watching all the girls go by . . .

High school sports activities and sometimes-strenuous part-time jobs gave us the exercise we had formerly gained by following the sidewalks. Jobs offered some income to feed our new need for dates and exploration with the opposite sex. We didn't always have access to the car, in my case a 1936 Chevrolet, so we walked slowly home from a date with a girl. The walks were slow and a great part of the date experience. There were flowering bushes, delightful smells and small gardens everywhere. Flowers were generally in the front yard and vegetables in the back. We stole a kiss somewhere in between.

Dates and "going to the show" took on great importance. There was no such thing as an "allowance" in our household. The allowance was that we could go out and earn whatever we needed for entertainment, clothing and the like. Pa did the best he could, but we knew that the responsibility was there again to "pull our own wagon." If we wanted popcorn and a movie, we needed to find our own way.

Walking under the girded elms of Broadway, down Grand Street to Lake Boulevard or following cemented Wabasha from Winona Street to South Baker, we were with Dean Martin "On the Street Where You Live" when he suggested:

I have often walked down this street before
But the pavement always stayed beneath my feet before
All at once am I several stories high
Knowing I'm on the street where you live

Gene Kelly took us down a puddle-filled sidewalk while *Singin' in the Rain.* The blockbuster movie of 1952 is frequently described as one of the best musicals ever made. Kelly's performance as a singer and dancer in the song is now considered iconic. He memorialized dampened sidewalks as a glowing gift to a generation of walkers. We were there with him—with that same feeling for our special girl. We just couldn't dance (or sing.) In 2008, *Singin' in the Rain* was placed on *Empire's* "500 Greatest Movies of All Time List," ranking at number eight.

Dean Martin didn't mention the sidewalks of Winona. But he must have been there again, along with the fine young men who served our country in World War II and Korea, to thankfully return to the safety and stability of their hometown neighborhoods. Like each of them, he was "Walking My Baby Back Home":

Advertisement for *Singin' in the Rain*, 1950s. (Photo courtesy of ebay.)

Gee but it's great after being out late
Walking my baby back home
Arm and arm over meadow and farm
Walking my baby back home

Sidewalks took us off the front porch and into the greater world. Throughout life we walked through the smells and scenes of adored experiences and relationships.

Reasonable Expectations of a Spoiled Generation

We are the most spoiled generation seen on the face of the earth!" So stated the checkout clerk the other day at the local Fleet Farm.

Garrett, a young man I knew from my visit as a psychology class substitute teacher a couple of weeks ago, remembered me. He was finishing his junior year. Like many other students in our burgeoning suburban community, he had become accustomed to my presence in the large neighboring high school. We shared a friendly greeting and a mutual respect for one another after three years of my showing up occasionally in his classes.

As he checked me out at the store in this after-school moment, Garrett was reacting when I suggested that at mid-May it was time for dock repair, trout fishing, and my gardens. I was about fixing the broken cable on my boatlift at the moment. As I handed up the thirty feet of steel cable, I said that I was done teaching for the year. He suggested, "Who wouldn't be, after putting up with spoiled children? We are the most spoiled generation ever seen on the face of the earth!"

I assured him that was a misperception. He knows I hold kids of today in high regard. He heard my pep talks over the years and understands that "the old guy" genuinely likes the couple hundred kids he faces in a day—if they follow reasonable expectations. And they do! The word is out—"Don't mess with this guy. He likes us!"

I complimented Garrett on securing his good, responsible summer job. He would be working twenty-seven hours per week to gain the things he needed. Working at it over the summer and into his senior year, he would be better for it—held to expectation and skill by chief clerk, store manager, and customers. He needed to satisfy all those folks to keep his job. He knew it and performed accordingly.

Other students I know wouldn't seek the job. They're too busy, or too "above" working at a menial job in a semi-hardware, clothing and supply store. They wouldn't get the job if they applied, since their attitude would show right through. Their parents accept their inabilities and let them lounge at home—staying on the couch indoors with their cell phones and continuous texting.

Rather than forcing their entitled young out the door to learn of the real world as Garrett did, parents leave their children alone to grow their attitudes. The absence of expectations from parents and teachers in their lives causes them to lose hope. They are learning a negative perception—and will live up to it. We need to affirm them continually—and hold them to high expectations.

Seems to me the last several presidents of McDonald's started out their careers as teenagers "flipping burgers."

After fifty years of working with young people, I sense there is a need in many of today's teenagers to be understood and to create with them a life theme. More than a few of the young people I observe have been coddled and left alone (read: ignored), with a natural retreat to smartphones and videos. They are afloat without a paddle.

They have not been asked to think or act or work or do—for eighteen years. They have been left alone to find their way. No wonder they stumble and avoid general communication. Nobody has said "Hello in there!" to them. According to parent reports, they are capable of communicating all day long via text messaging, but are absolutely fearful of making a phone call—even to order a pizza!

A mother of a teenage daughter whom I know was driving the daughter and her friend home—and noted they were texting and not involved in common conversation and courtesy. When asked whom the daughter was texting, the response was that it was to her friend—seated right next to her. What's wrong with this picture?

For these teens and others, I attempt to assist. They need simplicity. They need clarity. They might even need a few minutes "out behind the wood shed" of the past. It doesn't take complex steps or statements, only sincerity.

Garrett's on the right path.

Last night I visited my senior high granddaughter's "Pop Concert" at her small semi-rural high school, a couple of dozen miles (and possibly several light years) from my suburban home. I saw in the evening performance again (since we've been at a bunch of his concerts over the years) the dedication of a teacher with high expectations.

In that small school, whose student population numbers in the hundreds, there were two back-to-back, sold-out, reserved concerts put on by the choirs. More than two hundred kids from grades nine through twelve were dressed in like black t-shirts, jeans and sneakers. A single-strand beaded necklace, if chosen, was the only adornment.

Everyone participated—big kid, small kid, physically handicapped child, small farmer, big football player, homecoming queen, and precocious ninth grader. Probably fifty percent of the school enrollment was there on stage, with the rest in the audience wishing they were. Many had individual, short solos, with remote microphones being passed from one to another like a "hot potato."

The only differences that appeared were in their talents and experience. With succeeding years, their personalities and skills grew from the success of managing high-class music, hip-hop and learned teacher expectations. At concerts, the teacher was their encouraging leader—backed by a volunteer community, semi-professional pianist and musical orchestra. The adult musicians were well off-stage and behind, in order to enhance every aspect of the quality, featured performers.

There were no high jinks. Not a whisper of misbehavior. Perfectly choreographed and understood, quiet sneakers on their feet allowed a quiet exchange of groups on stage in seconds. There was full expectation to detail, including "the fifty times we reviewed a three-line stanza until we got it right," offered by a student representative at the end of the stage-filled, multiple choir performance.

Students acknowledged and showed, "This is our business. We are here to perform. Do your part. Don't screw up or waste our time." So simple. So effective. So well understood.

And were parents (and grandparents) ever so proud? Wow! Wow! Wow!

Each of their children had persevered, succeeded, learned quality of performance and their "place in the sun"—all due to the firm (and caring) expectation of a truly dedicated and accomplished teacher.

In Garrett's home school, a single band director similarly leads three hundred and fifty students in his marching and associated bands, as he has done for more than thirty years. Kids and teacher are there for Friday night football games, summer practices and parades, marching practice on the streets in the fall snows of Minnesota—and performing in Pasadena's distinguished New Year's Day Rose Bowl Parade.

There are similar teachers and effective parents sprinkled throughout the landscape. For the betterment of all kids, these effective role models need to band together, assert and expect. They owe it to their children.

There's nothing wrong with today's kids. They simply need parents to set expectations and hold their feet to the fire. They also need school staff members at every level to hold them to consistent, realistic standards.

A single teacher, a single parent can all make all the difference. Each one, teach one.

Garrett would agree.

Chapter Two

Tomatoes Free for the Asking

There was a time in the 1950s when we all had vegetable gardens. Tomatoes were in abundance and almost free for the asking. Stanley Newman had the greatest garden, right next to the glorious fishpond he had built in his backyard. Every day and night after work, he could be found in his garden or tending to his fishpond. He welcomed our kid visits where we fed the fish, talked with him as he polished his truck or focused on his precise rows of vegetables in his sixty-foot lot on Grand Street.

A gentle soul, Mr. Newman drove his like-new 1930s Ford stake truck slowly down Grand Street to and from work as a telephone/railroad controller. He was located daily in a small raised building at a railroad and street juncture of the C&NW Railway across from the Westfield Golf Course on the way to Prairie Island of the Mississippi River. From his tall, painted shed, he controlled some of the train movement in west Winona and dropped down the mechanical standard to stop vehicular traffic.

(Photo courtesy of the author.)

Having spent all day in his enclosed railroad shed watching trains and cars, he was delighted in late afternoon and after supper to talk in his backyard with kids and fish and vegetables. He enjoyed the tomatoes, onions, cucumbers, Swiss chard, leaf lettuce, beets, carrots, and snap beans growing in neat rows. His zucchini was in the corner of the garden alongside the Keeler lot.

The Keelers had only a small garden, but made up for it with a bounteous and beautiful Concord grape vine. The aged vine produced profusely. Easily picked, walnut-sized purple orbs hung on and across the trellis of the back porch. They were constantly tempting, as if in residence in the Garden of Eden. We were invited by Gil on occasion to sample the luscious fruit. We honored his invitation by not including the grapes in our midnight raids of neighborhood backyards. Mostly we sought pears, kohlrabi, and apples.

At our house down the block, Pa had his own garden, running the width of our sixty-foot lot along the neighbor's fence. Onions, tomatoes, cucumbers, and carrots were specialties of his summer garden, with squashes as our fall crop. Lettuce never seemed too big on the list for our family of seven. It would take a lot of it to feed us all—and we weren't into "side dishes" like salads and fluff. We were mostly meat and potatoes, goulash, sunfish, squirrel, bean soup, peanut butter, and buckwheat pancakes kind of people. Lots of fresh tomatoes provided afternoon snacks and graced our supper table.

Pa had a second garden down by the lake at a city-owned and leased piece where he grew corn, squashes, and potatoes, with the occasional melon added in the fall. Pa's gardens were for family sustenance all summer long. They also provided gunnysacks of root crops to the cellar to help us make it through the winter.

Along with greening apples and wild cherries, gunnysacks of carrots, potatoes, rutabagas, and beets were stored in the cellar for winter use. Garnered from Pa's lakeside plot and Uncle Arnold's fields near Lewiston, seven mouths were fed through the frozen winter months of Pa's unemployment. His background on the farm taught him the way.

Gardens were always a part of the backyards of the hearty European stock that settled in their new country. They were, after all, peasant people of the land who settled to create the hillside and valley farms within our beautiful, dolomite limestone Mississippi River bluffs.

A Desperate Need

Home gardens took special, front row notice in Winona and other cities and villages across the nation when the United States entered World War I in 1917. Food was desperately needed to supply European civilian and military allies. President Woodrow Wilson's posters and signs proclaimed, "Food Will Win the War."

Herbert Hoover was appointed to head the U.S. Food Administration and launched a campaign to conserve food. Americans were urged to voluntarily stretch the food supply by cutting waste, substituting plentiful for scarce ingredients and participating in the food-conservation program popularly known as "Hooverizing," which included wheatless Mondays and Wednesdays, meatless Tuesdays, and porkless Thursdays and Saturdays.

The Food Administration sponsored a program to educate the people about nutrition and food preservation to help persuade them that eating less would not be harmful. Signs and posters also pitched what became known as the "Doctrine of the Clean Plate."

–University of Wisconsin Digital Collection

A fellow Winona writer remembers the times and the efforts of children during World War II. He offers:

Every Monday Jamie gave his teacher a short note, signed by his mother, affirming that Jamie had eaten all the food on his plate at every meal for the previous week. Prominently displayed in every classroom was a poster noting each student's "clean plate" achievement. A gold star indicated those who were members of the Clean Plate Club.

–from *Sandbar Stories*, Jim Lackore, 2011

As part of the effort to conserve food, the War Food Administration created a National Victory Garden Program, which set five main goals.

1. Lessen demand on commercial vegetable supplies, thus making more available to the Armed Forces and to lend-lease programs.
2. Reduce demand on strategic materials used in food processing and canning.
3. Ease the burden on railroads transporting war munitions by releasing produce carriers.
4. Maintain the vitality and morale of Americans on the home front through the production of nutritious vegetables outdoors.
5. Preserve fruit and vegetables for future use when shortages might become worse.

–University of Michigan, Bassett, 1981

Victory gardeners in the 1940s. (Photo courtesy of Wikipedia.)

These Victory Gardens, initiated in World War I and utilized throughout World War II, were also called "war gardens" or "food gardens for defense." They were planted by citizens in their backyards and in the public parks of the United States, with the United Kingdom, Canada, and Germany doing similarly.

These were vegetable, fruit, and herb gardens that were used, along with food stamps, to reduce pressure on the public food supply. It was emphasized to American home front urbanites and suburbanites that the produce from their gardens would help to lower the price of vegetables needed by the U.S. War Department to feed the troops. Money was thus saved and could be spent elsewhere on the military. "Our food is fighting," one U.S. poster read.

Fully one-third of the vegetables produced by the United States were from Victory Gardens. A "conservative estimate" of one war year stated the value of Victory Gardens easily exceeded one billion dollars off the nation's food bills, with an average saving of thirty dollars per household.

In addition to indirectly aiding the war effort, these gardens were considered a civil "morale booster"–in that gardeners could feel empowered by their contribution of labor and rewarded by the produce grown. This made Victory Gardens become a part of daily life on the home front.

Amid regular rationing of food in Britain, a poster campaign ("Plant More in '44!") encouraged the planting of Victory Gardens by nearly twenty million Americans during the course of World War II. These gardens produced up to forty percent of all the vegetable produce being consumed in the USA. A British poster suggested, "Sow the Seeds of Victory–Plant and Raise your own Vegetables." Another said, "Dig in for Victory." At home and abroad, all dug in!

Winona's Paul Watkins Victory Garden Club was to enter the "governmental contest of canning prowess" in 1918 for "National Capitol Prize Certificates." Didn't get the results. Still waiting.

Gardens at Home

In a county-wide campaign of 1943, one hundred Winona's Swift & Co. meatpacking employees signed up for Victory Gardens, with each receiving the pamphlet "How to Have a Better Victory Garden" from the county committee. If that wasn't enough information, they could receive divine guidance on Sunday at the Salvation Army or the Assembly of God Church, where sermons included "A True Victory Garden" and "The Victory Gardens of Scripture." Across the Mississippi River, Trempealeau County officials established their own Victory Garden Council in 1942.

Interesting to note that the products of Pepin Pickling Company of Winona made it to the front lines of World War I and World War II, where Pepin pickles and sauerkraut were seen as easily transportable and notable additions to a soldier's diet. Not part of the Victory Garden movement, the historic company nevertheless gathered and processed vegetables for the war effort at their eighteen salting stations around the Winona area.

Winona County drivers of 1943 were given "extra mileage" allowance from the Ration Board to care for their gardens. All gasoline was being rationed. To gain the extra allotment, the "applicant must show that his garden consists of at least fifteen hundred square feet and be devoted to the production of vegetables."

By 1944, the "Big Three" of vegetables were tomatoes, carrots, and beans. So many beans were being grown and canned that they "could potentially be knocked off the ration list."

German prisoners-of-war (POWs) may have raised some of those beans that year. Of two hundred German aviators imprisoned at Whitewater State Park's prison camp, some were transported daily to Winona to establish and maintain a large public garden in Goodview, on the site of the current park and community center.

In rural Minneapolis in May 1943, "Victory Gardens (Are) Damaged by Horses and Dogs." Adjacent stable owners contended, "Parents permitting children to ride mounts they board(ed) are the source of the trouble."

In that same area in the same year, a neighbor's sons pushed a dog under a fence into the garden of Mrs. Elmah Conley, age seventy-eight. She "threw a broomstick at the dog (bulldog) hitting (and killing) it," causing her to be charged with cruelty to animals. She was "exonerated" by Judge Harold Rogers. Whew! It's hard to have a garden.

Chief of Police A.J. Bingold at the same time offered a stern warning to Winona citizens. All were urged to keep their dogs tied or on a leash. He said, "It is unpatriotic for dog owners to allow their dogs to roam free through the city—and damage flower and vegetable gardens."

President Harry Truman assisted and encouraged all with gardens in 1945, stating, "The need for food is greater now than ever before. We must do everything in our power to produce all we can this year."

One who was there said Winona authorities "plowed up a section along Lake Winona and assigned Winona families small plots of ground on which to plant Victory Gardens. Vegetable seeds of all sorts—green and yellow snap beans, cucumbers, leaf lettuce, carrots, peas, winter squash, watermelon, and muskmelon—went into the rich loam every spring and early summer."

In Hershey, Pennsylvania, in 1943, "fellow Victory Gardeners looked at State Policeman William McMillen's tomato plants and marveled. The tomatoes were bright red while theirs were still green.

They looked again and chuckled. For a joke, he had substituted red Christmas tree ornaments."

Dowling Community Garden of Minneapolis remains active as one of the last surviving public examples of gardens from World War II.

Free for the Asking

The tradition of gardens continued into the 1950s and beyond at our house. Daily sustenance from the garden was enriching and joyful. There was (is) nothing as delicious as sitting on the front porch with a little salt and a fresh garden tomato or cucumber on a warm July day.

We learned early to use the "spade." Young legs and arms toiled to push the shovel into the black garden dirt to give a heavy, high lift—dropping the load to break up chunks. A study of 1942 urged that a "Spading of a Victory Garden is Good Exercise." Pa's personal study also said it was good for the souls of five young boys growing up without their mother, who had passed much too early. We also got some exercise in Grandma's garden—thrilled to be the official dirt-turner, planter of seeds, and cutter of asparagus shoots in springtime.

At home, after planting, hoeing and weeding, the watering and spraying followed. Pa did the watering (called "sprinkling") in his garden—his relaxation after making "supper at six." He also took sole responsibility for manning the Watkins dust powder sprayer. Pa used his Watkins hand pump sprayer to dust the various crops with powder, most probably DDT.

DDT (dichlorodiphenyltrichloroethane) was the recommended poison of choice to attack all the buggy invaders. A colorless, crystalline, tasteless and almost odorless organochloride known for its insecticidal properties, it was first synthesized in 1874, and has been formulated in almost every conceivable form, including solutions in xylene or petroleum distillates, emulsifiable concentrates, water-wettable powders, granules, aerosols, smoke candles and charges for vaporizers and lotions.

Watkins duster. (Photo courtesy of the author.)

Few gardens in our neighborhood were untouched by the strong chemical offered by hometown and international Watkins Products Company, headquartered in Winona. From 1950 to 1980, DDT was extensively used in agriculture—more than 40,000 metric tons were used each year worldwide. It has been estimated that a total of 1.8 million metric tons have been produced globally since the 1940s.

In the U.S., fifteen companies including Monsanto, Ciba, Montrose, Pennwalt, and Velsicol manufactured it. Production peaked in 1963 at 82,000 metric tons per year. More than 600,000 metric tons (135 billion pounds) were applied in the U.S. before the 1972 ban. Usage peaked in 1959, at about 36,000 metric tons.

Interesting to note is that the Swiss chemist Paul Herman Muller received the Nobel Prize in 1948 "for his discovery [in 1939] of the high efficiency of DDT as a contact poison against several arthropods." We must have enjoyed his discovery, eating tomatoes nearly every day in season. Guaranteed we didn't wash every one off.

In 1962, the book *Silent Spring* by American biologist Rachel Carson was published. It catalogued the environmental impacts of indiscriminate DDT spraying in the United States and questioned the logic of releasing large amounts of chemicals into the environment without a sufficient understanding of their effects on ecology or human health. Its publication was a seminal event regarding the environmental movement—resulting in a large public outcry that eventually led, in 1972, to a ban on the agricultural use of DDT in the United States.

The Beauty of Bloom

Ah, the colors, the flavors!

Peppers, herbs, cucumbers, lettuce, spinach, peas, beans, corn, summer squash, zucchini squash, and Brussels sprouts (as the snow comes) are surrounded by the ubiquitous, luscious and delicious tomato. I can hardly wait for the strawberries. They're late this year, but will be fun to pick on the Fourth of July. I pace myself by picking single leaves of lettuce each morning as the sun rises, looking for the first of the cherry tomatoes and the occasional pepper.

Today's tomatoes are dusted with a safer powder. Washing is now a constant in our home for all vegetables. I give away bags of leaf lettuce, summer squash, and cucumbers. Long carrots of my garden give a special autumn treat—and build strong teeth and bodies. I yet make runs to my favorite orchard for bushels of apples from October leading into December.

I am enriched by the paring, slicing and sometimes dicing of the treasured Honeycrisp, McIntosh, Fireside and Haralson apples that I gift to others in pre-measured, pie-ready freezer bags for winter apple pies. It is for me an extension of the garden experience throughout the winter. Activities and seed selection from historic catalogues take me full circle toward the opening of trout season and first shoots of asparagus in late April.

I carry on a portion of the tradition of self-sufficiency shown by earlier Victory Garden workers. I thrill with sunshine, marvel at the beauty and growth of Brussels sprouts and the tiny lettuce seed. There's something enthralling about carrying into the kitchen crops raised in a home garden. I occasionally set them up in the soft rays of morning in old wooden bowls to capture the beauty of bloom with my camera, as I do with burgeoning peonies, wildflowers, geraniums or roses. These are elements of God's treasure presented to us.

An example of a Victory Garden poster from the 1940s. (Photo courtesy of Wikipedia.)

Stop by for a tomato or two. They're "free for the asking."

In March 2009, First Lady Michelle Obama planted an eleven-hundred-square-foot garden to raise awareness of healthy food practices.

Time for a Cushman: My Motorcycle Adventures

Allyn Morgan, the jeweler's son, brought the first motorcycle to Winona in 1905—a Glenn Curtiss experimental model.

As a boy, Allyn had won the half-mile fairgrounds bicycle race in one minute and twenty-four seconds. An inveterate bicycle rider across the Midwest, "he wore out fourteen bikes as he traveled to road races as far away as Detroit," said grandson Kent in a recent interview. Allyn may have met Glenn Curtiss on the bike race circuit, since Curtiss had begun his career as a Western Union bicycle messenger, bicycle racer and bicycle shop owner. Maybe Allyn rode it home.

In 1901, with only an eighth grade education, Curtiss, at age twenty-three, developed an interest in motorcycles. Internal combustion engines were then becoming more available. In 1902, he began manufacturing motorcycles with his own single-cylinder engines. His first motorcycle's carburetor was adapted from a tomato soup can containing a gauze screen to pull the gasoline up via capillary action.

In 1903, he set a motorcycle land speed record at sixty-four miles per hour for one mile. When E.H. Corson of the Hendee Manfacturing Company (manufacturer of Indian motorcycles) visited Curtiss in his hometown of Hammondsport, New York, in July of 1904, Corson was amazed that the entire Curtiss motorcycle enterprise was located in the back room of a modest shop. "Hell Rider" Curtiss, in an endurance race from New York to Cambrige, Maryland, had just trounced Corson's well-known motorcycles the week before.

Glenn Curtiss in 1907. (Photo courtesy of Wikipedia.)

In 1907, Curtiss set an unofficial world record of just over 136 miles per hour on a forty-horsepower, 4410 cc, V8-powered motorcycle of his own design and construction in Ormond Beach, Florida. The air-cooled F-head engine was intended for use in aircraft. That motorcycle is now in the Smithsonian Institution. Curtiss would remain "the fastest man in the world," to use the title the newspapers gave him, until 1911, and his motorcycle record was not broken until 1930. Curtiss's success at racing strengthened his reputation as a leading maker of high-performance motorcycles and engines.

By 1910, Curtiss had moved on to aviation. He won prizes with his biplane, created a flying boat and headed toward transatlantic flight. In May 1910, he flew 137 miles, the first long-distance flight between two major cities, winning a $10,000.00 prize provided by publisher Joseph Pulitzer. Curtiss went on to a long-term relationship designing planes for the U.S. Navy, passing away in 1930 at age fifty-two.

In the late 1940s, I heard the loud *putt-putt* of the big Harleys from Yeske Bros. Harley-Davidson Shop on East Belleview Street as they coasted down the streets of town.

At age fifteen, I rode my first "hands-on" motorcycle—Jan Wieczorek's Czech-built Jawa 250. Seating one comfortably, it was a bit bigger and a little

Deeren Motorcycle Shop, Winona, 1915. (Photo courtesy of Steve Deeren.)

faster than a Whizzer. But not as big as another popular 1950s machine—the sedate, big-seated Cushman used by plumbers and workmen. It was available at the shop of Pontiac auto dealer C. Paul Venables on Main Street.

Around the corner from Venables in the Morgan Block, Allyn Morgan had a highly successful store, a career in jewelry and two restaurants. As another sideline to this "Man of all Seasons," he took on the Indian motorcycle dealership in his magnificent home on Lake Drive in the 1950s. All I could do was "ooh" and "ahh" as I saw the colorful Indians cruise by with their fluttering handle grip plastic ribbons.

A year or so into high school, I was owner and driver of a green, two-toned 1950 Nash "bathtub" when I encountered my first "real" motorcycle. Motorcycles like the Triumph T120 Bonneville 650 cc were highly desired for action. I was thrilled to trade the "folding seats" of my Nash vehicle one evening for the Triumph. Lee, a local, dashing, James Dean lookalike who owned one, could enjoy the comforts of my lumbering Nash and I would figure out how to run the gears of his shiny new one-hundred-mile-per-hour steed for a few hours. I was a capable driver and gear-shifter, but the sheer power and speed made my eyes water.

It wasn't until I began teaching a few years later when Neil, a fellow math teacher, let me take a brief autumn afternoon ride in the Minnesota River Valley on his Norton 650 cc. It was a ride to remember, occasionally challenged by the soft sand of the roadway. It was akin to riding a bull out of the gate at the Texas rodeo, with me barely hanging onto the saddle—for all the power.

My return from Texas in the 1970s saw us with a new and safe 1972 Chevrolet station wagon with three seats and a stereo that blasted the Beach Boys' "Endless Summer." Settled into suburbia on a relatively strong career track and still having an itch for adventure, I bought a friend's used, off-road Honda 175. He had inauspiciously dumped it in a Portland Avenue intersection, creasing the fender, gaining a leg wound and ending his career as rider. It was high and strong and powerful enough to get me started. For my own "endless summer," I took it to the rustic hills of West Bloomington waiting for development.

Each summer night, I cruised to the open, undeveloped and roadless mounds a couple miles from home and spent my time making twists and turns on uphill and downhill loose dirt and rocks. "Suicide Schildknecht" of Winona motorcycle fame had done similar twists and turns in the 1930s, when he led motorcyclists to four hundred feet of limestone height "on the old birch trail" of the undeveloped Garvin Heights Road.

His sidekick, Ernie Yeske, entertained himself and the crowds at local fairs "making broad jumps with motorcycle through flaming hoops, a flaming board wall and through a fifteen-foot "Tunnel of Flame" in the next decade. I could do no less (but I skipped the flames) in learning balance, control, and safety of a motorcycle, albeit in a relatively safe environment. Once ready, I would then hit the streets with my few small scrapes to body and bike.

The new Honda 360 of 1974 brought me more power and speed than I thought I could handle. The first twist of the throttle at Burnsville Motor Sports told me that my training regimen had been essential. From that point on, I had power and speed in my hands.

Trusting my newly developed skills of balance and safety, my wife joined me for a few early rides. In the summer of 1976, we went to see realtor Bill, who was to show us our potential new home being built on Lake Marion. Janet was on the back of the 360. No doubt, with that auspicious arrival, he figured this to be a "no sale.' But, in fact, the gorgeous split-level became our three-car garage and residence over the next forty years, serving as taking-off point for my machines. Motorcycles of 650 and 750 and the large, fully loaded 1100 took me to work and back—and took us camping and traveling up and down the river. With son in tow I traveled and camped across Canada and into the north woods of Minnesota.

A couple of years later, riding a 750 cc Kawasaki twin, I took the day-long motorcycle safety course for instructors for a week in July, some seventy-five miles from home. On the course, I again returned to a 175 for carefully choreographed instructor moves. I definitely learned to "cover the clutch," balance my bike at every speed in every turn and make a continuous sweep of traffic and potentially developing situations.

Riding a motorcycle is the ultimate lesson in defensive driving. As a certified and experienced driver training instructor for young people, I was aware. But I needed to kick it up a notch. A rock in the roadway, a loose board flying off someone's trailer as they headed off to the cabin, behemoth semi trucks ten feet off your tail at sixty-five miles per hour, crosswinds, rain, oiled surfaces, potholes and totally distracted drivers suggest that one should do one's motorcycle riding in the undeveloped hills of West Bloomington. Danger lurks at every turn—and there are no seat belts, metal auto bodies, or air bags to protect you.

I have spilled the bike twice—with wife and son on separate occasions. Traveling into the soft, shifting sands of a turn on a northern Minnesota sand

The author with his son in 1981, heading to Winnipeg and Kenora. (Photo courtesy of the author.)

prairie road at twenty miles per hour dumped my wife and me into sugar sand. The green moss of rocks in a deep-valley, trout-filled stream of southern Minnesota slid the wheels out from under my son and me as we followed the trail across Beaver Creek to our campsite. We were dumped, got wet and thanked the Lord. On both occasions we were thankful for slow speed and helmets.

After having camped with my thirteen-year-old son at Ely, beside the untouched beginnings of the Mississippi River at Schoolcraft State Park, and within a baseball's throw of the very southern Minnesota, spring-fed Beaver Creek emerging from a limestone hillside, we began to plan a week-long cruise and campout around Lake Superior. On an early August trek, every moment was spent outdoors. It was hot chocolate in metal cups, hamburgers over a wood fire, sunset bedtime in our pup tent and riding challenges of rainy days. We loved every moment!

The exquisite North Shore, the historic trading post and settlement at Thunder Bay, the rainy days, rocks and gorges on the north edge of the lake and the soft, sunny eastern sands of Pancake Bay brought us full circle and one thousand miles to arrive at the Sault Ste. Marie Bridge and its challenging metal-grate roadway surface. Crossing it reminded me of my first queasy ride in the soft sand road of the Minnesota River Valley.

We enjoyed the final night of our journey on the shore of Lake Michigan with steaks on the grill. Our final cruise across small-town Michigan and Wisconsin the next day was especially memorable for its welcoming atmosphere, natural beauty, and ride toward home. Once we hit the front drive of home in our worn, week-long jeans and flannel shirts, we decided we should change clothes, shower and head out again.

The last comparable rides I made were to Wausau with a partner (who recently sold his Gold Wing) for a night of pyrotechnic marvel and again to Ely, following the Wisconsin "two-laners" up to Superior. Wet and cold, we were challenged by a harrowing, rain-filled and buffeting wind as we crossed the heights of the Duluth-Superior Bridge.

The John A. Blatnik Bridge carries Interstate 535 and U.S. 53 over the Saint Louis Bay, a tributary of Lake Superior between Duluth and Superior. The bridge is 7,975 feet long and rises nearly 120 feet above the water to accommodate the seaway-shipping channel. It was "white-knuckle time" for me from the peak of that one-hundred-twenty-foot bridge to the boggy flats and forests of Northeastern Minnesota as we negotiated twisting roads in pea-soup fog toward Ely. We could only hope that a moose wasn't standing in the middle of the road.

My rides on today's "one-up" Suzuki Volusia 800 are superb and motivating. After over forty years and forty thousand miles since my roadless rides in West Bloomington, it is a time to call it quits. My wife quit riding with me more than ten years ago. I have traveled on my own a bit, started and led a Senior Center Motorcycle Riders Club for a couple of years on twice-monthly rides, but lost interest when the politics of people overshadowed the beauty of the ride.

Montana and the Mississippi still beckon, but I'm not prone to take off alone. I content myself with brief twenty-mile rides in the nearby countryside. But the flavor is gone. Harsh reality (and my wife's constant concern) says it is probably not safe for me to be out there amidst eighty-mile-per-hour multi-lane traffic, ubiquitous cell phones and the crazy drivers of every day. The reflexes of my high-school basketball jump shot have probably slowed down a bit as well.

Cushman. (Photo courtesy of the author.)

Maybe I need to get a Cushman.

Gandy Dancers, Life Lessons, and Intersections: A Railroad Story of Winona

The position of Winona on the River is one of great importance, and when her Transit Road is pushed out to the bend of the St. Peter's, and the North and South Roads connect, must make her at many seasons of the year, almost the head of navigation.

–*Winona Argus*, first issue, September 1854

Winona was the epicenter.

Immigrants were arriving. There was a need to move the timbers that had been floated as logs down the Mississippi River, now refined as fresh lumber by gigantic Winona mills, to villages and farms of the west. A simultaneous and reciprocal need was to move bounteous wheat harvests of the west to the mills of Winona for refining and shipment down the Mississippi. To fill the needs, railroads were soon rolling, evolving and connecting.

Commencing in 1854—only a few years after Winona's settlement in the shadow of Sugar Loaf—a charter was granted to prominent Winonans to create the Winona and St. Peter Railway. In 1862, the railroad brought its first carload of wheat from Stockton to Winona. Officially opening in the spring of 1863, success was seen as imminent. A *Winona Republican* issue of 1864 said of the railroad:

> Even now, in the infancy of enterprise, the gigantic proportions which it is yet to assume are foreshadowed. The stripling is already called upon to do the work of a giant. It will be the part of wisdom to confer upon him, as occasion demands it, the strength of a giant.

By 1864, they were hauling at capacity of their rolling stock. Over thirty miles of railbed had been completed, soon reaching Rochester. By 1868, they were at Waseca. Then 1871 saw them completing the one hundred sixty-five miles to New Ulm—to continue on to the Black Hills of South Dakota. And 1879 saw them as a strong force in Rochester, Mankato, Zumbrota, Chatfield, Plainview, Redwood Falls, Tracy, and Gary on the Minnesota border, with a gross income of nearly one million dollars in freight and passenger revenue. For years thereafter, "Long trains of lumber left this city for the west."

Strong revenue also came from the land grant properties associated with the owned track lines. Over 150,000 acres of land were offered for sale by the railroad in 1865 in Winona and ten other counties, including advertised "Wheat Land" of southwestern Minnesota.

The Winona and St. Peter lasted until 1900, to be subsumed by the Chicago and Northwestern Railroad. Early incorporators of the Winona and Southwestern Railroad heading south to LaCrescent were historic figures of Winona in 1872. R.D. Cone, A.B. Youmans, Henry Lamberton, and William Windom, among others, were lumber barons and early designers of the city. Windom went on to greater designs as a Minnesota senator and secretary of the treasury of the United States. When the sparks were settled and their line was built, the president of the corporation was local resident William Mitchell of Minnesota law school fame.

Venturing Home

On my walk home on a wind-driven late afternoon of the 1950s, the sun was setting on another harsh day. It was a good day for the flight of northern bluebill ducks into our beautiful river valley. Along the way, I ventured from school to Wayne's house for a few comic book moments.

In these late October days, we sometimes enjoyed an outdoor basketball shootout on the playground. But the puddles had frozen and the wind was whistling. Better to head indoors for stove heat and hot chocolate.

The welcoming, barracks-like room that Wayne shared with his three brothers had been built in the fashion of a summer kitchen, as an add-on to the small house. One brother, Donnie, recalls the exposed ceiling rafters. He said it was "like having my own 'Jungle Jim' set from which to stretch and pull." I remember the great warmth and the pungency of kerosene that greeted us as we stretched out on the line of single World War II U.S. Army surplus bunk beds.

After an hour or so of planning, palaver, and organizing, I headed home in the dark of 5:00 p.m. I stopped in the small outdoor barn/shed where Donald, Wayne's father, had dumped his gunnysack full of flyers (ducks) waiting to be cleaned—a beautiful sight at this great hunter's feet. Gathered by

Donald in God's surround of the Minnesota City Boat harbor, it was a bounty to behold and a great dinner for the family of seven.

Donald was an early morning trucker and milk hauler from area farms to dairy. Even though he had put in a full day of lifting cans and hauling by noon, he still found time and energy for afternoon duck hunting—especially on a blustery day when the north wind chased mallards and bluebills down from Canada.

A pull of the outboard motor cord and Donald was headed into the channel and off to his favored point where he spaced out his two dozen decoys on the wind-filled water. When not at work, the decoys rested in the dark of the truck box, on top of the freshly washed ten-gallon cans. Wayne and brothers joined with their pa for an afternoon or weekend hunt, as schedules and space in the small boat allowed.

After brief words and an ever-present smile from Donald, I headed for supper on Grand Street. As I left Wayne's dad and his passel of ducks, I was intercepted by a Milwaukee Road passenger train with lighted dining cars and real people passing by but feet away from the sidewalk. Directly across Belleview Street from Wayne's place lay the tracks of the Milwaukee Road, bisecting the city in a north-south fashion. With the additional Chicago and Northwestern Station on the river at Huff Street and the Burlington Way Station in the slough across the river, we had trains running day and night through city and neighborhoods—and up and down the river to St. Paul, Chicago, and places west.

As I waited for the train to pass, I observed the fine folks readying for dinner in the white tableclothed dining room, or otherwise lounging in the well-lit and beautiful club cars. They looked like the fancy folks from California whom I had seen pictured in the *Saturday Evening Post.* Having had a classroom field trip on the same train to LaCrosse and return, I had a real feel for the ornate furnishings and the comfortable seats—rivaling the comfort of a 1951 Buick Roadmaster backseat in which I had once sat.

These Milwaukee Road tracks were less than two blocks from our front door—as contrasted to Wayne's one hundred feet or so. All who grew up in the neighborhood did so with a wonder of the world passing by—and a learned fear of the tracks. Open intersections of street and track and merging of tracks at crossover points meant potential death. There was no fallback. A stuck foot between rail and stone was nothing to be messed with. If we walked the tracks (which we often did), we jumped from tie to tie, since tie spacing was irregular to our foot beat and stride.

Speeding trains criss-crossed our city of one hundred intersections without warning lights or drop-down barriers. Common sense for pedestrian or driver was the only real rule. Our reality was the "City Traffic Box Score" shown at the bottom of every crash story in the *Republican-Herald*—a ghoulish statistic.

Milwaukee Road passenger train, 1950. Photo courtesy of the Winona Historical Society.)

The Gandy Dancers

In early days, track needed to be laid. Manpower was the answer. Once laid, with spring floods and ill-defined levees, the cities, small towns and railroad tracks along the river were continuous victims of massive floods. Crews were employed locally, urgently and often from a transient population to work the rails. My brother Bob, living on the farm, remembers that our Grandpa Frank (Franz) Voigt came off the farm daily for a couple of years in the late 1930s to be employed in the Dakota (Minnesota) section of the railroads. He was a "gandy-dancer"–a skilled worker who drove the pins in to hold the rails in place.

Before work was done by machine, the gandy dancer and laborers laid and maintained railroad tracks. "Gandy dancer" is a slang term used for an early railroad worker, for builders of railway lines, and "platelayer" for workers employed to inspect and maintain the track. In the U.S. Southwest and Mexico, Mexican and Mexican-American track workers were colloquially "traqueros."

The term is sometimes described as specific to those workers who built the track. Often, the job of the gandy dancer refers to "track examiner," ascribing responsibilities of checking ties, bolts, track, and roadbed for necessary repairs. Most sources refer to gandy dancers as the men who did the difficult physical work of track maintenance under direction of an overseer.

There are various theories about the derivation of the term, but most refer to the "dancing" movements of the workers using a specially manufactured five-foot "lining" bar (which may have come to be called a "gandy") as a lever to keep the tracks in alignment. Others suggest that the term was coined to describe the movements of the workers themselves—the constant "dancing" motion of the track workers as they lunged against their tools in unison to nudge the rails, often timed by a chant, as they carried rails, or, speculatively, as they waddled like ganders while running on the railroad ties.

A May 1938 article in the *Republican-Herald* describes a scene repeated up and down the river by Franz and his associates.

> There are citizens who think a circus is "The Greatest Show on Earth." This is because they've never seen a couple hundred soaking wet men, the big bosses and the gandy dancers, doing a piece of old fashioned railroading.
>
> And this kind of show has been going on a few miles above Hastings at the Mississippi River's edge since it was discovered early Wednesday that flood waters, imprisoned in a great natural pocket, had burst its rocky seams and, rushing out, pushed tons of soggy earth into the river leaving 150 feet of St. Paul railroad track swinging in the air as if it were a Chinese foot bridge. The tracks of the Burlington were washed into the river.
>
> To repair the damage, work was begun at once to put a foundation under the hanging rails and to rebuild the washed away track. Officials expected to work most of the night to finish the job.
>
> The drama, and it has many of the aspects of setting up a circus, is going on in a wild setting. On one side, with a camp train of ten cars at its feet, is a rocky bluff; on the other the swollen Mississippi. On the ground, and it is a mucky, swollen mess between these boundaries. The work went on all day Thursday and through the night as leaders assumed the responsibility for putting the railroad back together again."

Grandpa brought home several pieces of railroad track that he cut with a cold chisel. After marking the rail with hammer and chisel all the way around the track piece, he then struck with a maul to break off the piece. According to Bob, these twelve- to fourteen-inch pieces were used on the farm as tie stakes for a horse or cow. The animal could pull the piece on a rope to the fresh grass, but could not pull it too far to escape from the area. I have one of those pieces in my garage, still in use today. It was used at home on Grand Street some sixty years ago for the splitting of walnuts and hickory nuts and assorted tasks, like nail-straightening within the old shed.

Only a few miles upriver from Dakota at Winona Landing, in " a lonely section of Burlington track a mile south of Winona Junction," a section crew like Franz's worked hard to restore river damage in June 1943. The newspaper reported, "Section Hand Dies in Bunkcar Fight." After a full week in camp and on the rails, a fifty-two-year-old worker from Butte, Montana, arrived home to the bunk car drunk and disorderly at midnight Friday. With all the crew asleep, he was told to "Shut Up or Leave."

Belligerent, he attacked and was struck by fifty-six-year-old William Jackson, "an old-timer in such crews" with an iron bar. He said, "I grabbed the iron bar in my two hands and swung in the dark at his head." Jackson was charged at Alma, Wisconsin.

The *Republican-Herald* reported; "It is the story of a grim battle in the dark, a dramatic chapter from the lives of three homeless men who toll day after day to maintain the roadbeds of transcontinental railroads–the gandy dancers."

The tracklayers continue through this day, with college-age youth finding long hours, hard work, and good pay for their labors. Machines do the heavy lifting, but the torque of human bodies and independent muscle is essential. It is for each to become intimate once again with the frequently walked railbeds of youth.

In the Neighborhood

We were often "first responders" to auto and train crashes of the neighborhood. We heard the crash, jumped on a bike and were there before police, newspaper photographer "One-Shot Kelley" or the tow truck operator from MerKohn, Borzykowski or Owl Motor. Open intersections and the Box Score of deaths and injuries were constantly with us; not unlike the listed deaths and wounded of area youth in the Korean War, published weekly in the *Pioneer Press* Sunday edition.

Railroad track piece. (Photo courtesy of the author.)

From Milwaukee to Minneapolis, the story was the same. A cursory search for "Milwaukee Road crashes" of a nearly one-hundred-year Winona newspaper database instantly yielded one thousand stories to review. Big town or small, it mattered not. From the 1901 crash at LaCrosse, to the crash at Weaver with no air brakes in 1908, to Milwaukee's home yard crash in 1927, to the death of three and injury of four due to an "open switch" and collision of a freight train and a "crack Milwaukee Road passenger train" in 1929, the headlines run into one another. Derailments, death and injury of brakeman or fireman or both are documented. It was dangerous space where trains traveled, often leaving a "car sheared in half."

In Winona, we had crashes at Garfield (death of six-year-old boy) and Dacota and Laird and Winona and Chestnut streets (and every street in between.) Our twelve-year-old playmate died as he crawled under a boxcar that was "bumped ahead" in a neighborhood railroad yard. Observers watched from the train station platform on Center Street as a sixty-four-year-old resident living his life one hundred yards from the track ignored a train whistle–to die within sight of his home on Winona Street.

In February of 1954, there were two reported collisions within a two-hour period. In the first accident, a seventeen-year-old Minnesota City boy died at the Johnson Street crossing. The Box Score listed his truck's value at fifty dollars. We had more information than we needed.

Our "home street" of Grand brought death to a Minnesota City man in May 1951, "the fifth crossing accident of this year." Progress of clearing the crash scene was "hampered by the presence of the large crowd." In the dark of a February supper hour of 1954 a couple of blocks away on my paper route, a housewife of the neighborhood had her auto pushed one hundred and sixty feet by a train backing up at Dacota Street–to earn herself only "minor cuts and bruises." Auto-train crashes were grisly entertainment in our neighborhood.

1950s railroad crossing. (Photo courtesy of *Pieces of the Past*, Winona Historical Society.)

An experienced, forty-year conductor of Milwaukee Road trains on these very rails during the heyday of open intersections was interviewed for this story. Five team members (engineer, conductor, head brakeman, rear brakeman, and fireman) were constantly fearful of crashes as their trains passed through Winona in the 1960s.

Larry reports, "We would literally hold our breath as we traveled through Winona. We could see stop signs being avoided, people darting across and accidents to come. Meeting of another train on the heavily used 'double tracks' installed from St. Paul to Chicago increased the accidents. As one train went past in one direction, the hurried driver would cross onto the track—into the direct path of an oncoming train from the other direction!"

From the 1930s through the '70s, traffic was unbelievable. Nearly fifty trains per day (passenger and freights) passed over the tracks of the Milwaukee Road, Chicago & Northwestern, Burlington and Green Bay & Western near or through Winona. Numbers of trains of today are not known. Most intersections have been somewhat protected, although single road entries in rural areas are still troublesome—as are drivers who choose to drive around controls and pedestrians who walk between stopped cars about to engage. The double track was removed throughout the "River Division" in 2005, with single track and computer-controlled long sidings taking their place.

The Hobo—HOmeward BOund

The freight trains didn't have windows, but they held a lot of interest. We saw people even closer, these riders of the rails—the hobos of America. Night and day they passed by and stood in the doorways. Sometimes we would have a hobo or two drift down the street to someone's back door seeking a handout—but always in exchange for offered work. The hobo was one who was down and out, but hadn't lost his pride. More than anything, he wanted to work and find a home. A bum was a bum.

Hobos rode the rails into the heart of our small city along the Mississippi River—and into my heart.

Daily arrival of freight trains in the 1940s and 1950s brought us these open-air riders. Often seen standing in the open doors of the multitude of train cars passing through town, they sometimes chose to stop. Approaching a small home or two of the neighborhood after World War II, they entered or knocked on the screen door of the back porch, asking for a gift of a tomato from the garden, an apple from the tree or a sandwich to spare—and quietly inquired if there was any work they could do in exchange.

As H.L. Mencken in *The American Language* (1937) wrote:

> Tramps and hobos are commonly lumped together, but see themselves as sharply differentiated. A hobo or bo is simply a migratory laborer; he may take some longish holidays, but sooner or later he returns to work. A tramp never works if it can be avoided; he simply travels. Apart from either is the bum, who neither works nor travels, save when propelled to motion by the police.

The Hobo Ethical Code of 1889 states in part: "Always try to find work, even if temporary, and always seek out jobs nobody wants. By doing so you not only help a business along, but ensure employment should you return to that town again. When no employment is available, make your own work by using your added talents at crafts."

The number of hobos increased greatly to an estimated one million or more during the Great Depression era of the 1930s. With no work and no prospects at home, many decided to travel for free by freight train and try their luck elsewhere.

Life as a hobo was dangerous. In addition to the problems of being itinerant, poor, and far from home and support, plus the hostility of many train crews, they faced the railroads' security staff, nicknamed "bulls," who had a reputation of violence against trespassers. Moreover, riding on a freight train was dangerous in itself.

Modern freight trains are much faster and thus harder to ride than in the 1930s, but they can still be boarded in rail yards.

Privately Operated Passenger Rail Service

The Milwaukee & Waukesha Rail Road was chartered in 1847. Before it laid its first rails in 1850, its name was changed to Milwaukee & Mississippi. In 1851, it reached Waukesha, twenty miles west of Milwaukee. The railroad reached Madison in 1854, and Prairie du Chien on the Mississippi in 1857. It was reorganized in 1863 as the Milwaukee & St. Paul.

The Milwaukee & St. Paul ("The Milwaukee Road") acquired in 1872 the St. Paul & Chicago, which had just completed a route down the west bank of the Mississippi from St. Paul to LaCrescent, opposite La Crosse. In 1873, the Milwaukee & St. Paul completed a line from Milwaukee south to Chicago. A year later it added "Chicago" to its name, creating the Chicago, Milwaukee & St. Paul Railway (CM&StP).

From the mid-nineteenth century until approximately 1920, nearly all intercity travelers in the United States moved by rail. The rails and the trains were owned and operated by private, for-profit organizations. Approximately 65,000 railroad passenger cars operated in 1929.

Passenger rails' popularity diminished with a series of pullbacks and tentative recoveries. Rail passenger revenues declined dramatically between 1920 and 1934 because of the rise of the automobile. In the same period, many travelers were lost to interstate bus companies such as Greyhound.

In the mid-1930s, railroads reignited popular imagination with service improvements and new, diesel-powered streamliners, such as the gleaming silver Burlington Zephyr and the steam-powered Milwaukee Twin Cities Hiawatha. Even with the improvements, on a relative basis, traffic continued to decline, and by 1940, railroads held sixty-seven percent of passenger miles in the United States.

World War II broke the malaise. During the war, troop movements and restrictions on automobile fuel generated a six-fold increase in passenger traffic from its low point of the Great Depression. After the war, railroads rejuvenated overworked and neglected fleets with fast and often luxurious streamliners that inspired the last major resurgence in passenger rail travel.

The postwar resurgence was short-lived. In 1946, there remained forty-five percent fewer passenger trains than in 1929, and the decline quickened despite railroad optimism. Passengers disappeared—and so did trains. Few trains generated profits; most produced losses. Broad-based passenger rail deficits appeared as early as 1948, and by the mid-1950s, railroads claimed aggregate annual losses on passenger services of more than $700 million (almost five billion in 2005 dollars when adjusted for inflation).

By 1965, only 10,000 rail passenger cars were in operation, eighty-five percent fewer than in 1929. Passenger service was provided on only 75,000 miles of track, a stark decline. The 1960s also saw the end of railway post office revenues, which had helped some of the remaining trains break even.

On Grand Street

Winona continues as an epicenter of railroads.

Coal trains dominate. Amtrak, which began in 1971, is a whisper of its former self. The Grand Street I walked so many years ago is today one of the open, gated, street-and-rail intersections of Winona. Those same tracks at Belleview Street remain—albeit protected. I can still stand on the same sidewalk and see Amtrak passengers pass in their daily journeys from St. Paul to Chicago, or vice versa

More likely, I will be met in my now-drooping, waiting stance by massive freight trains that are hundreds of cars long—soon to be controlled by a

The Pontoon Bridge

An interesting railroad side story on our piece of the Mississippi is of the Chippewa Valley Rail Line. Larry told me of railroad line vestiges seen and of rumors heard of a "pontoon bridge" from fellow railroaders. Research shows the line originated in Winona in the 1880s, traveling from Winona to Wabasha to Durand, with termination at Eau Claire.

The line's specialty was moving freight cars over the Mississippi River at Reads Landing on a pontoon bridge. As early as 1882 at Reads Landing, a few miles upriver from Wabasha where eagles circle and abound, was a railroad trestle. Operated by the Milwaukee Road, the trestle combined with an approach from Wisconsin via a floating pontoon bridge to connect the rails. The Chippewa Valley Switching Service was "Wabasha's biggest industry," with forty employees moving cars at Wabasha, Reads Landing and the switchyards.

Ice chunks coming from Lake Pepin with spring flooding frequently damaged pilings of the bridge. Annual maintenance costs were high. Original pontoons were replaced with a single pontoon in 1932, "the largest single-unit pontoon bridge in the world," to be floated upriver from its launch at Wabasha. The four-hundred-foot by fifty-foot behemoth served nearly twenty years.

In 1951, the "landmark at Reads Landing for many years" was declared "not economically feasible to retain." Wabasha fought hard for retention of its economic mainstay, to no avail. It was ultimately removed and sold for scrap in June 1953.

Captain Frank Fujina, an experienced river pilot on the Mississippi, wrote in his "Ol' Man River" column: "to raft [barge] pilots, the bridge was a nightmare. Fancy piloting was required to run the bridge."

He concluded that with the closing; "Pilots will rejoice."

single onboard railroad man and a computer control system located one hundred or more miles distant.

The hobos are gone, frozen out by the speed of trains and the design of closed cars. Train crewmembers are virtually absent, with hardly anyone to whom we can wave. As the trains cruise through the night and shake the walls of Wayne's former bedroom, the beat goes on—as it did one hundred years ago.

I no longer live on Grand Street, but am happy to report that safety at railroad intersections is a premier focus of railroad and city today. Living

Modern freight cars. (Photo courtesy of the author.)

yet with the fear of God, and of Engine Number 77052, kids still need to watch where they walk.

Thankfully, the Box Score is no longer a published statistic.

And Today

TRAIN AND VEHICLE COLLIDE; WINONA MAN INJURED

By Amelia Wedemeyer–*Winona Post* 5/5/2014

At 6:11 a.m. on Saturday, April 26, a Winona Police Department (WPD) officer in the area of Third and Ben streets heard a passing train applying its brakes. When he arrived at the train tracks at the intersection of Jackson and West Fifth streets, he noticed a vehicle that appeared to have been struck by a train. The vehicle had heavy damage to its right side. The driver of the vehicle, Jonathan Lott Freeman, 67, of Winona, appeared to be conscious and alert. Freeman, who said he had pain in his right leg, was the only individual inside the vehicle at the time of the accident. Freeman told the officer that he saw the railroad crossing with its lights on and its arms coming down, but he forgot that the tracks went diagonal through town and he thought he could make a left turn. An EMT arrived on the scene and Freeman was transported to a hospital for minor injuries. He was cited for failure to stop at a train signal.

Keystone Railroad toy rider from 1941. A safe choice. (Author collection.)

Chapter Three

The Mystery Girl of Midnight Music

Suzy approached the swimming hole on Dacota Street on her blue Schwinn bike.

Cutting down the dead-end dirt road two blocks to the lake on this shiny autumn Saturday afternoon was a little jog out of her way. Nevertheless, she was passing by and wanted to take one last look at the swimming hole before school activities set in and before ice covered Lake Winona.

What a day it was!

Leaves turning on hardwood trees in bluffs near enough to touch shimmered in the lake's reflection of the late afternoon sun. It was as if she was riding into a scene from the movie *Picnic* and all its sensual glory. With girlfriends, she had recently seen the small town, romantic movie starring William Holden and Kim Novak at the State Theater. The movie set and the vibrant characters resonated with her feelings of hometown—and with her own yearnings for romance.

She was on her way to high school this year—finally making it as a Winhawk. By the time she reached this sophomore year, Suzy had stretched out a good measure—becoming a tall, willowy blonde attracting attention in a new way. In but a few weeks, she was cheerleader, class officer and the friend of many.

Acclimating to the ways of the school, to teacher expectations and to the full rush of meeting all the kids of the near county, she was no longer in her previous, separate comfort zone of junior high neighbors and buddies. Beside today's senior girls and farm boys in all manner of mixed classes and hallways there was new opportunity and challenge. Huge football players passed by as she reached into the tall metal locker on the second floor of her new three-year home.

As Suzy walked by already-clumsy teenage boys finding their own new growth, it seemed they often tripped over themselves. She was on her way into a new world—and sensed she was a part of creating it.

She met old friends from town for school lunch in the cafeteria. With friends new and old, she made an occasional legal noon escape to the Varsity Inn—"the Vars." Without Mom's permission, Suzy could see friends, grab a booth and enjoy a fried burger for a quarter, with a nickel Coke in paper cone cup held by a metal holder. It was all served up at the counter by "Howie," ever-smiling master of the grill and "the Vars." A fun escape, she was back in class within the allotted thirty-minute lunchtime.

Suzy was always full of it. At age four, she rode the bicycle she was riding yet today. By kindergarten, she was twirling the sidewalks around the block with playmates on roller skates and soon leading her neighborhood gang to adventures of hide and seek, tag football and apple raids in the night.

By age ten, she had won her share of races, played with the girls on occasion, but especially enjoyed playing the hardscrabble street hockey, football and dodgeball of the boys. She was invited, successful and capable of holding her own with them—even taking or giving an occasional punch. She could outrun most of the boys; one of whom remembered her well.

I was one of the many who had the freedom to bust out for nighttime play with an expectation that whatever I did, I would behave. We weren't a "gang." Rather, we were a semi-leaderless mix of individuals with separate and appreciated strengths. Suzy was probably the closest thing we had to a leader.

Suzy knew the neighborhood like the back of her hand. She swung from the rope to splash into the deep hole in the lake. She rode her bike on streets in daytime and ran the backyards at night. One shimmering winter night in this first year of high school, Suzy was introduced to the darkened end of Dacota Street not previously seen or considered.

On a first date of tenth grade, a boy took her to the school dance, then to the Steak Shop for a burger—and for a late night drive along Lake Winona. He made a slight detour to the west off Huff Street toward moonlight and huge cottonwoods overhanging the circular, dirt parking space of Dacota Street. With curfew of 11:00 p.m., Suzy didn't stay to visit too long, but did enjoy the *Music 'til Midnight* show on the radio as she snuggled in the moonlight.

Suzy's 1950s were the heyday of music on local KWNO radio. The day started with the *Choate's Musical Clock* at 7:45 a.m., moved into *Two Tips and a Tune* by Neville's Clothing Store and continued on with *Morning Music* by

Edstrom's Music Store, beginning at 10:30 a.m. After the noontime news, Dale Simons and the Blue Denims took over at 12:20. *Songs of the Night* by Edstrom's came back in the evening, leading into *Cedric Adams News* (on WCCO) at 10:00 p.m. and finally into KWNO's *Music 'til Midnight.*

"Music 'til Midnight," 1950s. (Photo courtesy of the Winona Newspaper Project.)

A staple through the 1940s and '50s, the late night, small town show was the musical domicile of teenagers enjoying the likes of Elvis's "Heartbreak Hotel" or "Hound Dog," Frankie Lymon's "Why Do fools Fall in Love?" the Platters's "Magic Touch" or the mellow "Lonely Girl" by Julie London. Music in the dark while heading off to sleep made for moments to remember.

By 1954, *Music 'til Midnight* was on the airwaves every evening from ten thirty to midnight. Varying hosts led the charge in the night. "Your Man for Good Music"—Ken Douglas—was at the controls in 1955. Larry Rubilashek brought the spinning 45s and his sidekick "Ole the Swede" to the airwaves in 1956, when Ole kept surreptitiously slipping records onto the turntable (records like *Spike Jones and His All-City Slickers*), disrupting Larry's mellow mood.

By the end of her sophomore year, Suzy had established a great reputation with all the kids in school. Every morning she seemingly needed to walk a gauntlet of boys hanging out on indoors school steps—and into the hallways where they interrupted traffic flow. It seemed as if there were more people in her way than there were students in the school. Wherever she went, there seemed to be a convergence. She didn't recognize that she was at the center of the maelstrom.

With her many talents and connections, someone suggested the station manager of KWNO contact Suzy. Although she already had a part-time summer job at McVey's Ice Cream Shop going into her junior year, she was asked to be a guest on *Teen Time with Choate's* for an occasional Saturday morning chat. From there, it didn't take long for station management to recognize her talents and invite her to a Saturday evening date with *Music 'til Midnight*, where song requests had become a big part of every Saturday's show. They poured in. Someone needed to organize them and verify their veracity, so as not to embarrass either listener or radio station.

For the next two years of Saturday nights, staying in the background of the show, Suzy became the unidentified "Mystery Girl of Midnight Music"—offering tidbits to announcer and listeners. She would suggest who was seen with whom at the Friday night, post-football game dance in the Jefferson School gymnasium. She would vaguely identify the "fool who fell in love," seen in the second floor hallway outside Mr. Zilliox's chemistry classroom. She visited the junior high to keep eighth and ninth graders in the loop—and in her ever-growing audience.

She was astute, attuned and a remarkable leader of peers. As broadcaster, analyst, and contributor to the *Music 'til Midnight* show, she was heard in small segments to blend and weave together comments, observations and requests for songs. When she had her own Saturday evening or weekend commitment, she would pre-record messages to be deftly slipped into conversation by the announcer. Couples who were seen at the Friday dance, the "Star of the Week" in sports or Suzy's suggested "friend to others" awards each week were instant hits for the well-known "mystery girl" of midnight music.

Mr. Stoltman, speech teacher and friend to Suzy, recognized her talents. He encouraged her to consider a college major in theatre and journalism as she left the hallways of the Winhawks. At her chosen eastern school, she again basked in the limelight. Surrounded by friends and admirers, Suzy continued to lead peers.

She was a star of theater productions, and a dedicated friend in helping others with parts in plays and in their personal development. Her learned lessons of leadership on the streets of Winona as a child formed a base of wisdom from which she drew continuous strength. She simply was not afraid to step out and offer quiet suggestion on how to proceed—in life or on stage.

By her junior year of college, Suzy secured a summer internship with ABC in New York City. As she had done with Mr. Stoltman, she was held to "face the fire." With her experience of Winona radio and the continuous support of peers and mentors, she soon became a most effective on-air reporter, excelling in the corporate organization.

With charm, expectation, and a major in theater production, Suzy's creativity was challenged in organizing and creating college productions. Her innate mathematical skills, refined by Miss Pallas, everyone's favorite high school math teacher, had seemingly been set aside. But as she moved forward in her senior year, she found the new world of computers, applied mathematics and an intriguing world of systems analysis.

By graduation she had secured a position with the burgeoning IBM as choreographer of new productions and programs to serve a larger world. She loved the challenge and potential impact of solving problems by machine to serve the greater needs of people and organizations. Each problem was "as a dance"–threading her way through people, problems, and organizational needs to arrive at solution.

Suzy's return to her roots and to her high school class reunion twenty years later at the Westfield Country Club saw her as wife, mother, MBA and vice-president of one of the world's largest computing organizations. The "Mystery Girl of Midnight Music" had brought Winona roots to the larger world.

On the Saturday afternoon before the reunion dinner, she once again rode her bicycle back to Dacota Street. Stored these many years in her mother's basement, she pedaled the few blocks–and eons of life–to remembered beginnings.

1950s Schwinn bicycle. (Photo courtesy of ebay.)

Author's note: Suzy is an amalgam of all the Winona girls met in the author's journey of life. She represents the very best–as playmate, housewife, friend, artist, teacher, nurse supervisor, secretary, television commentator, or IBM director.

Each girl provided her personal (and Winona) values to a larger world. Each is to be celebrated for her gifts.

A Sidebar for Ole—Just for Fun

Lindley Armstrong "Spike" Jones (December 14, 1911 to May 1, 1965) was an American musician and bandleader specializing in performing satirical arrangements of popular songs. Young Lindley Jones got his nickname by being so thin he was compared to a railroad spike. At age eleven he got his first set of drums, soon playing in bands he formed himself. A railroad restaurant chef taught him how to use pots and pans, forks, knives, and spoons as musical instruments. Ballads and classical works receiving the Jones treatment would be punctuated with gunshots, whistles, cowbells, and outlandish vocals.

Spike Jones and his City Slickers toured the United States and Canada under the title The Musical Depreciation Revue. In the 1930s, he joined The Victor Young orchestra and got many offers to appear on radio shows, including Al Jolson's *Lifebuoy Program*, *Burns and Allen*, and Bing Crosby's *Kraft Music Hall*.

From 1937 to 1942, he was the percussionist for the John Scott Trotter Orchestra, playing on Bing Crosby's first recording of "White Christmas." Spike Jones was part of a backing band for songwriter Cindy Walker during her early recording career with Decca Records and Standard Transcriptions. Her song "We're Gonna Stomp Them City Slickers Down" provided the inspiration for the name of Jones's future band, the City Slickers.

The City Slickers developed from the Feather Merchants, a band led by vocalist-clarinetist Del Porter, who took a back seat to Jones during the embryonic years of the group. They made experimental records for the Cinematone Corporation and performed publicly in Los Angeles, gaining a small following. The original members included vocalist-violinist Carl Grayson, banjoist Perry Botkin, trombonist King Jackson and pianist Stan Wrightsman.

Ole was wise to slip a few of Spike's recordings into the *Music 'til Midnight* mix.

A Flower for Your Thoughts: The Florists of Winona

Winona's First Florist

John Wonder grew flowers on the side hill of Sugar Loaf in 1857, long before the hill had been mined off. The beauty of John's flowers and his bounteous crop of "walnut-sized strawberries" begged this German settler to take them to downtown market. His Sugar Loaf Gardens endured for years, bringing gracious color to the lives of many.

He continued actively in the flower trade and Winona community for many years. He was the chosen Republican delegate to a county convention in 1867. He was also frequent award winner at the county fair of Rochester. In 1886, he "won fourteen premiums on flowers," with his major competitor Smith and Darling winning twenty.

In 1885, Wonder charged that the fair awards won by Smith and Darling of Southside Greenhouse of 120 to 132 East King Street were fair; but the "manner of obtaining them is a just subject of criticism." He added, "No florist would crow over such a victory." John headed the Decoration Committee for the Memorial Service held at the Philharmonic Hall in 1888.

Sugar Loaf in the 1890s. (Photo courtesy of *Pieces of the Past*, Winona Historical Society.)

Smith and Darling's flowers continued to bloom. Methodists of the city also appreciated their "frescoing and ornamental painting"—an advertised secondary business. The Methodist Episcopal Church was given "a very handsome appearance" by the talented florists/painters in the interior remodeling of 1882. The German Methodists were next in line, "about to inaugurate" their own facelift, with Smith and Darling as selected purveyor.

These main players in flowers continued a healthy sparring match over the years with Wonder's shop offering wedding, funeral and cut flowers as "a specialty, " while Southside offered "roses and plants." They did team up for a sumptuous dinner at the Huff House in 1888, provided for a team of visiting Sioux City businessmen. There were decorations at each table by the floral competitors. Both of the competitors offered to send a bouquet for any event or occasion, including "Sweet Violets."

Sweet Violets,
Sweet Violets,
Covered all over from head to toe,
Covered all over with sweet violets.

—Dinah Shore, 1951, © Joseph Emmet, 1892.
From *Fritz Among the Gypsies*, 1882.

West End and Beyond

The folks of the West End Greenhouse came along in 1891 to send their own bouquets—first by cart and horse and later by enclosed, chauffeur-driven truck. They offered "Violets at Kirchner's" in 1912 for twenty cents per bunch. A sample full bouquet may have included white snaps, red roses, white pom-poms and greens.

Ed Kirchner and son did a beautiful job for twenty-five years. Ed created a new fourteen-thousand-square-foot greenhouse at 802 West King Street (at Minnesota Street) offering "cut flowers and plants, designs and bouquets." Throughout the 1900s, the West End Greenhouse was the place to visit for beautiful flowers, skilled personnel, and a warm feeling from the experience of being in the actual greenhouse.

"Carrying out a corsage of fresh carnations to my favorite girl for the prom, selecting a respectful plant for my mother at Woodlawn Cemetery or bringing roses for a holiday to extended family members was a special experience," said one who had been there many times over the years.

Along with Mrs. Voelker's aging 1880s greenhouse on the tracks at Huff Street, the West End Greenhouse in 1915 became part of the Winona Floral

Company, operated by Joe Orlowske (Huff) and George W. Hartner (West End). Coming from Owatonna with vast experience, they were "men of more than ordinary experience in the florist business." They were purveyors of floral beauty for many years. Their company grew to operate the grand space of the West End, as well as to create two new thirty-by-one-hundred-foot greenhouses on Huff Street.

Delivery card for West End Greenhouses. (Photo courtesy of the author.)

By 1929, Joe, as single owner, built his new greenhouse. He brought his sons Joe and John into the year-round operation of the new greenhouses at Huff and the tracks, where "Orchids, gardenias, roses, and mums are all growing in profusion under glass." To achieve blossoming of an orchid takes seven years of loving care, warmth, and patience.

Coal-heat furnaces were first used for heat in the greenhouses, requiring frequent shoveling of fuel by employees. Oil-fired furnaces took their place, reducing labor costs substantially and giving consistent heat and care to the flowers. Orlowske and Siebrecht's, a friendly competitor of the 1900s, together "grew more orchids than any other Minnesota florist, except for the Twin Cities." Joe, Sr., managed the greenhouses and wholesale business until turning the business over to his sons in 1946.

Joe's former partner became florist of the Woodlawn Cemetery upon dissolving the association, assisted there by son George W., Jr. Mrs. George W. Hartner (Mina) became proprietor of the Winona Floral Co. store at 114 East Third Street, assisted by son Clarence. All six of the Hartners, including Edward and Dorothy, who employed elsewhere, lived above the store.

George W. sold the business to Clarence in 1949. By 1957, Clarence moved back to his father's heritage as florist of the West End Greenhouse, with George W., Jr., becoming superintendent of Woodlawn Cemetery. Winona greenhouses operating in 1957 were at the Huff Street site, West End, Siebrecht's on Highway 61 and the Hy-Way Greenhouse of West Gilmore Avenue.

Call Siebrecht's to See

Siebrecht's was to become a Winona floral institution. Along with Hartner's Floral and Pet Store and the West End Greenhouse, Siebrecht's was a tasteful shop at which to get outfitted for prom or wedding—or to send a dozen roses.

> "I'm sending you a big bouquet of roses,
> One for every time you broke my heart.
> And as the door of love between us closes,
> Tears will fall like petals when we part."
> ... I'm sending you a big bouquet of roses ...
>
> –"Bouquet of Roses," Eddy Arnold, 1948
> Words and music by Bob Hilliard and
> Steve Edward Nelson (Hal Leonard)

Starting in 1897, the Siebrecht's greenhouses, farm and "Columbia Gardens" created natural treasures offered for sale in their beautiful downtown shop at 66 West Third Street in the prestigious Morgan Block. Their greenhouses, located on Old Homer Road across from St. Mary's Cemetery, employed twenty employees who serviced local customers and shipped to many more. In addition to quality service to individual store customers by six employees, Siebrecht's also provided daily fresh flowers for the Garden Gate and Candy Box restaurants next door.

Charles's cousin, German-born florist H.C. Siebrecht, owned a greenhouse on Fifth Avenue in New York City, where Charles left him. Charles established his first greenhouse in Winona in the 1880s at Howard and Washington streets, moving soon to Wabasha and Zumbro and thence back to 626-630 East Sanborn, and finally building greenhouses to serve the thriving business in 1922 on Homer Road.

As with the traveling greenhouses, the downtown Siebrecht shop traveled—beginning in 1913 at 66 West Third, to 60 West, to 58 West, and finally (again) to 66 West Third in 1923. Charles, Jr., succeeded his father upon his death in 1913 to lead the company into the booming 1950s. In 1957, Charles Siebrecht was president and treasurer with Josephine Schneider as vice-president and Mrs. Kate B. Beth as secretary. Charles's brothers and cousins were also active in the family business, establishing floral shops in Rapid City, Aberdeen, San Diego and Palm Beach—all a long way from Winona and their family origins in New York City.

One of the longest-term arrangements of advertising and sponsorship on the local level was a Siebrecht collaboration with the popular Oaks Supper Club of Minnesota City. Chef Walter Kelly and Mr. Siebrecht arranged from the early 1950s through the early '60s to offer a "Free Orchid by Siebrecht's on Saturday evening" for each guest at the marvelous Oaks dining room.

The hometown growers liked to suggest in their ads in the *Daily News* of the 1960s and early '70s that, "Flowers from Siebrecht's have more impact, more originality—and they are fresh!" They suggested further that, "there is a difference in flowers. Call Siebrecht's to see." They were also proud to announce, "If it's sold here, it's grown here."

Siebrecht's closed the downtown store after more than fifty years in 1966, opening a new store at their 2200 Homer Road site in September of that year. In 1974, they re-opened their "garden house" on May 15 to serve local gardeners. Unfortunately, for lovers of fresh flowers, the growth of the vocational-technical school and adjacent housing consumed Siebrecht land and removed the greenhouse panes that had encapsulated floral beauty for nearly seventy-five years.

The Glass Is Gone

The Huff Street greenhouses were closed and dismantled in the 1970s to make room for Winona State University student housing. The last of the Orlowskes (Joe and John) ended their part of the nearly one-hundred-year West End Greenhouse era in the early 1980s. According to descendent Mike Orlowske, a now-retired Winona Prudential agent: "Even in the 1950s the heating costs were astounding." (Eight to nine thousand dollars per month.) "With previous coal heating, we had a night fireman who spent the night firing the furnaces at Huff Street and the West End—and removing all the clinkers." With gas and oil firing in latter years, the high costs remained. The economic challenges were too great, necessitating the closing and removal of the west greenhouses and their loads of transite (a bedding material of hazardous waste including asbestos). Senior housing apartments were soon built on the greenhouse space across from the old Bourne Cash Grocery, later known as Ferdinandsen Grocery.

Thanks to All

Flowers are yet available from a variety of small shops in Winona. With greenhouses gone, few of the flowers are grown in the city. The imported plantings may rival in kind the likes of flowers from the Hartner's, Orlowskes', and Siebrechts'. But the personal growth, pride, and presentation made in growing from bulb to blossom are absent. Sufficient to say, there are no free orchids at the Oaks on Saturday evenings. A time has passed.

A long-time Winona resident and relative aids me in my verification of places and people in town for my stories (he's ninety or so). He would suggest that the best place to get fresh flowers today is at Hy-Vee. "They can accommodate any need—and deliver per your request. They have a large space dedicated to flowers that are always 'extra nice.' I would go there to buy them," he recommends.

Mike likes to recommend Flowers on Broadway, located in the old Broadway Theater and Grocery building of East Broadway near the famous Bloedow Bakery.

Next time you are down that way, treat yourself to a donut and a sweet violet.

Kent Stever presented the best of Winona's flowers to his high school sweetheart. He's wishing today he could visit that West End Greenhouse again—to bring home a well-deserved bouquet to that same girl, now in Lakeville.

Steamboat Days: "Happy Days for Many"

Steamboat Days—the ever-glorious, five-day summer festival of July.

We saved our nickels for the arrival of the "carni" (carnival) for rides, nickel-tossing at plates and the Penny Arcade. We were thrilled to be a part of the Grande Parade on a steamy Saturday afternoon with thirty thousand viewers and a thousand participants. Most came from within a fifty-mile radius of Winona—from Spring Valley, Arcadia, Lewiston, Kellogg, St. Charles, Caledonia, and all the little towns along the river in between.

LaCrosse and Minneapolis and other big cities sent us the best of their bands and their marchers, including the St. Paul Boy Scout Hi-Lex Drum and Bugle Corps and Hi-Lex Gnomes with their curly-topped helmets. We had calliopes, floats, and six-foot-tall bicycles. Shriners showed us their motorcycle tricks. Others of them shimmered in tall, colorful and festooned fez hats as they marched in step to their rousing brass band.

In 1953, the Lanesboro Daughters of Norway float won first prize, with the Bub's Brewery "Pirates" float in second place. St. Martin's Church sponsored the Lutheran Radio Hour Program float. Clowns of the Chatfield Clown Club touched the crowd, leaving a balloon and an impression. The Morgans (senior and junior) rode their 1900s-era high-wheeled bicycles along the parade route.

The Mahlke Baking Company brought Uncle Remus to town to read his stories to children on their float. Fountain City sent us their delightful American Legion German Band. And the Jacob Schmidt Brewery of St. Paul offered the colorful Schmidt's Indian Band. At the end of the "gigantic" hour-long parade, with an assortment of saddle clubs and horse drawn wagons, there were "Horse, horses, and more horses."

Motorboat races on the river woke us on early Sunday morning, causing us (with sand in our eyes) to grab a bicycle and head for the levee. A full day of noise, speed, hydroplane boat mishaps, and free adventure awaited us, ending at dusk of Sunday evening. In 1953, with an atomic bomb-like blast as finale to the evening fireworks show from the bathing beach directly across the river, we ended an enjoyable, full day from our grass seats on the levee.

The night before we had enjoyed a Hollywood-like show and queen coronation at the program platform built out over the river at the foot of Center Street. On Sunday afternoon, it became the high-above-the-river starter's gate for motorboat races. Green flags, red flags, checkered flags, Sno-Cones, friends, and Art Sultze's delicious popcorn made our afternoon and early evening complete. Art hollered across from his parked trailer's sound system speaker as we passed, "You buy the popcorn, we'll put the butter on free!"

The Upper Mississippi has a long history of steamboats, paddle wheelers, and trade. David G. Bates piloted keelboats in 1819 to Galena, Illinois, to haul lead from the mines. He also piloted the *Rufus Putnam* in 1825 to Fort Snelling, the first ever to supply the fort by boat.

Joseph Throckmorton came to trade with Native Americans in 1824 in the Red Rover. He purchased the *Winnebago* and later the *Warrior*, and spent over fifty years on the river, owning ten boats.

Daniel Smith Harris was a "cub-pilot" to Captain Bates in 1829. Harris built the first steamboat of Upper River construction, the *Joe Davis*, and piloted twenty others. He ended his career with the sinking of the *Grey Eagle* at Rock Island in 1861.

There wasn't a popcorn stand on the levee in 1851, when Captain Orrin Smith landed his steamer *The Nomonie* on Wapasha's Prairie. He may have landed on the sanded flat with some early settlers. By the spring of 1852, however, he landed upriver a bit with three hundred and fifty immigrants coming from New York to claim land at Rollingstone. Captain Frank Fujina, experienced river captain in Winona, claimed in "Ol' Man River," his news column one hundred years later, that the route may have taken Smith past the levee's Indian mounds, Wild's Landing and the Stone House to bypass Fountain City, passing through Dark Slough onward to Rollingstone Slough and landing at the base of the Rollingstone Dam.

Captain Hunter in his tenure particularly liked the steamer *Mark Twain*, but served part of his forty years on the steamer *Capitol*. The *Capitol*, "the fastest boat ever on the upper river," came for an original "Steamboat

Day" on July 27, 1920, transporting hundreds from Maiden Rock to LaCrosse and back. Passengers were thrilled with a four-hour stopover in Winona for shopping. The downriver trip from Winona to LaCrosse in the late afternoon would rival their record two hour and fifteen minute turn of the paddlewheels. It was stated that, "In comparison to railroad fares to Winona, the [round trip] rates are ridiculously low."

The steamboats didn't make it to the levee for the first Steamboat Days, save for the simulated paddle wheeler *Avalon*; offering its "last cruise of the year" just before Labor Day of 1948. The huge and realistic *Avalon* was a frequent visitor to river towns. Sedate daytime cruises were offered, as well as evening cruises on the shimmering river.

Adults liked the one-armed bandits and gambling available once the gangplank was lifted. Teenagers liked to join the moonlight cruises for $1.50 each. The offer of exciting company and the promise of illegal beer (not included in the ticket price) served at mid-river was too much to resist.

In the first Steamboat Days Celebration of 1948, Captain Walter Hunter of Bellevue, Iowa, the dean of Upper Mississippi River river men, gathered with Captain Frank Fujina and others for a banquet. He stated that "the river is a young man's field; the river doesn't need old men." He would know, having started as deck hand in the 1870s at age thirteen at Pepin—where he landed "after being kicked out of school in eighth grade at Menomonie." His starting pay of thirteen dollars per month was raised to thirty dollars per month as watchman and then beyond three hundred dollars per month as the captain with a master's license in the 1890s.

About the time of our first Steamboat Days, my adventurous, one-legged, seventeen-year-old brother raised on Grandpa's farm at Dakota took a run at being a deck hand on the *Alexander MacKenzie*. Like Captain Hunter had done at Pepin, Bob joined onto the crew

A steamboat at the levee. (Photo courtesy of Pieces of the Past, Winona Historical Society.)

at the boat's downriver stop at Dresbach Lock and Dam Number Seven. Walking the narrow, high and greasy catwalks day and night took him forward and back on the many barges. It was too much of a physical challenge through his six-hours-on, six-hours-off schedule. His artificial leg was discovered. The captain a short week later at Rock Island, Illinois, graciously released him. Bob grabbed a bus back to Dakota and reports today, "It was an interesting week nonetheless." Wow!

From its inception in 1948 by the Winona Activity Group, the new "Steamboat Days" was a hit. Events were created, buttons/badges were sold and folks came from far and wide. The first event was seen to be a "warm-up show to the 1949 Minnesota Territorial Celebration."

And celebrate they did. The listing of events over a typical Steamboat Days five-day period included nightly band concerts and vaudeville entertainment at the levee, fireworks, Grande Parade, carnival, dog trials at Prairie Island, Country Club card tournament, bait casting, archery, photo contest, Tommy Bartlett Ski Show, dance and golf contests. Three hundred square dancers did their called "eights" or "squares" in front of the post office on Main Street on Saturday evening.

Becky Morgan and her baton twirlers were pictured performing in the parade while passing by Archie's Fine Foods on Third and Main. Wally Valentine of Wally's Dinner Club in Fountain City joined the "flyers" in the motorboat races, along with Winonans Dr. John Tweedy, John Bittner, and Rudy Ellings. With 15,000 fans, waters churned with hydroplane twists and flips, power surges, and sharp turns. Local community leaders and regular boaters joined on calmed waters for the Sunday evening boat parade preceding the fireworks, and then anchored at mid-river for the bombastic fare.

John Foreman, illustrious musician and salesman of Edstrom's Music Store, was chair of the beard-growing contest of 1951. The female quasi-judges declared John's effort as "kinda like seeing a blond beard." Charles Berry was "like a much-beloved Santa Claus" and others were described as "dapper and distinguished, charming, so well trimmed, and Paul Bunyan-like." Howard Clark, erstwhile contestant and local insurance agent, was found to be "one of the eight best." Prizes totaled thirty-five dollars, with intent to have "pioneers" start their beards six weeks in advance to "emphasize the neatly trimmed, smart numbers," according to John Foreman.

The first event, in 1948, was also the year of "two queens and two attendants"—one for home activities and one to represent the city at the Minneapolis Aquatennial Parade and queen contest, also in their beginning years.

A hydroplane racer in the 1950s. (Photo courtesy of the Winona Newspaper Project.)

The only evident criticism of the first event of 1948 was by "Steve," a well-known resident sage and writer of letters to the editor. Well-meaning, he just wondered why "there are no steamboats evident."

Merchants of Winona decorated store windows throughout the downtown area in contest for best prize. The air was electric in the fashion of the carnival's cotton candy expanding before our eyes. From morning 'til midnight, streets were filled with shoppers and visitors and partygoers. It was a festive time for the entire community, with so much to do, so much to see.

True to their roots, Siebrecht's Floral Store on Third Street won first place in the downtown window-decorating contest of 1951. Their miniature river, with the steamboat *Southern Belle* passing through, was set amidst "home-grown" greens and fresh flowers. Not to be outdone completely, Winona Paint and Glass around the corner won second prize of fifteen dollars for their "mermaids in an underwater scene, surface water sports and a carnival scene."

The real carnival scene of 1949 was set on Main Street. My first ride on the Ferris Wheel had me observing the alleyway and the second story over the Hurry Back Billiard Parlor containing Kegler's Bowling Alleys. The only condition Main Street merchants requested of the city council was to ask "management to prevent carnival crews from living on the street." At the

The Tilt-A-Whirl was just one of many attractions available at Steamboat Days. (Photo courtesy of the author.)

tented carnival, with corn diggers, dart-tossing at balloons in a small booth for teddy bear prizes, shady side shows, a nickel toss, merry-go-round, Tilt-A-Whirl, and Caterpillar there was more than one could handle—especially if the nickels were limited.

The Steamboat Days' spell was there when, with younger members of the audience hanging from trees and others gathered on plank seats set up on Center Street bricks in 1949, "Over 5,000 Hear Concert." The one-hundred-fifty-member Winona Civic Chorus "owned" the entertainment platform, the evening and the audience. Covering one hundred years of music at the Levee Park concert, it was "A Grand Night for Singing." The beauty of musical offerings was occasionally "punctuated by the staccato sounds of motorboats in the river and the cries of pop-corn and soft-drink hawkers." It was the same year that the Tommy Bartlett Show skiers from Florida returned for a second time for their free (to viewers) water ski show of layered performers, ski jumps, and stunning, huge and powerful ski boats.

In 1951, the *Republican-Herald* announced, "Two Rivermen Named as Steamboat Days Royalty." Representing the river skippers of so many years past, Skipper Howard Clark and Mate William Thurow took their years of experiences as river and safety leaders to guide us. Skipper Clark came from a background in the U.S. Navy, becoming the first of Winona's trainers of U.S.

Coast Guard boating safety classes. Clark and Thurow would spearhead a meeting with sixty-five other experienced river men at a noon luncheon at the Hotel Winona.

Many of the shows over the years involved Winona talent, but occasional appearances by professionals punctuated the offerings. The ten-member female cast of *Vogues of Manhattan* brought us their Chicago-based stage show in 1954. Local artists often performed and drew huge crowds for evening events. The only concern expressed on the still, warm nights at riverside in the valley was for "mosquito control."

The Steamboat Days celebration has now continued for over sixty-five years, with iterations, changes of venue and additions and contractions. The current committee offers a parade down Broadway from St. Charles Street to Main Street. There is excitement and opportunity with a "Carnival at the Levee," boat races on Lake Winona (recently removed from program), a beverage tent or two, car show, queen contest, softball games, road race, "Kids' Power Pedal Pull," kids' fishing contest, craft show/flea market, tennis, buttons and the still beautiful fireworks. But the pull of the crowd to downtown and to the river is somehow absent.

The river men and downtown merchants appear to have folded their boats.

How I loved watching it all—the river, the events, the people, the parade and the overall five-day scene. It was about a mood, a festivity, and a joy of life. "Lefty" Himes, "Voice of the Outdoors" columnist of the *Republican-Herald*, offered in 1953: "the river affords an ever-changing view that often reflects satisfactorily the mood of the watcher." Observing a passing towboat in July, he continued, "Dreaming perhaps of the adventures steamboat men experienced, the lad on the dock has completely forgotten his fishing," as the darkly colored towboat *Socony* passed by the levee.

He spoke for many when he offered: "The river with its far-reaching spell is the thing that makes Steamboat Days happy days for many."

Chapter Four

Crossing the Monkey Bars: Seeking Purchase at Hillside

In the woods too, a man casts off his years, as the snake his slough, and at what period soever of life, is always a child. In the woods, is perpetual youth. . . . He who is not everyday conquering some fear has not learned the secret of life."

–Ralph Waldo Emerson, Nature, *1836*

We were on our way to the woods.

The sun was shining brightly with a promising blue sky all the late July day. It was another day for hiking over and around the bluffs of our beloved Mississippi River valley. It was a day to carry a canteen on a belt holder and a rucksack grab bag of essentials on my back, tied with a rope across my chest. I needed both of my hands free for grabbing and climbing in the high hills.

Davey was similarly equipped since we had together gained our outdoor essentials at the U.S. Army/Navy Surplus Store on Second Street. Mr. Roberts, the owner, let us buy all manner of World War II military items returned (often unused) from across the seas. In our cellar stash we had a machete and hand grenade (welded shut), knives and rope, helmets, hatchet, tent and carriers, record and plot books and self-assigned military decorations of rank–along with *G.I. Joe* and *Sad Sack* comic books. Mr. Roberts's daughter Shari was a special friend who made our hearts do flips in fourth and fifth grade classes–and on the playground.

Davey and I shared the same German-Lutheran Wisconsin Synod church, school, neighborhood, classrooms, and teachers. With added after-school forays into his underground cellar, entered only through the outdoor folding "trapdoor" leading down a short cement staircase, or into the old shed of my backyard, we were forever together.

His house was easier to get to after school, since it was right across the street from the school playground and kitty-corner from Deilke's Grocery Store, where we often hung out for a Pepsi or popsicle. His ma was always at home after school to greet us and offer a peanut butter sandwich or cookie. She was a strong woman—with an even stronger smile of welcome that put son and visitor at ease.

We were talking about Shari again as we started across the lake. We stopped at the lake bridge opening between the east and west parts of Lake Winona to take a look at happenings, of which there were usually none—unless some lucky duck hauled in a northern pike. It was the place where we usually fished. Best to be there, or at the end of Dacota Street under the big cottonwoods, early in the morning or near sundown, when mosquitoes usually kept us company.

Today was going to be a hot one. Our first stop was at the hand pump across the lake at the base of the hill known as Garvin Heights. In Bluffside Park, we filled our canteens with the cool water hand-pumped from the underground depths of limestone. Our intended trek for the day was to follow the old trail of crumbling cement steps from the park to the top of the hill.

The winding, narrow, two-lane road could be followed, but the straight-up path someone had created fifty or more years ago was the less traveled path. It was a real, unmet challenge—even to strong ten-year-old muscles. Our goal was to get to the top, take a look at the city from our four-hundred-foot perch and then explore the backside of the hill. We would be fortified by a few of Davey's ma's cookies, a can of Vienna sausages and a couple of Schumacher's wieners (each) to be roasted over a small fire built upon achieving the crest of the hill.

The first steps up the hillside were relatively easy. The lower third of the steps was a shortcut up to the road. Thanks to frequent use, it was relatively free of brambles. Having reached about one-third of the height of the hill, we crossed the hill road to continue our path upward. By the time we entered the sumac and brambles of the upper side, we were in for a significant challenge. Weeds were overgrown. Steps had become more deteriorated and covered with fallen limestone scraps. Our climb seemed steeper—and a bit treacherous.

We were virtually standing straight up, while simultaneously getting a grasp and bending our scrawny legs around growth to push-pull our way upward. We hadn't made thirty yards upward beyond the road when we virtually ran out of breathing room, steps and handholds. The cool summer breeze of lakeside had been replaced by an open-furnace, high noontime heat coming off the limestone facing.

How anyone could have built the original trail and steps was inconceivable. Washouts and limestone leavings left us with few solid stepping stones. Striding upward was soon replaced by hand-over-hand pulls up the slope, not unlike crossing the monkey bars of the school playground. The only difference was that we were now hanging on a couple of hundred feet in the air. Davey took one slide downward about ten feet or so, resulting in a strong scrape across his nose.

Using twisted limbs and unsteady foot holds, we managed to take a break on the top of a large rock outcropping. As we sat, I reminded Davey of the pictures of workers we had recently seen crossing the faces of Mt. Rushmore of the Black Hills of South Dakota. In a display on the second floor of the Winona Public Library, sculptors appeared to easily move—vertically and horizontally—in chorus with a tangle of ropes and block and tackle attached from above. No doubt they had some steel-toed boots. Our U.S. Ked "tennies" just weren't doing the job. We needed those heavy boots and a hundred-foot rope attached to our belts that was pinioned on the upper shelf of the hill. Where was our "go-to" plan?

We were reaching a point of no return. Previous experiences in the woods had us sliding on our backsides as we tumbled and slid down and through the snow. We had slipped on a trail of vegetation, leaves, and mushrooms on a dewy morning in autumn woods and slid downhill for a ways to stain our corduroys in tall grass. But we were relatively unhurt. This was a different kettle of fish into which we had ventured. We could not gain purchase by going upward—and our climb/slide down was nearly vertical. We were truly between a rock and a hard place.

Ralph Waldo Emerson (one of our favorites) said that fear needed to be faced. Author Judy Blume more recently observed what we already knew at age ten: "Each of us must confront our own fears, must come face to face with them. How we handle our fears will determine where we go with the rest of our lives—to experience adventure or to be limited by the fear of it."

We knew it intuitively. This was to be a learning experience not in the books and teachings of our third grade teacher, Grace McLeod. She kept our nose to the grindstone in arithmetic and cursive writing, but did little to spark the interests of ten-year-old adventurers. She certainly wasn't about ropes and Keds and high places. We were on our own.

As we sat, we established a target. About fifty yards to our right from our rock seat, we could see a draw with small trees seemingly growing out the sides of the hill and leading downward to the road. We needed to do a sideways venture. As we approached the draw, we could take the ropes from our kits, toss the kits downward for later recovery and tie the ropes together to give us flexibility and support as we moved downward.

It would be a shared mission of joined hands and tossed ropes. Coaching and apprising one another, we drifted sideways to reach toward our target cut out of the limestone facing. The shared rope length was good and sufficient as we tossed it over a branch at a time and lowered away. Once gaining a foothold, the rope was tossed to the other. And so we worked for what seemed an eternity—steadily teaming and encouraging and knowing our downward path. The greatest joy was to drop the final eight feet or so to land in the soft limestone ditch at roadside.

As we munched on hot dogs made over the fire pit of Bluffside Park, we were pleased with our effort. Even though we didn't reach the pinnacle, we had learned a lesson of value. Crunching Ma's cookies, we were affirmed again by our friend Emerson when he offered: "When a resolute young fellow steps up to the great bully, the world, and takes him boldly by the beard, he is often surprised to find it comes off in his hand, and that it was only tied on to scare away the timid adventurers."

Kent O. Stever wanders yet the hillsides and woods of his youth. He likes Emerson—and sometimes thinks of singer Bette Midler's song "The Rose" as he pushes and pulls through life.

"It's the heart afraid of dying, that never learns to dance; It's the dream afraid of waking, that never takes the chance; It's the one who won't be taken, who cannot seem to give; And the soul afraid of dying, that never learns to live."

Winona's Flying Liberators: The B-24 in World War II

Recently pondering a 2007 issue of *Big River Magazine*, I ran across a story that brought "World War II to Lake Pepin," or so the title suggested. Bob Parrott of Lake City wrote of the crash of a B-24 Liberator bomber being ferried from St. Paul to Kansas City with a three-man skeleton crew in 1944:

> It was a cold, snowy Friday afternoon, and a brief, squally snowstorm had kicked up over the lake. Less than half an hour into its flight, the plane circled low over Pepin, Wisconsin, and turned westward, possibly in an attempt to reach an emergency landing field at Frontenac, Minnesota.
>
> On December 15, 1944, there were no bombs falling or bullets flying—at least not in Minnesota—but the war was on everyone's mind. The front-page banner of the *Lake City Graphic* newspaper read, "One Week Nearer Victory."
>
> Full-page ads encouraged people to "buy at least one extra $100 war bond over and above your regular purchases." Meat, butter, sugar, fruit, and alcohol were luxuries, and the local hardware store was suggesting practical gifts. People were planning for another wartime Christmas.
>
> At about 2:00 p.m. the plane went down, struck the ice and exploded in a mass of flames. It plowed a quarter-mile-long hole in the two-inch-thick ice, extending upstream from the point of impact. The plane was demolished by a second explosion as its wing tanks blew up.

A 1976 *Winona Daily News* story offered that the bomber, having left the St. Paul modification center after being turned over to a ferrying crew from the Thirty-third Ferrying Command at Kansas City, "hit the thin ice about three-quarters of a mile from the Pepin shore, burst into flames and sank in about twenty-five feet of water."

A descriptive eyewitness account of the crash cited:

> The plane came from the direction of Stockholm traveling down river. As it passed over Pepin it appeared that trouble had developed as the huge craft was losing altitude. Near the east outskirts of the village the plane momentarily appeared to begin working properly as it pulled up in a sharp climb.
>
> Like a wounded bird the plane seemed to stagger, stand motionless for a brief instant and then go into a slow spin, which increased in speed as it fell. The craft dived nose down into and through the ice.
>
> As it struck there was a loud crash followed by an immense explosion and flames which shot into the air 100 feet.

Big River reported that L.M. Potter of Pepin, Wisconsin, made a statement to Major Maynard Bauer, Army Air Corps Station Accident Officer on December 16, 1944. As recorded in the Army's report of the accident:

> The plane seemed to be climbing and when it was about one-half mile off shore, it began banking to the right, and the bank and turn kept increasing and the ship just kept spiraling down and crashed through the ice.
>
> It made a terrific crash and immediately after it hit, there was another explosion and smoke and flames erupted from the spot.

"The ship" was the B-24 Liberator. Introduced to the world in 1939, it ended World War II as the highest production heavy bomber of history with over 18,400 units, half of which were produced by the Ford Motor Company—at the rate of one every fifty-five minutes. The B-24 holds the distinction as the most-produced American military aircraft.

With a wingspan of 110 feet, length of sixty-seven feet, height of eighteen feet and top speed of 290 miles per hour, the B-24 carried a lot of Winona-area crewmembers throughout World War II. It moved into the Korean War of 1950, and was soon to be replaced by the B-29. The crew initially consisted of

A B-24 Liberator. (Photo courtesy of Wikipedia.)

eleven—pilot, copilot, navigator, radio operator, bombardier, nose turret, top turret, ball turret, two waist gunners and a tail gunner. Of the lost Lake Pepin plane, members were three: pilot, flight officer, and flight engineer.

Along the way, I discovered some of the brave young men of the Winona region who were touched by the B-24.

- Adolph Bremer, Winona's "Outstanding Young Man of 1950," served as bombardier on the B-24. City editor of the *Republican-Herald* and a B-24 veteran, he was shot down over Belgium, landing behind enemy lines to find his way home to safety. Wounded in action, he received the Purple Heart. At home, he served as district commander of the American Legion.
- Master Sergeant Irvin W. Schildknecht of Winona served as B-24 navigator. Attaining the rank of major, he returned to permanent rank as master sergeant and served as the air force recruiter of the LaCrosse area in the early 1950s.
- Captain Gerald Baarsch of Spring Valley was pilot of a B-24 heavy bomber in the European theater, participating in the Berlin airlift. He earned the Distinguished Flying Cross and Air Medal with three oak clusters.
- First Lieutenant Bill Brown of Omaha, a Distinguished Flying Cross and Air Medal recipient, was a frequent visitor to and relative of Winonans—

and new team leader as pilot of his B-24. He remembers his thirty-five missions over Germany as a member of the 93rd Bombing Group, also known as "Ted's Traveling Circus." He graciously verified and documented personal experiences for this story at age ninety-three.

- First Lieutenant Walter Mimetz of Arcadia piloted the B-24.
- David Morse of Winona was B-24 gunner for thirty-six months in the Fifth Bomber Group. Crashing in Luzon, Morse received the Silver Star and Purple Heart for his wound and for leading survivors out of enemy territory.
- Sergeant Hubert Mrozek was a flight engineer in the B-24 and B-29, stationed in the South Pacific.
- Ray Meyer, amiable host of Winona restaurants, was B-24 pilot for thirty-five missions.
- Al Francois of Peerless Chain was a B-24 commander.
- Dr. James Kahl, veterinarian of local note, was a pilot of the B-24 in the Eighth Air Force, England, leaving active service as a lieutenant colonel.
- Dr. Cleve Gruber, Goodview chiropractor, completed forty-three missions as navigator.
- Jack Ollom, chief pilot for Watkins, Inc., served with the Eighth Air Force in England as commander of a B-24 Liberator squadron from 1939 to 1945. After earning the Distinguished Flying Cross with two clusters and Air Medal with five clusters, he joined Watkins as chief pilot of their twin-engine Beechcraft. While at Watkins and after "more than a million air miles," he nearly met his maker in a 1951 scene—not unlike that of the B-24 crash of Lake Pepin with a "nightmarish escape out of a crashed airplane and a subsequent three-mile trek to safety across the icebound Mississippi River near Dresbach." Soon thereafter, Ollom and Watkins took delivery of a reliable DC-3 for worldwide executive travel.
- Lieutenant Colonel Robert Foley of Wabasha flew the B-24, B-25, and B-29 after his beginnings at St. Thomas College in 1939 and Air Force training in 1940. By 1955, he was appointed to command the South Air Material Area of the Pacific (based in the Philippines at Clark Air Force Base). His son Michael was appointed to the U.S. Air Force Academy in 1959, to carry on the Air Force heritage and tradition. Robert was caught in a railroad car in LaCrosse in 1933 with another fourteen-year-old, having apparently hopped a train to ride the rails from Wabasha to LaCrosse. His well-known brother, Eugene, also of Wabasha, served his military time and headed for Washington. Their brother Dan gave many years after his service, eventually

serving as national commander of the American Legion. During World War II, three of the boys and father John, Sr., were all in the military service. John had married and settled in Wabasha as county attorney in 1915.

- Colonel Edwin Ambrosen, native Winonan, became pilot of the Liberator after training in 1940. He flew fifty combat missions and gained four thousand flying hours after stints at Purdue and the University of Minnesota. He became commander of the 455th Bomb Wing. By 1966, Colonel Ambrosen commanded all Air Force Reserve units in seven southwestern states. In active service, he earned the Distinguished Flying Cross, Air Medal with five clusters, Silver Star and Air Force Command Medal.

This is but one small story of a named few who gave years of their lives to protect our freedom. They were the Liberators. Thousands from our area served, others gave their lives—all needing to be recognized at lakeside bandshell ceremonies, in our stories and in personal, quiet moments.

The dedication and expertise of Winona's young men in the B-24 (and others like them on ships and in battlefields) led us to final victory. We are proud of their contributions, the heritage they engendered and the legacy we find hard to duplicate.

World War II indeed came to Lake Pepin and to Winona.

Our "hometown heroes" protected our freedom, and must be remembered for their unparalleled dedication and personal sacrifice.

Ted's Traveling Circus—The B-24 in Battle

In 2013, former First Lieutenant Bill Brown spoke gently of leading his "lucky crew." The W.M. Brown crew, serving in the Eighth Air Force, stayed together for the duration of their assignment from July 1944 through March 1945. They were in the Second Wing, 93rd Bomb Group, 328th Squadron of B-24s. They were "lucky" in that none of the eight members of the crew received a Purple Heart in their thirty-five combat missions over Germany.

The 93rd Bombardment Group (Heavy) originated in 1942 at Barksdale Air Force Base, Louisiana. Sent to the newly constructed Hardwick Air Base five miles west of Bungay, Norfolk, England, their first mission of October 9, 1942, was a strike against a locomotive manufacturing facility in Lille, France, led by Colonel Ted Timberlake. From that point forward, the 93rd went on to three hundred and ninety-six missions, ceasing operation on April 30, 1945, with the total

Eighth Air Force stand down and the end of the war. Victory in Europe (V-E Day) was declared on May 8, 1945. The 93rd returned to Sioux Falls, South Dakota, Army Air Field to be converted into a B29 group.

According to Lieutenant Brown, the "original loss rate [of planes and crews] was forty-five to fifty percent." Twenty-five combat missions was the required standard for pilot and crew. In 1944, General James Doolittle, leader of the Eighth Air Force, increased the requirement to thirty missions. Doolittle earned the Medal of Honor for his valor and leadership as commander of the Doolittle Raid over Tokyo in April 1942, while a lieutenant colonel. He is also noted for initiating instrument-guided flying. According to Lieutenant Brown, "the mission requirement was soon raised to thirty-five. Some chose to fly more."

Bill flew his "brand new ship" (which cost one-quarter of a million dollars) to England to be stationed in "the Bulge" or eastern part of England at Norwich-Hardwick Air Field. Lieutenant Brown had to sign for his plane upon leaving Topeka. He "traveled the North Route to Manchester, New Hampshire; Goose Bay, Labrador; Iceland and Greenland and on to Valley, Wales—where they "took my new plane away." He needed to turn in the plane upon arrival. Bill "demanded a receipt—and received one."

Plane 44-10511, which Bill flew from Topeka to Valley, Wales, in July, lasted only until September 27 of the same year, when it was shot down—with the pilot and three gunners killed in action and the remaining five crew members listed as prisoners of war.

Due to frequent travel, the 93rd Bomb Group was informally called Ted's Traveling Circus. One notable and "most dangerous mission" from Africa of the 93rd was the low-flying bombardment of the Ploiesti Oil Fields of Romania by one hundred and seventy-seven bombers, with many dangerous flights to Italy thereafter. At Ploiesti, nearly one-third of the planes and crews were lost. Total casualties for the mission were six hundred seventy men killed in action (KIA) or missing in action (MIA.) Traveling back and forth between England, Africa, and the Mediterranean, "the Circus achieved an unparalleled record."

The original B-24 crew had eleven members. Bill offered they had ten, which was cut back to eight (pilot, co-pilot, engineer, navigator, radio, nose gunner, tail gunner, upper turret gunner). The bombardier and belly gunner were eliminated before they arrived in England, with the switch to "pattern bombing." Lead planes of a strike force had smoke bombs attached to their wings and a bombardier on staff. When the lead planes dropped their smoke bombs, all dropped their payloads.

Lieutenant Brown completed thirty-five missions as pilot on February 23, 1945. He earned a Distinguished Flying Cross and Air Medal with five clusters. Bill's flights took him to approximately twenty-five distinct German cities, with seven doubles and one triple to Magdeburg. Bill remembers them all, but especially the "pea soup fog" takeoff to Hanau with a runway marked only by the headlights of radio Jeeps. The trip to Hamburg gained him a tree limb in the landing gear, a smoking engine, and "twenty-some holes elsewhere in the plane."

The Distinguished Flying Cross citation reads;

> For extraordinary achievement while serving as Pilots of B-24 airplanes on many bombardment missions over enemy occupied Continental Europe. Displaying great courage and superior flying skill, these Officers have materially aided in the successful completion of each of these missions and their actions are an inspiring example for their fellow flyers. The courage, coolness and exceptional skill exhibited by these Officers on all these occasions reflect the highest credit upon themselves and the Armed Forces of the United States.
>
> Signed Francis H. Griswold,
> Brigadier General, 25 March 1945

Lieutenant William Brown in 1945. (Photo courtesy of the author.)

His trip to Cologne caused him to return at diminishing altitude over the North Sea "on two and one-half engines" after taking heavy flak from the target area. "Three engines were replaced before this plane flew again," it was noted. Another incident caused him to land on three engines at a distant airfield. The next day, he was asked to take off to his home base on those three.

He agreed, but only if his crewmembers were sent ahead in another plane and if the flight leader requesting the flight would volunteer as co-pilot. After starting takeoff with locked controls and a smoking engine, causing his new co-pilot to scramble, Brown offered, "You can bet after that I never allowed anything except an item-by-item use of the takeoff check list."

Paralleling the experiences of many, a recent obituary in the local paper tells the story of a Lakeville B-17 gunner shot down in November of 1944 over Germany. Taking anti-aircraft fire, "The airplane caught on fire and we couldn't seem to get out. We were leaking fuel something terrible. There were so many holes in the wings, we expected to blow up. The pilot ordered the men to bail out before the engine fell out, and the pilot and bombardier remained in the plane when it crash-landed in France."

The parachutists bailed out over Nazi Germany, to be captured and placed in a POW camp. The co-pilot, a man of Jewish heritage, "was found by a German police officer who hung him [for being Jewish] in front of the men—a horrific scene that haunted the gunner throughout his life."

The gunner landed in a tree and broke both legs—never to receive treatment from his German captors. The Germans stripped the men to their underwear, interrogated them with threats and at times put one or the other in solitary confinement (a hole in the ground with boards covering it). Returned to the United States in April 1945, the ninety-pound, twenty-year-old gunner "had relied upon his faith to survive."

Awarded the Purple Heart and the Bronze Star, the young man went on to recover from his injuries and incarceration. He founded a gas station and successful Mack truck dealership and major diesel repair business, serving drivers of the Midwest. He was "a man of his word whom customers always knew followed through with his promises" and "the best father you could ever have."

After the allies took back Paris, they took my group out of combat temporarily," Bill told me. "Wood racks of flooring were built into the bomb bays of planes of the 93rd to fly loads of flour to Orly Air Base (Paris)." He said he was "a flour deliveryman." When the war ended and Bill was attending four-engine instructor school, all personnel were assembled and "told to raise our hand if we wanted to stay in the service." About one-third chose to stay. Bill stayed a while, going on to earn certificates as a pilot instructor in instrument training and four-engine training.

Bill fondly remembers his crew and their shared purpose of mission. The responsibility shown by his group of young men over the course of thirty-five harrowing missions was exceptional. Three members, including Bill, were senior at age twenty-four, with the balance of the crew even younger.

During an interview, Bill was asked whether he had considered being a commercial airline pilot. His response was, "People get killed in those things, you know." He returned to Omaha and to a secure position on the ground as an auditor for the Union Pacific Railroad.

Although seldom mentioned, war experiences were paramount in Lieutenant Brown's life. Reunions with fellow members of the 93rd Bomb Group across the nation have been highlights of his abundant life. He so enjoyed frequent trips after war years from Omaha to Winona, enjoying the beautiful entry toward Winona past the Arches and over Stockton Hill.

He is honored to have served his nation.

Helicopter Down

It was a good day for a nap. My injured back needed a rest.

So about noon on May 24, 2011, I took a few minutes on a beautiful spring day to lie down in the air-conditioned comfort of a lower bedroom of our comfortable lakeside abode. We have lived in the same glorious space for nearly forty years—a rustic, simple home in the midst of the burgeoning Twin Cities metropolitan area. We can leave our ski boat at the dock and be at the Mall of America or international airport within fifteen minutes.

A garden on the side of the house faces east, and a lake is background to our personal, south-facing hundred feet of lakeshore. An untouched, twenty-five acre swamp and personally created "park" sits across the street. We are in the heart of a setting not unlike that of the 1981 hit film *On Golden Pond*. My wife and I probably mimic today the cantankerous behaviors of Henry Fonda and Katherine Hepburn in their roles as Ethel and Norman Thayer.

Mr. Fonda and Ms. Hepburn each gave one of the greatest performances of their long, truly distinguished careers, and received Oscars. We don't perform, but we have the same love for our similar space. It is where we have had all manner of child raising and continuous outdoor enjoyment.

The cause of the back injury was overstraining from moving thirty-two-foot dock sections into place by myself—as I had done for so very many years. Who was to know that the muscles and back would finally rebel against the twists and tortures of weightlifting?

In my welcome mid-day rest, I always drift off to sleep after reading a chapter or two of another mystery. I had completed only the first several pages and was about to drift off when I heard the reassuring and comforting *thwap-thwap-thwap* of a helicopter flying over our house at treetop level. It was a sound to which we had become accustomed.

The arrival of the highly skilled pilot of the Metropolitan Mosquito Control District helicopter with his attached aerial sprayer is a near-weekly occasion through the rainy season. Enticed by it all, we drop our rakes or slow our lawnmowers to watch the exhibit of loops and turns across swamp and house and light poles. His is the dance of the two-winged barnstormer of another era. The skill in aeronautic maneuvering of his "Whirly-Bird" is consistently intriguing. With those nasty biters (the mosquitoes) having a travel path of over fifteen miles, reduction of their nests in our area and in nearby lakes and ponds is critical to the comfort of the much larger populace of the south metro area.

We are so fortunate to live on Lake Marion of Lakeville. With five hundred acres of water in our backyard (and sometimes more), we enjoy the wildlife—fox, deer, rabbits, turtles, opossum, raccoon, mink, doves, and birds at the feeder, muskrat, eagles, ducks, Canada geese (too many), and an occasional coyote join us from sunlight to midnight. We don't like the red squirrels, however.

We started early years with a little wooden paddleboat for two-person rides and for my personal, early-morning excursions to an offshore duck blind. Our power ventures began with an old four-horsepower Johnson motor and a twelve-foot Montgomery Ward fishing boat. We graduated to a fourteen-foot Alumacraft and new fifteen-horse Mercury after these many years. The main difference of the new version over our old motor(s) is that with advanced electronic start, I no longer take the skin off my fingers as I had done in pulling and pulling to start early, fix-up models.

We cycled through a stable of snowmobiles for winter rides that required similar starting issues and skinned knuckles, with a couple of runabouts for waterskiing used for training our four kids. We have now settled into a sedate, plush, pontoon boat style to take us on leisurely cruises that would suit Ethel and Norman Thayer. The boats were at rest at dockside as I rested inside on this soon-to-be eventful May day.

As I rested, my momentary repartee between sound and movement and accomplishment of the helicopter and its pilot was rhythmic and enjoyable. Dropping low over the house and lines, he let loose the spray of pellets into the swamp from treetop level to do a seemingly weightless turn to head back in the opposite direction with the power engaged. Having seen and heard the ballet so often, I was used to the cacophony of sounds. And then it stopped!

As the "chopper" was making its turn, the *thwap, thwap, thwap* of the rotor went soundless. Hobbling from my cot with my compressed back disc, I checked through the front window to see if the craft was falling from blue sky into the swamp had caused the sudden quiet. Not there. Turning around and heading out the sliding door to the lake and dock, I found the chopper's rotor sticking up out of the water about one hundred and fifty feet off shore—within fifty feet or so of our dock.

As neighbor Richard and I looked out simultaneously, he, with phone in hand, called 911. As I walked out on the dock, the pilot struggled through the water toward the dock's end and to me. I called to him and simultaneously waved at a passing speedboat filled with young adults. As they approached I waved them over to the pilot who, although injured, had been able to escape his underwater plexiglass bubble. He was yet able to semi-walk in throat-high water. Fortunately, he was quickly in water shallow enough to begin his struggle toward the shoreline.

Within minutes the wakeboarders, including two trained nurses, entered the water to secure the injured pilot to a wakeboard and the large back entry platform of their full-size ski boat. They were able to maneuver near shore where they transferred him to a two-inch by twelve-inch, ten-foot cedar plank I shoved out to them, giving support as he was floated to shore.

In moments to follow, paramedics and what seemed like every police official in the county arrived. Paramedics were quickly at work to secure the pilot and transfer him to the hospital for care of his injured back. In the next hour, every television station sent a broadcast truck and crew, as well as their

The helicopter's rotor in the lake. (Photo courtesy of the author.)

own helicopters, to film the scene. Our yard was overrun with medical and police officials, neighbors, visitors, and television crews. One could have set up a stand for concessions.

The Bell 47 helicopter piloted by Kevin Rossan, age thirty-seven, of Michigan, had engine failure as it turned out. Visiting the backyard nearly a year after his recovery, Rossan stated he needed to aim for the lake to avoid crashing into one of the houses surrounding the swamp. In other words, "When it became clear that a crash was imminent, the pilot aimed the Bell 47 helicopter toward the lake to minimize harm to the neighborhood," according to Dakota County Sheriff Dave Bellows.

The day was filled with extraction operations led by FAA officials—ongoing until well beyond the dinner hour. Visitors were many and frequent to our backyard, with some setting up lawn chairs to observe the operation. The helicopter was floated and pulled through the water by a large boom truck operating off our shoreline. It was ultimately lifted by a huge, second wrecker truck. From the shoreline it was carried to the street by the wrecker and transferred to a flatbed for transfer to facilities for further FAA review.

For several days thereafter, divers searched for parts of the aircraft and for any evidence of harm from the pesticide tanks. Fortunately, there was no imminent danger to lake or persons, with all tanks having been intact and secured.

Extracting the helicopter from Lake Marion. (Photo courtesy of the author.)

The Top of the Pole

Helicopters were crashing regularly in the 1960s, with the Vietnam War creating the bulk of the crashes. Forty-one were killed in a crash into a mountain in Vietnam in 1969. In addition, a rocket grenade brought down thirty-two American soldiers in a fifty-foot, fourteen-ton Chinook troop transport helicopter at Fire Base Judy near the Laotian border in 1970. With fifty-two killed and three hundred and fifty-eight wounded in battle that week, it was the first time since 1966 that American war dead was less than sixty for a week.

Chicago's "Copter Traffic Officer [was] Killed" in 1960, while broadcasting traffic conditions to drivers for radio station WGN. KSTP Radio of Minneapolis nearly lost reporter Stan Turner and Photographer Jerry McEowen in 1969, as they hit a wind gust upon landing at Red Wing's Prairie Island. They were "shaken up," with the pilot unconscious, but safe. At Los Angeles, the tragic loss totaled forty-four lives over a three-month period in 1968. Two commercial helicopters flying to Disneyland were lost on separate occasions.

Astronaut Eugene Cernan, backup commander of the Apollo 14 flight, was alone on a solo training flight when he crashed his helicopter in the Indian River of Florida in 1971—and escaped injury.

As with Captain Cernan, pilot Bill Dundas of the "Hell Thriller Act" at the Minnesota State Fair in August 1958 "hoped to get a new helicopter" in order to resume his work for state fair record-setting crowds. His act was for the precise placement of acrobat Darrell Hornbeck, twenty-three, of Dallas, on top of a one hundred twenty-five-foot pole in the grandstand. The crowd of eight thousand in attendance didn't know Dundas crashed after setting Hornbeck atop the pole, since he "landed on a darkened dirt stock car track away from the lights."

The grandstands where he crash-landed were filled the next day with a sellout crowd for a "100-mile stock car contest." It wasn't reported whether Hornbeck had been left on the top of the pole.

I had to wait for the next day to continue my nap. It was of necessity, having stayed up for all the television stories on the late news. Pictures I had taken were but a few of those to appear, having been transferred immediately from my camera to computer to television audience.

It was an interesting day for "Helicopter Down."

Chapter Five

The Circuitous Route: A Memoir

Do the Job

I was recently asked to begin an accounting of my life. It seems unbelievable that anyone would want to know the life story of a truck driver and educator—a consummate worker and decision-maker throughout life. Actually, I have a great deal to say. When asked about a topic of interest, I can literally go on for hours. All you have to do is ask me. Favorite themes seem to be about life, hobbies, family, and philosophical meanderings.

Somewhere I learned the expectation that the way to achieve and to provide for a family was to work hard. Whether in work of a physical nature at home, running the streets fifteen miles a week for years or being in the intellectual world of academia, I have done my work.

I remember a friend, Larrys, a shop teacher with whom I worked, who had a theme for all he encountered—students or others. They were to "Do the job." It wasn't anything complex or learned in a scholarly way. It was a message of simplicity to move ahead without excuses and get the job done. Whatever the job in life, I have lived a similar theme since childhood. It's the ability and interest to "do the job"—and to receive resultant wages for that day's work. A simple guidepost for me, work is good.

My counseling of students over the years, discussions with children at home, motivational techniques in developing new or old teachers always have taken the same steps. Do the job. Believe that you are special. Make a beginning. Stretch yourself. Whether facing an adversity of life or staring at a seemingly unattainable goal ahead, one can do it with perseverance, inner strength and support from others who make the difference in our lives.

In my conversations with kids, my own or others, I have discussed themes of "No excuses" and "Take the hard way." It is my thesis that the hard way takes us on a more circuitous route than the easy way. There is more to learn and more personal gain if we dip ourselves into the reality of life, the long way around. When combined with the adage of "One step at a time," we move toward achievement of our own volition.

In dealing with kids at school, my theme has always been, "It isn't Mother or Dad who decides our future. It is up to each of us. Parents can drop us off at the front door of the school, but each of us will decide how we interact with every person from that point on. If we choose to be into avoidance, we cut out. If we choose to be scholarly or thoughtful, that is our choice. Nobody tells us which way to turn, which way to respond." We personally need to do the job.

Where Did It Begin?

I really don't know. It's been a mystery for me over all of my life. Did it begin with seeing an older brother accomplish a goal through his own efforts and my following his lead? Did it begin with the teacher who told me that I performed well with speeches and presentations when I was in twelfth grade? She had high expectations of me.

Or did it begin with a mother I hardly knew? She could have been the greatest influence in my life. Messages implanted by her at age two or three or five seem to have become the guiding themes of my life. With her death at an early age, I may have already had a good beginning, to be reinforced by a father who raised us throughout the years. Whatever the truth, I am delighted to be at this point in my life where personal strength is all that I have to offer.

Some people around me looked for the easy way. They thought the world owed them a living, that it would all just fall into place since they were smart and life had been easy. They may have missed the message that for success to occur, one needs to blend attitude with ability—in other words, "do the job."

Over fifty years have passed since beginning a career in education. It has been a life of challenge, opportunity, hardship, and accomplishment. Did I really make a difference for others in holding to tenets of belief and commitment and response learned in my teenage truck-driving years? Was I wise in having "done the job"—accomplishing for self and family and organization?

Simply to Be

We are here for a reason. God placed us here. He provided us with a mission. The mission is often unclear, but if we step back and acknowledge that God will provide, then our sense of being will come into focus. We are not to decide, know or control all that has happened or is to happen. We are simply to be.

Teachers provided me with some themes. They were often supportive and encouraging. One of my earliest teachers, Miss Kjome, was with me in first and second grades. She encouraged and prodded and expected our best in reading and academics and behavior. When I left her classroom, the third grade teacher took over with a similar set of values, although the delivery was a bit more defined. Miss Kjome remained a lifelong friend.

My father's expectations were even clearer. A written warning on a report card sent by my third grade teacher about my "attitude" was immediately and directly clarified. I never needed another reminder. The teacher-coach who gave us a start in basketball after school in the gym, the parent Cub Scout leader, the neighbor ladies for whom we raked leaves, the sixth grade teacher all made a difference. They were teachers in a very real sense. Whether they were in the classroom or the neighborhood, their lessons were clearly defined, understood and appreciated.

Today we hear a lot about the "assets" youth need to possess in order to have sufficiently strong egos to make it in the world. These strengths are neither rocket science nor a new invention. Parents and teachers and neighbors shared their common values as we were growing. They used common sense and declared boundaries of behavior and expectation in combination with courtesy and respect to mold us in a form their hearts knew best. They built our assets.

I think of these traits as some of the characteristics that I took with me as teacher into my senior high classroom at age twenty-two. Those "children" were but a few years younger than I. Their needs were no different than mine in high school. I simply needed to remember how special I felt when the twelfth grade social science teacher complimented my speechmaking, presentation and organizational abilities.

Lessons of college teachers of mathematics and pedagogy and deviant behavior and earth science weren't lost. They were the required academic strengths that needed to be brought to bear on the lessons of the day. But in dealing with one hundred and fifty high schoolers per day, it wasn't the mathematics that was to get one through. It was simply to be.

The author as the principal of Lincoln High School in 1980. (Photo courtesy of the author.)

After thousands of days of working with young people in their teenage years and environments, I am often asked whether things have "gotten tougher" over generations. I think not. The issues have certainly changed, but the same basic emotions and behaviors prevail. Quality teachers are still doing excellent work. Student needs remain fixed. Less than top-notch academic students can still be brought forward with encouragement and prodding and love.

"What you see is what you get." "Be what you are." Kids are keen observers of people and the depth of care and respect shown toward them. They want to be challenged and led to limits—and complimented for the good that is within them. They see who we are.

In my early days there was a support system built around me by teachers who cared. It was extremely important to my development and to other children I knew. Teachers cared and exemplified. I saw them, heard them and listened.

Many times in my career I have been faced with experienced teachers in high schools I served who were teachers of biology or mathematics or typewriting. Those several didn't seem to share in the perspective that they were teachers of children. Rather than following the ways of the heart, some teachers followed the learnings of university professors who hadn't gone "eyeball to eyeball" with a teenager in the whole of their career.

I think these teachers (and professors) were afraid to step out and let their personality show through. They were afraid to be vulnerable in losing a few inches of power off the pedestal they had built for themselves. If you didn't meet the pre-determined line of the teacher, you were cast off.

If you were a troublemaker, you were gone as quickly as possible. If you skipped class, you were removed for lack of attendance. These were processes and procedures common and strengthened through conversations by teachers in faculty lounges on a daily basis. The demise of difficult students was assured.

It isn't about "winning" through subject memorization. It's about nurturing and developing young people.

A Vignette—On the Road

Today's meeting is at 6:15 a.m. Last night's meeting lasted until 10:45 p.m. With a commute home and a moment to read the daily mail, it had been a short night of slumber. Even though it is a pattern created over more than twenty years, it is still exhausting. A schedule of early morning meetings, full days of managing a thriving senior high school and late night conferences take their toll. Enthusiasm for helping others and the excitement of building one's own school and environment are often bridled by the realities of cumulative stress.

Today is crisp and clear. With the temperature in the single digits, it is a typical winter day in Minnesota. The driveway crunches as my vehicle takes me on an early morning drive in the dark. Slowly driving off around the frozen swamp in the neighborhood, I am delighted with the sight of a winter hare at the roadside.

Each of my days starts with the beauty of this countryside, the natural treat of deer cautiously peering out on early morning headlights, of frost on cattails, of geese sailing off for an early morning feed, or the smells of the country. These are special moments in my day—enriched by the simplicity of natural renewal. More often than not, my morning drive to the freeway is calming and therapeutic.

The thoughts of personal matters ahead are pushed back as nature prevails. These are moments to be savored at the beginning of each day. Ahead lie new adventures of personal enrichment and challenge. Each day is new in the issues presented for consideration. I look forward to the 6:15 meeting.

Resiliency

It's a new day. I begin again. This is not a statement of fact as much as a philosophical belief endured throughout life. Experience has shown me that our spirits are inherently renewed with each new day. The degree of ability of a person to endure the issues of the previous day and yet be able to renew after a night's rest is astounding. We simply go out and hit it again.

That essence of renewal is resiliency. Our ability to rebound, to recoil and to become again buoyant in the face of a new day is within us. It is a belief that "This too shall pass." We will renew ourselves again. We can endure challenges and hardships and difficulties to the point of breaking and, remarkably, awake refreshed and ready to do it again. If one can understand and practice the belief that rest and resiliency take over to renew us when we complete a particular day or challenge, then our growth will continue.

Resiliency is a visualization experience, incumbent upon the belief that you will continue, you will endure, you will persevere in a reality of positive outlook. Somewhere it came to me. Bills will be paid. Challenges of children and work relationships will pass if one has an inner strength to let go of today's worries and have a higher belief. It is so basic.

God will provide. The good will out. There has to be a bottom-line that good will prevail. Good is measured in the quality of work that we do. To do less is to cheapen oneself. Good is measured in the way that we treat people—all people. We are not to be selective in forming relationships only with a certain group or social strata. We are intended to meet all people as equals.

My earliest thoughts of that demonstration of equality and internal self-management came to me from the way that I was treated as a child—as an equal in every way. Rich or poor, each of us had the opportunity to succeed. Fast or slow, there was always merit in who we were as people.

Grandma treated us as equals; there were no favorites. The barber, Dick, made one feel like a very special human being when we sat in his chair at the earliest of ages. Next to his shop, Mr. Schumacher the German butcher welcomed us to his meat market as "the kids in the bald-headed row." He joked and spoke and radiated joy in having us in his presence. The bus driver on the town bus line treated us more as friend than as customer or "kid."

The folks to whom we delivered our newspapers and from whom we collected the bill respected us as young businessmen with a job to do—and offered rewards for a job well done. The owner of the small grocery store let us "hang out" outside the store with our eight-cent Pepsi or purchase of penny candy—or even no purchase at all. Pa entrusted us to clean the shed or paint the house and prepare our meals. There was not shouting or criticism or "put-downs" by adults in this environment.

A focus on resiliency began my thoughts. It has led me to the understanding that we are resilient because we have cultivated an inner strength. That confidence causes us to take on (and not avert) the hardships. It's just putting one foot in front of another. With inner strength and belief, we can do the next thing. Running a marathon or skydiving or creating a major planning document for a school district each has a common element, knowing that we can do it—and getting started.

A Vignette—Closing the Door

This is the last time to turn the key in the door of my office, my last day to be "in charge" of anything official—after thirty-five years of doing so. It is a rainy day on the second day of summer, the second day of my retirement yet to be "official" on July 1.

As these new days begin, I experience my "last" moments in public education: my last day in the office, the last quiet evening rest on my office couch before beginning my last presentation to the board of education. These are moments that cause me to reflect upon the many times that I have been at the office, the multitude of evening meetings, the early morning rise to get there ahead of everyone else—as a beginning math teacher, as an ambitious young assistant principal, as the new principal in charge of three separate buildings and programs over more than twenty years, and as a research director intent upon creating a new "data-driven" design for the entire school district.

How Do They Decide?

Throughout the years, I have regarded myself as a teacher and parent first. The learning necessary to accomplish budgets, operations, systems and dealing with personal and emotional issues of the school environment have been grounded in the simplicity of caring for kids and families. None of the procedures or systems have been complex. The complexity has been in trying to find ways to connect with kids and their needs on a personal level, in supporting families with needs and in finding ways to motivate the sometimes-unmotivated students and teachers.

The question on my mind as I woke today relates to the violence of schoolchildren. Where did the anger and violence and death generated by them come from? Who is the culprit that put semi-automatic guns into the hands of young people? What developed emotionally within them that caused mayhem and destruction of schoolmates, parents and teachers? Why is their intent of destruction directed to the very people who are friends—there to help and guide and nurture? Is there something that I know? Could I offer an insight that would explain it? Does the answer have anything to do with my experiences and with the place called school?

I am not a trained psychologist with a plethora of theories and models of explanation. Like those professionals, I have studied the theoretical, taken the coursework, read the texts, gained the degrees and calculated the statistics. Fortunately, for my own wellbeing and application of everyday realities, I have concentrated more on the goodness of grandmothers than the theories of Dr. Spock. I have not dwelled on the data or looked for the answers within books and charts and Ritalin applications. I have simply looked next door or out the window.

When the young neighbor boy pushed his mother into the bathtub at age ten or so, I knew something wasn't right. When I heard the words out of the mouths of girls in the hallways of the high school at 7:00 a.m. and had them repeated outside my front door by neighbor kids at night when they should have been at home under parental care, I knew something wasn't right. As I counseled the young man or young lady the next day in my office who was referred after others hadn't resolved an issue, I heard that parents weren't there, that teachers didn't care or that kids "just want to be bad."

I knew something wasn't right. When I conversed with some of the most troubled kids and attempted their resolution and integration back into a school where they didn't fit, particularly after their ten-week drug treatment program, I found these young people often had a greater depth of life awareness than the parent or teacher with whom I counseled the hour before or after. What's wrong with this picture?

The problem today, yesterday or so many years ago hasn't been the kids. In recent, retired years I have yet been in the classrooms with them—as many as fifty days a year. As a continuous teacher for fifty years and the guide to thousands of young people as a junior and senior high principal, I will state unequivocally that kids haven't changed at all. They are as pliant and interested and motivated as they have ever been.

They are warm and caring and delightful, one at a time or in groups of thousands. They will go where we lead them. They will learn what we teach them. That is not to say that they don't have minds of their own. Indeed they do, and we should honor the individuals and his or her collective strengths. And what should we teach them? That's up to us.

It's the Teachers

As teachers, we often insist that the subject matter being taught is the do-all, be-all of life. It's the stuff of life of many secondary school teachers. Having observed and evaluated hundreds of teachers over my career, it is safe to say that there are just too many who teach the stuff of their curriculum as the manna of life.

Selected students in front of these teachers are bored, disinterested and uninvolved. They are neither motivated nor encouraged. Other students who "get it" are the featured ones who are brought forward as samples of success. The others simply fail, skip class and get kicked out of class and school because they don't attend or behave. And why should they? Who cares? The teacher gains a more suitable class environment when they have excluded enough of these troubled youth.

I am reminded of the time that I was speaking with one of the leather-jacket kids from the high school headed for his "vo-tech" classes at mid-morning. He stopped by my office for a moment to express himself. He was livid. He had just left the office of his school counselor—an intended (and experienced) liaison and representative for the vo-tech kids and their issues. In spite of the student's jewelry hanging from his exposed body parts, he was able to express himself clearly with words that would shock the gentry.

Expecting comfort and support, he had been totally rebuffed by the words and actions of that counselor. Most telling to me was the statement that college-bound students who visited this counselor were offered a seat in the office, whereas vo-tech students were expected to speak from the doorway—and not offered a seat. I often wondered why I had so many occasions over the years when I was a resource for students who had been rejected by their learned teachers and counselors, who were trained specifically in handling those student needs—and in being their first-line advocates.

Teachers (and counselors) will insist that this doesn't occur within their classrooms or offices. Of course it doesn't—in the classrooms of the truly professional teachers and guides. They are nurturers and intellectual trail guides who deserve the very best we can offer them in the way of support and reward. One can just feel it when you are in the presence of one of these true professionals. They are worth their weight in gold.

But children at all levels will tell you that it is with too-great frequency that the opposite is the reality. Do we listen to these unmotivated, disinterested, difficult children? Of course not. Instead, we listen to the teachers, through their powerful unions and legislative compatriots, who encourage teachers to gain even more "power," often used to exclude the most challenging, difficult students and make it a school for teachers—but not necessarily students.

It's the Parents

Our kids see us (and hear us) everywhere. From earliest moments of rising to moments of bedtime stories with little ones and late-night discussions with teenagers who arrive home late, our every movement is engaged and being observed. Kids can see right through us. They will tell us, and we well know, that it isn't just what we say. It's as much about how we say it and who we are over time. The words alone don't make the impression. It's our manners, our mannerisms, the words unsaid.

One former secretary told me that she believed she knew how I felt on a given day, simply by observing the way that I walked down the hall. Children observe us similarly: where we walk, how we talk, and what our body language means to them and to others with whom we have contact. They know if we like someone who stops by the door. They know, too, how real we are when we stop by their table to chat when they're doing homework or when we give one a pat or tap while seated in church. We're constantly communicating.

And what are we saying? What is our real communication with our children? Do we tell them we care about other people? Do we show that care by offering a can of food for the school food drive or by committing a moment or a dollar to our local church? Do we tell them how much we care for them and yet never take them for a quiet walk or a family camping trip or something equally simple?

Do we tell them to respect others and then have them hear us sounding off about the cop who gave us the well-deserved speeding ticket? Do we make real time for them, day after day, year after year? Our communication, verbal and otherwise, is about principles, consistency, fairness, encouragement and depth of relationship. We are not apart from them. We're among them. Choices made by and for our children along the way cause them to learn what is valued and what is not. From every occasion, every interaction, they carry away an impression and an understanding of the value we have for them.

Do we really buy these oversize houses and then set our kids off away from us in their own rooms with smartphones, videos, computers and Game Boys ad nauseum, so that they are never in our way? More than one child has talked about the loneliness in their own home—whether parents are there or not. They are just never invited to engage, so they find their own way.

I sometimes see it occurring between children in the same household. One is favored, tracked through activities, cheered on and held up as the "model." The other is virtually forgotten or ignored. How can this be? Why does this happen? Each wants to be inclusive in the family—for every day from birth to death. What will be the outcome for each of these children? Which child will be nurtured and successful in life and which might carry the gun to school?

Guns don't get into kids' rooms (or classrooms) by themselves. We allow them. "How?" you say. What have we done to allow it? By avoidance, we let them run, we look the other way and cause them to camp out in their own homes. Who would ever believe that a child of any age would choose to sleep in his or her own closet? It has happened more than once in my experiences with families. Why do we wonder what they do when we have set them off in closets of our own making?

As today's parents, we are expected to guide our children to give and care and understand their rights and responsibilities—or not.

They are just trying to find a way to survive. Does a gun surprise you?

Continuing the Pattern

This is the final and absolute last day of my education contract with the school district I have served for thirty-five years of my life. Beginning as a twenty-two-year-old with a wife of two years and a child of one, we moved to our school district of choice in the summer of 1963. What a heady time!

Little did we know that upon graduation we would embark on a journey of creating our own household over the next fifty years. We settled in suburbia with an older (age thirty-five) couple next door with a herd of kids. Ray and Lorene showed us the way to the shopping center, stores, and into the neighborhood gatherings.

We were thrilled with the welcome, but the young mom was also lonesome for home—and somewhat fearsome of the "big city." Many trips were made to the train station in downtown Minneapolis so Mom and grandchildren could continue to connect with home and parents.

Necessity caused by my first monthly teacher's paycheck of $283.00 net showed the need to reach beyond in support of family. Within but a few weeks, I was working as part-time salesman at the local Dayton's store—three nights a week and Saturdays. Necessity caused me to work the twenty-hour-per-week second job and join my occasionally train-traveled family in our hometown after completing work on Friday or Saturday evening. We were blessed to have the extra twenty-five dollars of income each week to move us up the scale from starvation to stability.

The ability and expectation for "extra" work was not unknown. Having worked all of my life, I knew that no one would provide for us. It was up to me to be gone too much—to allow us to survive. It wasn't at all a "poor me" kind of existence. We knew this was the way to personal success and to achievement. Others did the same.

Continuing the pattern, I was able to work at the store, teach driver training in summers and on occasional Saturdays and begin work on a Master's Degree within two years—all financed out of our usually empty checkbook. It seemed like the thing to do. The school district was encouraging, paying half of the tuition for courses completed. I seemed to recycle the money.

Complete a course, get fifty percent reimbursement, register for the next course and add the additional fifty percent. Somehow we juggled it—and paid for it all. Mom stayed at home with the first, second, third and soon-to-be fourth of the children. A Ph.D. program followed a similar pattern over five years beyond the Master's, allowing us the joy of a one-year sabbatical for study in Texas. The sun did shine upon our family of six in more ways than one.

The Tried and True

Six months into the age of retirement I sit at my computer at 6:00 a.m. pondering where all of this writing is leading. The days have been so busy since I left my regular work-a-day world. I have virtually not golfed or fished or written or contemplated the sunrise. Each day begins with a cup of coffee and a wonder of what I will do. By the end of the day I am exhausted from having done too much.

I build fences, wire in lighting in a crawl space or garage or work on the computer to prepare lessons, organize my life's finances or write my next teaching unit. An occasional breakfast out with Mom, a trip to Florida or Wisconsin or an activity to do for church keeps us in a state of perpetual planning and motion. Right now I am teaching three university graduate classes and looking forward to the completion of one or the other—to begin another.

I still seek a talent. At this age, I am still questing to prove that I have it in me to score more points in the game than the next player. I am reminded of the older gentlemen whom I have met along the way. I admire the way that they are still vibrant and vocal and have a life-force within them as they approach their eighties or nineties. It is my wish that my life will follow a similar pattern.

Writing seems to be a vehicle to do that. It is taxing only to the brain and to the backside as I sit at the computer and jot down my thoughts. It feels right to share these thoughts. Just yesterday I commented that it was forty years since high school graduation. Hard to believe, but we are now the chroniclers of the 1950s.

My wonderment is probably self-centered, rather than global. I know about the travails of the world, the changes that happen "too fast" as others suggest the realities of push-button remotes on virtually every device devised by man. But I am not troubled. I keep up. I set my own LCD clocks and figure out the pieces of technology I need to know, but I am not intimidated by it at all. These are just things that happen around us.

Just as grandparents watched the evolving of the automobile during the age of horses, we absorb these daily occurrences as part of the natural stream of man's need to seek and evolve. There's nothing to trouble us. People need things to do to make their lives meaningful, so they create new products

A Vignette—A Rut of Goodness

What was it like some quick forty years ago? What was important to us as we grew through the time of Elvis to the Y2K problem? Will the beginnings of the Social Security system originated during our lifetime provide a fruitful future for each of us as we enter the twenty-first century? Do we worry about it? Are we bothered by urban blight and the loss of serenity in the countryside of youth? What is important to us as we age?

Today I live with a grandmother. She has been a soulmate on the journey of life for nearly sixty years. Wow! Who would have thought that the years would have gone by so quickly since those idyllic teenage years in our small town of southern Minnesota? Who would have thought that we would be at this point those many years later, when, after all this training and life experience, we are really right back where we started. We are here with our own children, grandchildren and the realities learned from our parents and grandparents, our neighbors and teachers.

The theories and understandings that we gained individually and together from those we held near and dear have transcended the decades. Like our forebears, we believe that life is goodness and fairness and common sense. All the complexities of others' theories haven't done much to change our minds. We're stuck in a rut, I guess.

and configurations. Having watched it for some time, there is really not so very much change. Things just take different forms.

The tried and true are still with us. If we want good products, we seem to return to the tried and true of oak and walnut and steel and structural quality and integrity. Composition board or plastic window material in new homes does not dupe us. We know they are cheaper substitutes that get us through until we can have the solidity of the past. So, too, with our structures of belief and behavior. The composition board veneer of relationships and values just does not stand up to the weather.

Discussions with children and young adults in class suggest that they want the simplicity of structure and control in their lives. They are not interested in something second-rate or is a quick fix. To create a mind and body that will carry them into their future years, they still need to eat well and feed their souls with the values that forebears attempt to pass down to them. They want to know when they are doing well, when they are on track and what their limits are to be as they move forward. Possibly some of the stories I have to share will be of value.

Milk, Bread and Rest

Current awareness of psychological and intellectual development suggests we are nearly formed by the age of five. By then, we have learned the nuances of behavior, established the linkages of synapses within the brain and created the form for our physical, emotional and intellectual development. Milk, bread, rest, and nurturance aid in bringing about the body structure and the behavior patterns that establish us for years to come. It is also especially good for intellectual development to run, jump, chase and keep on moving.

In my childhood home, in spite of six kids, a dying mother and a father who faced unemployment in the cold Minnesota winters, there was always plenty of milk and bread. We rested well after the many tasks of the day. We must have had nurturing. My memories of those earliest days are limited, yet the feelings are integral to my being. There was a steady routine of positive expectation, of no "messing around" and of jobs to do.

Toys were limited, but wood-splitting chores, snow shoveling, Saturday cleaning and doing the wash all occupied our minds and bodies. My sense is that the challenge of putting the bread on the table for Pa, the grips of cancer for our mother, and the jobs we each had to do caused each of us to entertain ourselves and attempt to add to the good of the household, rather than languishing on a need for someone to entertain each of us.

As children of a household of expectaton, we each became "independent contractors" in finding our way. These blessings of order, personal limits and guided encouragement are lessons that stay with me today.

School Days

School days were our life; we needed to stretch our imaginations beyond play at home with our magnetically opposed black and white Scottie dogs, beyond the memorization of Sunday school lessons and beyond mathematics lessons learned at playing Canasta with our ailing mother. After her passing, the lessons of teachers and the readings of *Dick and Jane* became even more critical to the growth of six kids aged two to thirteen. Teachers became our friends, our mentors, and often replacement parents for the evolving needs of each of us.

From the effusive kindergarten teacher who guided each of us to the teachers of junior high, we were encouraged and challenged to build upon the lessons of hard work learned at home from a big brother. We built our educational skills upon that foundation to become recognized and rewarded for our skill and ingenuity.

We became the best readers in the classes, the most skilled mathematics pupils, and most generally the leaders in classes and extra-curricular activities. It wasn't long before we were the captains of the school safety patrol, the after-school assistants to teachers and some of the few students who took home special books for further study. Carrying these treasures of additional learning home from school was an honor and a source of pride for one brother or the other. With our big brother leading the way, we followed his model of genuine love for the process of education and of sincere appreciation for those who provided us with the opportunities.

It has been a good trip.

Exemplary Schools of Note
A Vignette—For the Lincoln Bears

Appointment to the position of principal of Lincoln Senior High School was a heady gift to receive on my thirty-second birthday.

The challenge and opportunity of becoming principal of the oldest and smallest high school in an otherwise growing and dynamic, suburban community represented a risk by the superintendent—and a one-year opportunity for me. Since I was replacing a veteran principal on leave for one year, there was an inside chance I could retain the position for years ahead if all went well. The school was a place of tradition.

From a cornfield-like background, the Bloomington community grew from truck, farm and country school environment in the 1950s to the point of being recognized as a leader in educational programs and corporate ventures in the state and nation by the time of my appointment in March 1974. Bloomington at the time was an "All-American City," home of major league baseball, hockey and football, and the Mall of America was on the radar.

At the heart and in the center of the community's educational growth was this old, original high school with its deep roots in the community. It was a stable environment with a lot of pride and a lot of need. It was seen as so stable that others in the educational community of Bloomington often viewed it as "the old folks home," since so many senior staff remained there over the years.

Upon arrival, I found a school with a heart, but also one a bit outdated with facility, program, and pride. All had been worn down a bit after having their facility overloaded for so many years as the rest of the district buildings were built. Folks were not defeated, just tired and in need of regrouping. These were, after all, World War II and Korean War vets who had lived sensible lives in community, school, and home. Their kids went to school there, too.

The school was by now the smallest of three, the people the most entrenched. The sparkle of their new building of the late 1950s had started to fade. It was time for rejuvenation of all aspects. The terrazzo needed shining, the air needed to be conditioned and the wooden seats needed replacement.

For this young principal it was a time of risk. Raising the community consciousness of the inequities that had occurred as the district went on its new-building binge, questions were readily apparent (to me) of funding equity, program opportunity, and renewal of facility. Through changes of internal leadership, procedures and awareness, we quietly attacked the Board of Education with questions of merit and intended equity. With mutual effort, our political action caused new enrollment boundaries creating greater equity for students, programs, and funding.

We challenged students with renewed and coherent expectations of curriculum and behavior—and they responded beautifully! We transitioned quickly to the new programs that staff put together. Soon there was a "flash" to the old place—a flash that came to all with new expectations, programs, rooms, and schools. We even marched the two-hundred-piece marching band through the halls on game days to shake the dust out of the ceilings.

The school became internally the most "together" group of 2,000 or more students, staff, and faculty I had ever seen or could ever imagine. It was the home of "synergy." Over time we virtually refurbished the whole of the organization—from attitude to furniture. With five years of perseverance, we completed the political action necessary to achieve nearly one million dollars in remodeling and enhancement to the core of the school, a library/media/career center.

We refined and restructured the curriculum to the point of being copied by our "new," sister schools. Together we created the single largest number of National Merit Scholars in the state of Minnesota in the same year as the school's closing, 1982.

Suffice it to say that there was a major loss in the heart of this community when the school of excellence closed its doors due to overall district enrollment decline and political action of the board.

Those who lived the life of Lincoln Senior High School never did lose, however. The memory lives on and grows even stronger—even as the building was sold off. We were in a special place in a special time with synergy in action! We knew it then. We know it now. The Lincoln Bear is yet out there, visiting some thirty-plus years later.

We are the Bears, forevermore!

The Lincoln Bear, Christmas 2013. (Photo courtesy of the author.)

Exemplary Schools of Note

A Vignette—An Accomplishment in the Oak Grove

The community and the school of the east side needed a place of pride.

For so many years, the "flash" and glow of the other side of town, the west side, seemed to suggest that the east side was "tough" or "poor" or lacking in educational skill, discipline, or student accomplishment. It was "too bad" that those kids on this side of town were perceived by some as not having the same skills or abilities to behave or do whatever the fanciful folks of the "prestigious" side of town thought they should.

For me, my placement as the new principal in a junior high (my first experience with junior high students and staff) on the east side presented a challenge. I had just come from the newly closed senior high, and had twenty years of high school experience.

With an image problem, a disparate staff and eighteen hundred seventh through ninth graders in the Oak Grove, it was a challenge made to try the strongest. With "best wishes" from those who saw me pack my bags and be "demoted" to a junior high school after being "up" in a senior high school, I arrived one cold, March morning (my birthday again) to take over a school that others believed was going to hell in a handbasket. I sensed a need, an opportunity to create a new environment and a chance that few get in their lifetime to share a vision and to go about implementing it.

I immediately told all staff to forget their previous conceptions of what had been, where they had been and where they thought we were going. Never had this school seen so many students. Never had there been so many disgruntled staff placed from their beloved senior high assignments to those of the junior high. Never had there been so many philosophies and different experiences in one room at one time.

Never had there been an inexperienced junior high principal before them. With many of the teachers coming from closed junior highs and some remaining from a past liberal atmosphere and program of the school in the late 1960s, as well as the displaced senior high teachers and principal, we had it all. The question was, what would we do with it?

Each was challenged to bond into a "new" environment, a new school, a new way of doing things. Through past experience, I knew it could be done. It was simply a matter of attitude, of perception, of visioning—and of hard work. We needed to get to the task—*our* task—of being premier educators, of giving our all as we had in our previous schools, our earlier environments.

Through restructuring of programs, staff, expectations, facility, and with substantial community involvement and pride, we went about the task to make Oak Grove Junior High into Minnesota's "finest junior high." As one wizened veteran said, "If I hear that often enough, I begin to believe it." Indeed they did. We became a significant community of quality, an environment that cared for rich, for poor, for emotionally disturbed, for gifted and talented, for old staff and new.

Suffice it to say that Oak Grove's National School of Excellence Award after only three years of our being together evidenced the achievement. Our action stimulated our east side high school to adopt the Oak Grove approach and become a National School of Excellence as well. Leadership and vision were the keys. Expectations were the force. Personal commitment over time was the methodology.

We made it happen!

Warriors Don't Shoot Reindeer

A pre-Christmas conversation with a four-year-old grandson led me to new understandings.

Cole claims that St. Nicholas (not related to Santa) has something to do with the death of old people. He told me I was going to die—apparently due to the "bad" St. Nicholas, since there's a good one, too. I wasn't going to die right now, though, since the good St. Nicholas was watching over me. This is St. Nicholas, the bear who's the good guy. I learned this as we rose from our nap.

After a busy morning in the Santa line (as number thirty-one in a crowd of hundreds), face painting, shopping for Mom's Christmas gift with Grandma at the community Christmas kids' store with a Santa helper, we topped it off with lunch at "McD's." We both needed a rest. Before lights out, he reminded me I was there with him for Santa's picture—and for his telling Santa that he wanted an iPad, even though he's never seen one. He has seen a drum set, though—his first choice.

Cole claims there are lots of bad guys in the video games of today. He doesn't play these games, not having any of the tools in his home. He does, however, attend day care—the learning land of today. Tyler, his video game-playing six-year-old classmate, seems to impart more learning than the day care provider and pre-school teacher combined. I didn't know about swords, karate chops, and slick, quiet moves in two-step across the room. But they must be true—since Tyler taught him so.

I learned all this stuff while coloring Christmas scenes at the kitchen table after naptime. As we often do, we spin around words and colors and choices. "Use the yellow. Does orange make a difference?" I offered. "Do warriors drive golf carts? (He likes to ride in my golf cart.) No matter how bizarre my comment, he has a comeback. It is amazing what that little brain has absorbed after only four years on earth.

I learned that blue is bright and purple is dark. He spoke of the warriors and I offered that each ran around with a bow and arrow to shoot the rabbits and the like. Since we had just visited the reindeer at Santa's petting park, I suggested that warriors shoot reindeer. He vehemently exclaimed: "Warriors don't shoot reindeer!" They only do good with their implements of war and attack, it seems.

He has not only learned some words. He's formulated concepts and feelings and learned what he can get by with. His attitude has been addressed since earliest days when I offered to him that no "Lippy Louie" could be at our house. He has learned that whining doesn't work. He's a great worker—with a red shovel that works equally well on the sand beaches of summer or the snowdrifts of December. He minds his Grandma and plays beautifully with neighbor kids, excelling at baseball and hockey.

We play the guitar, bat the ball, play catch and learn to dribble a basketball. Together we took his first climbing steps (at age two) on the high monkey bars in his park down the street. It's a beautiful city park with all the safest equipment that sees little use in our quiet neighborhood—thus it's "his" park.

Amazing that we spend days with Cole in such similar form to that in which we raised our four kids. Included are the basics of "eat your lunch," "be nice to Grandma," "take your nap" and "pick up the end" of a piece of wood seemingly too big. We share in fun and work and expectation that lead us through relaxed days together. On a recent day, we went deer tracking in the snow. From our lakeshore, we followed the tracks across the street and into the swamp. With his selected Indian tracking pole in hand, he soon led the way.

I'm not sure about iPads, video games, and the seemingly protected life of indoor children. I'm more certain of outdoor ventures and garage time. We seem to fall into new spaces, experiences, and discoveries. St. Nicholas, the good guy, watches over us—allowing us to enjoy every moment.

Chapter Six

Taking the Market Basket to the People: The Watkins Story

The Watkins Company originated with twenty-eight-year-old Joseph Ray Watkins. A manufacturer of health remedies, baking products, and other household items, Watkins, Incorporated, of Winona has a catalog including four hundred products. It largely relies on an independent sales force of twenty-five thousand people to distribute its products.

This sales force sells products using various methods, including the Internet, person to person, trade shows, party planning, and fund raising. In order to increase overall awareness for the brand, the company has begun offering a select number of products in national retail outlets.

The company was founded by J.R. Watkins in Plainview, Minnesota, where the young man began selling liniment door-to-door in 1868 throughout the southeastern part of the state. The new, all-natural liniment was manufactured in and sold from his Plainview home, where he personally concocted the one-of-a-kind pain reliever "with camphor from evergreen trees, spruce oil and extract of capsicum from red peppers and other ingredients." Still sold today, the Pain Relieving Liniment is 965 percent natural and uses eco-friendly packaging.

J.R. Watkins. (Courtesy of the Winona Newspaper Project.)

In 1868, J.R. "secured rights to manufacture and sell medicines compounded by Dr. Ward of Cincinnati, Ohio." He mixed the ingredients in the kitchen, bottled them in the woodshed and sold them via buggy to town and country folk alike. He "set the pattern" for merchandising his products. He sold the various medicines, including liniment, salves and extracts, for seventeen years in the Plainview area, before moving to Winona at age forty-five on May 1, 1885.

Beginning to find his way in Winona, he ran for Judge of Probate in November 1886, garnering one hundred thirty-seven votes and a third-place finish. The original Watkins "company laboratory" was located at 800 East Fourth Street.

His first assistant in Winona was George Smith, a fourteen-year-old who stayed with J.R. Watkins Company for sixty years. He was a complete friend and assistant, serving far beyond Watkins's passing in 1911. George was a pallbearer at J.R.'s funeral, president of the Paul Watkins Garden Club of 1917, and one of the organizers of the First Watkins Picnic (for five hundred employees and friends) in 1926 at the Farmers Community Park. George was recognized there with the oldest employee award—forty years!

By the time J.R. moved to Winona, he had in place a dozen men, known as "wagon salesmen," who covered the area. He had "agents canvas every farm house in the Northwest from door to door, leaving sample bottles of the remedies free." Foregoing local politics and the judgeship, he instead "knew he had something," having started the Watkins line and sticking to it. By 1892, "with the business increasing by fifty percent per year, the company soon had one-hundred and twenty-five agents from Minnesota to Oregon."

The remedies offered consisted of "Vegetable Anodyne Liniment, Egyptian Stick Salve, Vegetable Cathartic Pills for the human family, and Improved Condition Powders for horses and cattle. Suffice it to say that the liniment is invaluable in cases if cholera morbus, any kind of a sore throat or diphtheria, while it can be used externally with gratifying results for rheumatism, pains, burns, bruises, wounds, etc." Over the years, he and nephew Paul (president of the company after 1911) grew the business to over three hundred products.

By 1890, J.R. had become someone "of personal wealth," as shown in the *Winona Republican*. He was one of one hundred and thirty investors in the new Hotel Winona, along with J.A. Latsch, H. Choate, A.B. Youmans and a host of others. All had "personal taxes to the City of Winona over $10.00." Those same "Elite of Winona" attended "a dancing party for two hundred friends" at the Philharmonic Hall, sponsored by the Boalts and the Mitchells.

A Prosperous Institution

A July 1892 *Winona Daily Republican* story gave, "A Brief Resume of One of the Most Prosperous Institutions of the Gate City." Watkins stuck to his product line in the "Magnificent Medical Laboratory" and to "The Manufacture of Dr. Ward's Celebrated Remedies," advertising in 1893 for "Dr. Ward's Remedies and Extracts." Mr. and Mrs. Watkins took the Watkins story to the World's Fair in Chicago in June 1893.

In January 1896, Brown and Abbott challenged Watkins in a jury trial of Municipal Court. Specifics are not known, but it is rumored that Dr. Ward had sold the formulae to more than one agent—with overlapping territorial concerns resulting. The following year, Watkins Medical was assessed for the "street macadam and curbing" fronting lots six through ten of Plummer's addition—a total of three hundred feet.

The J.R. Watkins Medical Company asked the public in 1897 to "Try the Watkins Brand." They stated: "No mouldy, musty or damaged spices are ground by the J.R. Watkins Medical Co." In that same year, J.R. gave a "free sample bottle of Dr. Ward's Liniment and a free sample packet of Dr. Ward's Headache Tablets to every dwelling house in town." He also "delivered a copy of their handsome pamphlet called Dr. Ward's Guidebook describing the origin and manufacture of Dr. Ward's Extracts and Watkins Pure Ground Spices."

Dr. Ward's *Almanac*, 1910. (Photo courtesy of the author.)

The Board of Trade of Winona accepted the J.R. Watkins Medical Company as a new member in 1899. With the addition of the one hundred and sixty-four new members, the total membership grew to two hundred and thirty-five, including Charles Biesanz, Charles Siebrecht, John Von Rohr, Joseph Leicht, J.L.F. Dielke, Paul Watkins, J.W. Selover, A.W. Laird, R.D. Cone, S.W. Morgan, and H. Choate and Co.—all acknowledged Winona builders.

By 1901, J.R. was also the president of the new Winona National

Watkins Bank Lion. (Photo courtesy of the Winona Newspaper Project.)

Savings Bank on Fourth and Main, a part of the evolving Watkins vision, organization and financial success. Years later, I worked across the street at Owl Motor Ford-Mercury-Lincoln, another Watkins family venture, and cashed my paycheck in that very bank's vaunted interior—surrounded by the lions and tigers of the Watkins family's later expeditions to Africa.

In J.R.'s new hometown, many others emulated the Watkins model. By 1908, but a few of those competing companies were McConnon and Company at 326-328 East Third Street (kitty-corner from Watkins at Liberty Street), Schroer Medical Company of 110-114 Center Street, Watosa Company at 117-121 West Second Street, Dr. Koch's Vegetable Tea Company at 157 East Second Street, and Dr. W.F. Holden at 523 Huff Street. All offered "family remedies," with most moving into spices, extracts, and medicines, as well.

J.R. died on December 21, 1911, of "acute digestion" while on a cruise and visit to Kingston, Jamaica. In the company of Mrs. Watkins, E.L. King, daughter Grace, and Maude King, he became seasick on the cruise, and died within an hour of a family carriage ride around the island. The funeral was in January in Winona. Mrs. Watkins lived until 1924, with her burial alongside her husband in the Watkins Vault at Woodlawn Cemetery. Her home on 206 East Broadway, a full half-block lot, was vacant for several years thereafter, and owner E.L. King had the Watkins home torn down in 1928.

The Direct Marketing Approach

The concept of peddlers had been in place since Shakespeare's time, but Watkins refined it with communications, branches, sales training and diversification. He "took the market basket to the people." By 1893, he had a branch in San Francisco and added a number of products to his lineup.

Sales continued to grow, and in 1895, pepper, vanilla, and cinnamon were added to the product line, a line that quickly grew to include Petro-

Carbo Salve, Gen-De-Can-Dra tonic bitters, Oriental Nerve Tonic, Cathartic Liver Pills, and Hindu Pain Oil—all backed by Watkins' money-back guarantee and sold by troops of "Watkins Men" door-to-door from coast to coast. By 1915, Watkins had grown to be the largest direct-sales company in the world and had established the reputation for quality products that would keep the Watkins brand in homes and farms into the next century.

"From Ocean to Ocean" Watkins offered liniment, spices, extracts, automotive accessories, tires, soap, cold cream (including the Supreme Garda and Mary King lines of toiletries, which offered "exquisite daintiness that is distinctive and entrancing,") polishes, washing compounds, shampoos, animal compounds, dips, disinfectants, supplements, and remedies for human and animal.

At the Paris International Exposition of 1928 (World's Fair), the J.R. Watkins Company won gold medals for its vanilla extract, cinnamon, and black pepper. Watkins natural vanilla flavoring was derived from real vanilla beans, with little or no alcohol—usually less than three percent.

A Watkins Red Pepper can of the era shows the medal and suggests: "That same high quality you have noticed in Watkins spices and extracts is packed into every one of the 300 daily-used home needs in the Watkins line. The pick of the world's markets—first quality raw spices full of the natural oils, [are] milled by improved manufacturing processes," and were distributed through Winona's home base and branches in Newark, Memphis, and Oakland.

A recent study by the Direct Marketing Association reports that in 2010, marketers—commercial and nonprofit—spent $1533 billion on direct marketing, which accounted for 542 percent of all ad expenditures in the United States. Measured against total U.S. sales, these advertising expenditures generated approximately $1798 trillion in incremental sales. In 2010, direct marketing accounted for 83 percent of total U.S. gross domestic product, and there were 1.4 million direct marketing employees in the U.S. Their collective sales efforts directly supported 8.4 million other jobs, accounting for a total of 9.8 million U.S. jobs.

A strong case may be made that J.R. Watkins was one of the earliest marketers, with door-to-door sales his bailiwick, having spread his fifteen thousand salesmen across the United States.

Songs and Liniment

Dr. Richard Ward cannot be ignored. He started J.R. on his way, apparently from an earlier connection in Cincinnati. Ward created the liniment that became "The

World's Largest Selling Liniment," licensing it to J.R. Watkins of Plainview in 1867. Reported in the *Watkins Song Book* of the early 1940s were pages of personal testimony to the benefits of the descended Watkins Liniment—interspersed with twenty songs of the day, including "America the Beautiful," "Oh, Dem Golden Slippers" and "The Little Brown Church in the Vale." The booklet, offered free by Watkins Dealer A.N. Freedell of Owatonna and other dealers nationwide, advertised that "4,460,050 bottles of Watkins Liniment [Were] Sold in a Year."

The colored-page centerfold of the booklet stated: "Vaults in our Administration Building are filled with carefully treasured boxes of testimonial letters running into the hundreds of thousands, praising Watkins Liniment for its many uses." A cadre of twenty-nine female "special staff" is pictured on the first page of the booklet under the granite sign of the administration building with nearly as many huge sacks of mail as employees, suggesting, "Millions of Customers Can't Be Wrong."

- Max J. Wilber of Michigan wrote: "When I'm really lame and sore, with a pain I can't ignore, then this Liniment rubbed in, changes my frown to a grin."
- Thomas L. Bolte of Wisconsin is pictured in the booklet with his horse. Bolte attests: "Watkins Liniment gives quickest relief taken internally for colds, cramps and colic or used externally for sprains, bruises or muscular pains for man and beast."
- Rhina Austin of South Carolina offered: "Watkins Liniment does so much for me. I take it for stomach trouble, feed baby chicks to prevent diarrhea. It keeps hens laying regularly."
- E.A. Wurzbach of Texas even suggested: "I walked out to my barn this morning. I had cows, chickens and hogs following me. I didn't know what was the matter, and later discovered I had a bottle of Watkins Liniment in my hip pocket. That is why I like Watkins Liniment. It is good for every living thing on the place."

The 1919 *Almanac* of Watkins Medical yet bore the company name of "Dr. Ward's Medical Co. of Winona, Minn." It was suggested therein to "Buy two bottles of Watkins Liniment. Keep one handy in your medicine cabinet in the house. Keep the other bottle for use on pets or livestock."

New Leaders

In 1892, Paul Watkins of Lebanon, Ohio, joined his uncle J.R. as vice-president—to become president of Watkins in 1911, upon J.R.'s death. A former executive of Ohio Coal and Iron Company of Columbus, he was vital to Watkins's overall success. Paul led the organization to become "the ten-million dollar corporation of today," at the time of his death at age sixty-seven in December 1931. He was known as "a man of strong character and deep conviction," "lover of the aesthetic" and "a good man and good friend."

The evolvement continued to Memphis in 1910 and Baltimore in 1912—the soon-to-be Newark plant. In 1912, the company erected a ten-story manufacturing plant in Winona, joined by the exquisite administration building, completed in 1915. From that "finest private administration building in the world" was mailed in 1915 a Watkins-printed postcard shown here. The beautiful administration building on Liberty Street was designed by Prairie School architect George Washington Maher and is listed on the National Register of Historic Places. The front entrance includes a window designed by stained-glass artist Louis J. Millet, depicting Sugar Loaf, a local landmark.

By 1946, Watkins facilities were present in Newark, Memphis, Winona, Oakland, Montreal, Winnipeg, Vancouver, and Melbourne, Australia. A Birmingham, England, facility, established by Watkins vice-president Ralph Boalt in 1938, was bombed twice with "full fire-bomb attacks by the German Luftwaffe" in World War II.

J.R.'s only child, Grace Eleanor, grew in the early 1900s into a vivacious young lady with many talents. According to Paul R., a great-grand-nephew of J.R. whom I interviewed recently, her marriage in 1904 to "one-time sales manager for a typewriter manufacturing concern" E.L. (Ernest LeRoy) King "changed the course of the Watkins Family and the involvement of Paul's children." With the marriage, King became a vice-president of Watkins. He was president of Winona

Watkins World Headquarters, Winona, 1915. (Courtesy of the Winona Newspaper Project.)

National Bank throughout the years, with E.L. King, Jr., listed as president and treasurer of J.R. Watkins Company in 1931, with the passing of Paul Watkins.

King, Sr., was seen as a "genius," with talent for purchasing and selling properties from Houston to San Francisco to Florida. He owned a golf course in Daytona Beach and an estate at Homer (south of Winona several miles) called Rockledge. When he died in 1949 at age seventy-two, he was shown to be living at 209 East Fifth Street in Winona. E.L. King, Jr., and Mary Eleanor, for whom the Mary Kay line of cosmetics was named, survived him.

In the Neighborhood

Paul had purchased the former home of Dr. D.D. Stewart at 175 East Wabasha in 1904 to make a home for all the family. Rising above the neighborhood, it had a back window view of Sugar Loaf. With hardwood floors throughout, three fireplaces, library, and accoutrements, it was the forty-four by fifty-foot setting for all manner of social gatherings, weddings, receptions, and funerals.

Paul's sons Roderick Henderson Watkins, Joseph R., and William left Winona to be educated at Harvard, Harvard, and Andover, respectively. Daughter Florence was at Wells College and excelled, leading the senior class as president. Traveling as a family, they spent summers in the Florida Keys, making frequent trips to Europe.

Paul R. offers that there were several houses from 123 to 175 East Wabasha Street. According to him, the house at 175 was built three years before his grandfather Paul's death. The 1931 city directory shows William Watkins at 127, next door to Paul Watkins, at 175. The 1946 directory lists Roderick at 123 and Florence Watkins at 175. Apparently the Stewart Home had been taken down, with a new mansion built in 1928.

At home, Paul was president of the company and vice-president of the new Winona National and Savings Bank (with E.L. King as president in 1915). E.L. King, Jr., succeeded his father as president of Watkins (at age twenty-nine in 1944) and the bank, with other Kings to follow.

Paul was president of the music club, leader of the Salvation Army drive and contributor of many art works to the Winona Library and Winona State Teachers College. Grandson Paul Roderick Watkins and his sister, Ruth, later documented each gift. Notable was Paul's presentation of "First Step" by Salentin in 1919.

In addition, Paul was remembered as a man who "wrought well." Others "never knew how much he helped the poor of the city through anonymous charity," as Paul R. recalled. "He greatly appreciated Winona. He was distinctly interested in all its people." As chair of the 1931 Salvation Army appeal, he showed a bit of himself with the listed support of the Salvation Army to 1,659 families, providing "13,450 pounds of coal and serving 10,370 meals," along with other forms of relief in the midst of the Great Depression.

Florence, Joseph, Roderick, and families were there (with William nearby) for Christmas in 1931, when Paul passed quietly of a heart attack. All had lived elsewhere.

Joseph R., a World War I veteran and investment banker in Boston, was the "ad hoc" lawyer to Watkins. He was shot and killed in New Jersey in 1948 by a financier who had owed Watkins $72,000. He is buried in the family mausoleum in Woodlawn Cemetery of Winona.

Roderick resided in Chicago and later Winona, to serve as purchasing agent for many years. He married Gladys Anderson of Westby, Wisconsin, in 1938. He returned to Winona in the early 1940s.

William lived in Winnetka, Illinois, and Winona, and was a Watkins salesperson.

Accolades Abound

From the manufacture and sale of a single product, as "Your Good Neighbor for Four Generations, 1868-1955," Watkins dealers offered home and farm necessities including, spices, extracts, toiletries (notably the famous Mary Kay Line of products), medicines, feed supplements, insecticides, and more. The growing company had established its world-renowned experimental farm at Homer for visitors—flown to Winona in the company's DC-3 airplane captained by Chief Pilot Jack Ollom.

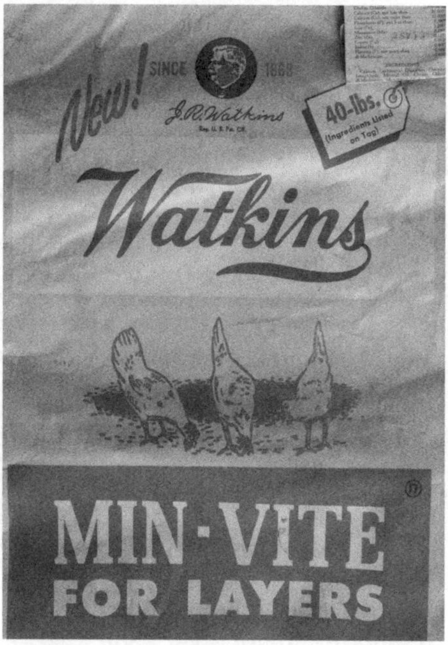

Min-Vite chicken supplement. (Photo courtesy of the author.)

J.R. got it all going. Accolades were evident as early as 1892, as seen in the *Winona Daily Republican*:

Few of our citizens realize or appreciate the importance of this meritorious institution. The large amount of capital invested, the number of hands employed and the scope of the proprietor's prestige [come] but to the city as well, as it spreads evidences of Winona's enterprise and greatness all over the country. We will venture to say that Mr. Watkins does more to advertise the Gate City abroad as any score of firms within its gates. He takes an evident pride in his institution, and well he may, as it is one of the most perfect and thoroughly equipped of any in the country, and too much praise cannot be accorded him. [. . .]

Mr. J.R. Watkins, the proud possessor of this meritorious establishment, is a typical Winona businessman. He has risen from the ranks of its labor to the ranks of its capital. His rise was due to no accident, no streaks of capricious fortune. Natural ability, innate thrift and indomitable pluck in the prosecution of his business, backed by meritorious remedies are the solo causes of his success.

He has been trained in the school of experience and knows precisely the methods by which a great concern like his must be conducted. He is a man of keen perceptive qualities, sagacious, tactful and resolute. He holds in the community an enviable position for his liberality and progressive spirit, and is a gentleman of pleasant and courteous manner.

Modern Day Leaders

By 1935, the children of Paul Watkins had been "drummed out of the company" by Grace and E.L. King, according to Paul's grandson Paul R. After Paul's death, a decision by King to stop paying dividends affected the Paul Watkins children and their mother. According to Paul R., suit was brought against the King family and settled in favor of the heirs of Paul Watkins. Unfortunately, it also removed them from any ownership in the company thereafter. Of interest is the Watkins-King subsidiary company of four hundred agents and branch facilities established in seven major cities in 1926.

Grace was at the forefront of family publicity—as a nationally recognized trap shooter. She continued to "show up" family and friends of Watkins in shooting competitions. She easily beat husband E.L. King and F.G. Jackson (of Owl Motor) in a Minnesota competition. In 1928, she set a world record with three consecutive shoots in southern states and Indiana, beating all the men along the way. The Kings often visited Hawaii and led safaris as big game hunters to Africa, gaining all manner of beasts for display at the Watkins-owned bank on Main Street.

E.J. Sievers, executive vice-president for finance, served for many years at headquarters. Along with a steadying hand at Watkins, E.J. Sievers was active in bowling, the Izaak Walton League, Winona Hospital Board and the Madison School (my home school) Zoo Fun Frolic. Along with other Winona notables like the Indalls, Doners, Kanes, Pletkes, and others, Mr. and Mrs. Sievers supervised the junior prom at the Winona High School gymnasium for one hundred and sixty couples in 1952.

Dr. M.H. Doner, entomologist of Watkins for many years, frequently distinguished himself as "monarch butterfly bander," bird club leader, garden and flower club organizer and patron of Winona State College. He was said to have the most extensive collection of mounted butterflies and insects in the state. He also led Sunday morning services for the Unitarian Universal Fellowship at the Winona Hotel. One of his selected topics was "Modern Concepts of Morality."

My only connection with the headquarters staff and employees of Watkins was to fill employee nickel-vend coffee machines of the 1960s on my vending route of Winona's businesses. I had also worked as a teenager at the Watkins Owl Motor facility—and visited their bank with the golden arches and the permanently docile tigers across the street. I knew the Watkins and King descendents from afar, and the employee families on my paper route who took pride in their employment and production. My affinity for Watkins products was learned early in Grandma's kitchen and at home on Grand Street. Vanilla extract on the kitchen shelf and in my brother Frank's "Upside-Down Orange Cake" was a delightful smell remembered yet today.

An Orchid Among Flowers, A Favorite Among Flavors—
Watkins Vanilla Flavor"

> Deep in the tropic semi-jungles (of Sumatra and Madagascar) a dainty, orchid-like flower blooms on a slender, clingy vine, reaching its way up into the darkness cast by the foliage of a great tropical tree. All around it other vines and flowers grow in a welter of jungle foliage. As these flowers wither and fade a slender pod develops and grows. From this delicately tinted growth comes the most popular and widely used of oil extracts or flavors—vanilla.

> Through drying, curing, sweating, packing and aging of the beans leading to percolation comes the aromatic, flavorful bottled liquid that led to the Gold Medal of Highest Quality at the Paris International Exposition. Discriminating housewives prefer Watkins Vanilla because baking does not drive out its full, mellow flavor. It is 'bake-proofed'–The Flavor Stays.
>
> –*Watkins Almanac and Home Book*, 1939

The award-winning vanilla was a constant essential, along with the spices in their extremely colorful cans, which added décor to simple, household kitchens of the 1940s and '50s. I have gathered many of those tins (some with product therein) over the years. Pictured below is my original salesman's carrier and supply of various Watkins products of the first half of the twentieth century.

C.K. Heberling, a Grand Street friend's father, was the national rural sales manager for Watkins in 1957. His father, G.H. Heberling, was one of five incorporators of the J.R. Watkins Company in 1894–including J.R. Watkins, Paul Watkins, N.H. Watson, W.H. Garlock, and Heberling. C.K. apparently supervised my friend Russell, who lived around the corner and down the block.

Russell Herbert introduced me to Watkins products, methodology, and the home-to-home marketing concept. Russell and I loaded his brand new

Salesman's kit and products. (Photo courtesy of the author.)

1949 Frazer car (of Kaiser-Frazer) through its folding rear door that opened up like a modern-day van or SUV.

A perfect Watkins salesman's vehicle, the Frazer was a "hit" in the flagship line of upper-medium-priced American luxury automobiles built by the Kaiser-Frazer Corporation of Willow Run at Ypsilanti, Michigan—where a new B-24 had come off the line every fifty-five minutes during World War II.

We packed the vehicle with all the spices for the housewife, all the offered poultry and cattle medicines and supplements and set out with a load of spices and delightful smells to visit the farms of Winona County.

Russell was first a salesman at Winona Motor Company, then the *Republican-Herald*. He found a special niche with the Watkins family in the early 1940s, where, like many of the other fifteen thousand agents, he stayed for many years. His daughter, Judy, was employed there after high school.

Russell's special smile and friendly greeting to all the farmers on our route is well remembered.

And They Carried On

By the 1940s, Watkins was the largest direct-sales company in the world. From northwest and Midwest, farmers and their wives "flocked to Winona like Mohammedan pilgrims to Mecca—sometimes 5,000 in one day!" In 1939, John Turner, a dealer of Tomah, Wisconsin, brought a "car caravan of 145 people." Other dealers on the same day brought forty-seven, twenty-seven, thirty-six, fifty, and fifty-one, respectively. In November of that year, the one-hundred-thousandth visitor was celebrated and recognized with a check and award from E.L. King.

Demographics and buying habits of the United States waned from the fabulous '40s, with major shifts in the following decades. In 1947, three million calendars were printed and distributed by Watkins dealers. However, the company did not keep pace with consumer buying trends. With King leadership, Watkins filed for bankruptcy protection in the 1970s and was purchased by Minneapolis investor Irwin L. Jacobs in 1978.

In 1996, Jacobs' son, Mark Evan Jacobs, began to take over day-to-day operations of the company. Since taking over the reins, he has controlled spending and introduced an enhanced compensation plan for sales associates. An extensive brand study led to introduction of products onto store shelves for the first time.

WalMart has carried about twenty Watkins products since 2003. Other nationwide stores including Cub Foods, Hannaford, Whole Foods, Rainbow Foods, Pik 'n Save, Schnucks, Hy-Vee Food Stores, Walgreens, Smith's Food and Drug, Target, Sunflower Market, Ultas and others are carrying select items, particularly spices, extracts, and personal care items from the catalog. Reception from the retail community has been strong.

A new all-natural line of personal care products was introduced to the retail community in the spring of 2008, in order to quickly gain market share against Burt's Bees and others. A new, natural home cleaning line debuted at Target and rolled out nationally in the second half of the same year. Sizes of the spice and extract line offered to the retail community are different from those offered to the consumer via the independent representative, allowing the independent representative to maintain an advantage in the marketplace. At this time, both channels are performing well.

The Famous "Watkins Man"

The unstoppable Bill Porter began his career as a Watkins man in October 1955, walking door-to-door in his Portland, Oregon, sales territory despite crippling cerebral palsy. He asked the first, hesitant supervisor to give him "the worst route" he had. Given the chance, Porter became the Watkins "Salesman of the Year" in 1989. His indomitable spirit and steadfast perseverance propelled him through a fifty-plus-year career with Watkins, inspiring others along the way.

Porter had been told for many years that he was not employable, but he threw all of his effort into working as a salesman for Watkins. Despite the pain of his medical condition, he would walk eight to ten miles a day to meet his customers. Porter was able to support himself and continued to work as a salesman until 1997, when he quit as the times changed and people turned more toward the Internet rather than door-to-door salesmen. In 1998, John Glenn presented a national award to him for being a model to the handicapped. In 2002, an Emmy award-winning television movie of his life, *Door to Door*, was created. The film was produced for the TNT cable network and nominated for twelve Emmy Awards, winning six. He had also been featured in countless news stories.

The Watkins Way

There were many Winonans and other national employees like Bill who devoted their lives to Watkins. They were packers, printers, bottlers, farm workers, accountants, secretaries, salespeople, and executives. Each has a story to tell. The familiar J.R. Watkins script logo appeared everywhere in our town—on trucks and products and bowling shirts. All celebrated their employment and camaraderie each summer with a company picnic for two thousand or more at the Farmers Community Park, "the Arches," near Stockton.

Every committed employee deserves mention. Here are but a few:

- Six Thurley family members, covering three generations led by Charles with thirty-one years, together gave "100 years of service to Watkins Co."
- Miss Rose Maas retired in 1969, with forty-eight years in the legal, rural sales and credit departments.
- Charles Kochta spent forty-seven and a half years as a compounder in the cosmetics department, retiring in 1961.
- Lead compounder Harry Wieczorek left in 1969, with forty-four years.
- "Six Watkins Employees with a Total Two Hundred and Fifty-Three Years," according to a newspaper headline of the time, left with an average of forty-two years in 1964.
- Miss Mary Paskiewicz spent thirty-four years "in the bindery."
- Harold Ziegenbein, production worker and packer, "went fishing" after twenty-eight years.
- Harry Meyers was in rural sales for forty years, with Tony Jilk in maintenance for thirty-six. Both left in 1969.
- Retired in 1964, Antone Guenther spent forty-three years as a compounder—mixing ointments, shampoo, soap powder, desserts, minerals, and spices. With his previous eight years with a chocolate company of Winona, he had the recipes for just about everything—after fifty-one years of mixing!
- A possible record holder, pressman Rudolph Maas retired in 1950 after fifty years of service. He said, "I was happy there. We were always pushing, always building up. I was happy when the presses were clanging." He offered, as well, "J.R. Watkins and Paul Watkins were our best pals." He especially liked lunchtime, when "We would walk home at lunch together and talk about the print shop. Yes, J.R. was my buddy."

The employees mentioned above are but a few of the individuals responsible for the quality and integrity of Watkins products. The door-to-door sales people were encouraged by the company "to be a friend and counselor to farm families." As independent operators, they were seen as "simple, kindly and having an independent nature." The *Saturday Evening Post* of May 1948 suggested that the salesman for Watkins "was his own boss." In-house employees were numerous across the nation–and especially valued.

The Product That Started It All

> From the beginning, J.R. Watkins has been committed to providing high-quality products and excellent customer service. Watkins first introduced the "Trial-Mark Bottle" and America's first money-back guarantee in 1869. Relying on door-to-door sales, Watkins gave customers a risk-free way to try his products by adding a molded "trial mark" to each bottle. [. . .]
>
> Watkins ordered a stock of specially made medicine bottles with a line and the words "Trial Mark" cast into the glass about a quarter of the way down. Use the product, he told the buyer, down to the line–if it's working, keep on using and buy some more. If it doesn't, use it down to the line, put it on the shelf and return what's left for your money back, no questions asked.
>
> –*Winona Daily News*

"The pledge wasn't chiseled in stone, but, almost as good, it was cast in glass." Watkins employees through the years have been assurers of the "trial mark" for every product.

Sources:
Winona Newspaper Project–Winona State Universitty
Winona Daily News
Watkins Official Website
Personal research–booklets, materials and experience
Interviews, Paul R. Watkins, 2014
Sandbar Stories, *Jim Lackore, 2011*
Plainview Area History Center Website

The Quest for Excellence

One of the great wonderments I hold is of that seemingly undefinable quality of excellence. Where does it come from? What makes us know it when we see it?

Why does a movie get our grand review as we wander out of the theater? What is it about a singer who touches our heart? Why are we drawn to one artist over another? Why is one business great, a school, and community all-inclusive while others do not quite measure up?

Yesterday I visited several automobile dealerships. Those with "Five Star" ratings seemed to show their stars with knowledge, friendliness, overall cleanliness, organization, and quality products. Does the Toyota organization have a patent on excellence? It appears through my limited research in the store, on the Internet and by being a fifteen-year, two-car Toyota owner that they have structurally quantified every action of manufacture and service in order to achieve zero defects. Their product shows the result.

They seem to have similarly defined the actions of salespeople, service writers, and automobile technicians through processes of lean design and Six Sigma (a methodology of removing defects and improving a business). My dealership continuously provides services and products that can only be judged as ten on a ten-point scale. The local agency has been President's Award Winner for nearly twenty consecutive years. I personally observed the owner of this huge dealership arrive at work one morning to remove a wrinkled cardboard sign from a new vehicle in the showroom—before he had taken off his coat.

We don't seem to know what specifically makes the difference in what we judge to be excellent. We see the difference between mediocrity and excellence every day at every turn—in the bank we visit, the church we know, and the stores we frequent. Could it be, like Izhaak Perlman, that individuals and organizations demonstrating excellence practice their processes no less than five hours per day? It may be part of the answer. But practicing redundant chords on my guitar day after day doesn't seem to make me Chet Atkins.

Cleaning the floor of the shop we own twice a day presents a nice, clean image, but what of the greeting and awareness provided by a sales associate or waitress behind the counter? Are their actions and practices consistent with an overall message of excellence and care? Do we practice the right actions? Do we have awareness that our every action results in a perceived reaction? Whether in the product we develop, service we offer or customer relations we create, we may not show a focus on star quality.

Maybe it's about training, or about careful hiring. As Bill Gates of Microsoft had done in his reign, he needed only to "hire the best" and continually train and direct their actions toward a goal of excellence. It is training, commitment and focus on quality customer service, product knowledge and a continued sparkle in all we do, all the time.

Whether in a Cannon Falls bank, a Texas school, or in our neighborhood metro copy service center, there's a common denominator. The best people are around us. We just need to nurture their souls, make them aware of the place they hold in the larger world and move all forward to excellence. Shop owners or leaders of nonprofits need to identify practices to get to the consistency needed in their chosen marketplace.

My thoughts suggest that the common denominator is leadership—another undefinable quality. What is it? Who has it? Where do we find the leaders who will make us more competitive as restaurateurs, software manufacturers, automotive dealers or non-profit organizations? Who will pick up the piece of paper on the floor?

We are they! I suggest that we begin to focus, define and clarify our total purposes as organization by preparing ourselves, first. As leaders and owners of entrepreneurial ventures we must develop our own knowledge base of effective leadership through reading, seeking and observing.

Through many years, I have attempted to identify the components of excellence in organizations. It has been a personal search that led me to conferences and conversation, to personal study, and to the application of principles I believe, heard and internalized. I was able to lead large organizations with the belief that, like Harry Truman, "the buck stops here." There was no one else to blame for success or error, no one to turn to for inspiration or grit in making tough decisions. Key to my belief was that it was my own integrity, skill and handling of very personal situations that worked to create the ethos and culture that bespoke the best.

It was my responsibility on whom to hire, how to organize and focus and whom to feature and nurture. My goal and outcome was to exemplify the best practices, establish the framework and then get out of the way. All players need to build the system for the common good. Once built, the leader serves as consultant, guide, and mentor. If effective, the organization will run on the skills and drive of those who understand their own very personal missions. Over the years, our schools have been fortunate to be recognized as national models of excellence.

Until we change our own definition of significance and focus to the greater good, we will never experience lasting victory and true excellence. Our actions speak so loudly that words can't be heard. We must decide who we are and act accordingly. No easy task. We must first identify the things and people from which to draw our identity. We must then renew our mind to the truth that there is a greater being who guides us, that our heart is at the soul of our business and that we want to lead.

Let me offer a three-part model of leadership.

I. Leadership Is a Construct

Philosophy is our bedrock to achievement.

We need to know who we are, what we care about and what we intend to do. To be successful in a leader role we must like people and envision their growth. We have to personally assess our commitment to people and product—and determine what we want to be our life's work. If we like only to work with numbers, then we should. If we care not for helping others, then don't. If we really want to focus on our people, community, and personal legacy, then we just need to roll up our sleeves and go to work. We will be those successful leaders who create environments of nurturing employees and customers to sustain a lasting culture of relationships, work, and product excellence.

Construct is concept. It must be our belief that we are destined to do well. As leaders, we must thoroughly understand our vision. We must prepare, train and understand, first of all, our own belief system—and then communicate those thoughts through our every action. We must become the model for the organization, the model of a life philosophy. As in the movie *Field of Dreams*, "build it and they will come."

We will not have Charley or Jane do it. We will demonstrate that we can and will do it. Whether it's grabbing a broom early in the morning before all others arrive, setting up a database to quantify our products and processes or defining a corporate model of mutual expectations, we must burn the midnight oil to verify both our skill and evidence our awareness.

Our modeling is under continuous observation by all with whom we work and know: "Wherever you go, there you are." We are observed by the way we walk, the personal contacts we have and the work we model on a daily basis. If we do not model personal excellence continuously, it will not be achieved in the organizations we serve.

The resilience we have as individuals has always amazed me. Every day starts fresh. Every Monday is a new beginning. After working a sixteen-hour day yesterday, how can I possibly awake refreshed and optimistic today to again make a maximum effort at organization, recognition of the good in others and the possibilities of the new day? It has to be that one has a genuine belief in the good of every person, in the ultimate belief that "good will out," that God will provide.

One has to get his or her head around one's own belief system, study the actions of those we choose to emulate and "just do it."

II. Leadership as Competence

We must recognize, like Toyota, that actions are quantifiable. Actions of the effective leader can be found in Stephen Covey's *Seven Habits of Highly Effective People*, in Carl Rogers's *On Becoming a Person* or in practices shown in multitudinous management books. Look at the leadership of Johnsonville brats, see what FISH! is all about; take a look at *Corps Business* to see how the Marines do it. The list is endless. Not one book has all the answers. We look at them all, extract what we will and create our own model of organizational and personal excellence. We will then be leading with soul.

I have been fortunate to assist hundreds of evolving leaders over the past fifteen years or so to create their own models of life planning. Using their personal metaphor of gardener or space traveler or coach or resource determiner, each has taken identified competencies, integrated them into their own "best practices" model and verified their experiences in each area to create a unique travel guide to success in leadership and excellence. They demonstrate, clarify and deduce the competencies they hold and then create the application of their model. We need to do the same.

Frameworks abound, but I like simplicity. Too many actions and responsibilities of the effective leader exist to be remembered in list form. Therefore, I ask each of us to find the three or four major groupings of responsibility that we know must be practiced to create excellence. As Edward Deming has suggested, "It's so simple." It may be as basic as these three areas:

A. Visioning

The effective leader will know that the key to success is visioning. Through integration, balance, judgment, self-awareness, problem analysis, policy decisions, and, ultimately, skill application, we will put our vision into practice. We will need to "measure twice and cut once." If we don't have an overall plan and vision of how things are to appear, then we need not measure. We just slap boards together.

But what of our final product? We must define the end first. What do we want our organization to look like in six months or five years? What do we envision for our product? What will be our corporate ethos? How will we be known? Who will hold responsibility in given areas, and how will they be accountable? How will leadership and people evolve? Oh, so much to do.

This is the area for our vision statement, our framework of belief, and the overall model of the organization. Doodling it out on a piece of paper, we look at our beliefs and attempt to create our own star and linkages. What aspects tie together to create our simple model that is easily understood by all—customer, employee, and community?

Rotary International believes in "Service Above Self," tied together with truth and fairness and goodwill and benefit to all. IBM says to "Think." Where do we want to focus our energy? Once determined, we set up the linkages to definable goals, performance standards, and measures of how we will know what we have achieved in each area. With three to five basic and specific goals created, we can then get on to achievement. These goals are extremely important. Although simply stated, they are the structures that drive our every move every day. They are not permanent. We need to be specific and get started, but as we proceed, we will look at the measures of our success and modify goals accordingly.

I like to think that I'm a good garage cleaner. I like the order and comfort that a garage provides me. It is my workshop, my home away from the office wherein I create my personal projects, store my tools and create the difference for self. Herman Hughes has suggested, "The difference between life and existence is the intelligent use of leisure." It's a small statement that has been on the wall over my workbench for many years.

I look forward to a sunlit spring day when I can get into the garage again and re-order the many parts and pieces of my leisure world. The most effective way for me to organize myself is to pull the items off the shelves, place them in the center of the large garage and replace them in the order that makes best sense for days ahead. I cast aside, hang on to the important and clearly understand what I have and what I need to do to give myself greatest efficiency and comfort.

So, too, with today's organizations. In mine, I would pull all the pieces off the shelf, take a look at them, understand their value and placement and put them back together in a new order. We must aim all the components toward the vision we hold and the job we have to accomplish. Once the garage is clean we can go about doing the business of our business. We must have clarity and focus and knowledge of how all the parts work together to achieve excellence. Once done, we begin to define.

B. Organizational Practices

A business plan is formed. Based upon our model, we isolate the structures that bring our vision into practice. No matter what our business, profit or non-profit, we need to know where we're going and how we will get there. We must shape the organization and be ready to facilitate change.

We must manage time effectively, establish events and cycles, create appropriate paces, design systems, identify staff development, and organize our measurement and evaluation. Budgets, financial processes, information collection, data systems, resource allocation, legal/regulatory responsibilities all call us to know the specifics of our business.

With these specifics of the organization, we establish a set of procedures critical to our success. How will we know when we have arrived? What are employee expectations? Manuals and guides must be established to verify consistency of practice. Employees must be trained. A quantification of all aspects is required.

The task seems daunting, but we can do it. Model business plans abound on the shelves of Barnes & Noble. We can easily go online and review successful models created by others. We can see how Shabby Chic modeled their worldwide enterprise, take a look at the vision of Oshkosh Motors or look at ISO 9200 standards. The "stuff" is there, we just need to borrow an idea from here and there and blend it into our own. Along the way, we will seek the counsel of successful entrepreneurs whom we know. It's amazing how easy it is to engage in conversation with successful leaders. They want to share. Just ask.

The effective leader takes the position of Jonathan Livingston Seagull in the book by Richard Bach, wherein he states, "he who flies highest sees furthest." As leaders, we are called to rise to a new level to see the whole landscape of our evolving organization. If we stay on the ground and in the fray, we will not see the whole picture. The effective leader is first the thinker, and then the doer. Laying out the structure is our unique province.

C. Human Development

We exist not to make widgets. We exist to serve. How will our widgets fit into the needs of others? Will our nuts and bolts be manufactured as tools to serve a larger world? Or do we envision their manufacture as simply a tool to the bottom line? Do we appreciate customers who use our product? Are we providing jobs to better the lives of our employees and society or are employees only tools themselves?

Our whole focus has to be on the capital of human development. Once we have that in our hearts, the sales and development of our organization will follow. A school exists to serve all—students, parents, community and employees. Our focus is on human development of every person in our organization. The tasks of learning and success of organization will follow. All of our organizations exist for service. Our challenge as leaders is to create the environment and nurture the people. Our reward comes from the service to others. Financial benefits will accrue naturally from our human focus.

For the leader, aspects of motivation and human need are to be known, acknowledged and foremost. The basic needs outlined by Abraham Maslow are the needs of each unique employee—safety, security, belonging and, ultimately, self-development. As employers, we are held to bring them to their highest possible level. As entrepreneurs, we need to know that all people have a style unique to their persona. It doesn't change from home to work to social setting.

We are the same wherever we go. Our goal is to recognize that each individual customer and employee is met where they are. Some are fact-driven, some are emotion-oriented, and some are more gregarious than others.

To be successful leaders and entrepreneurs, we must provide the best to each. We need to be able to discern their basic style and meet them where they are. Some will need just the facts. Others will need to "feel good." How do we meet unique employees and customer/client needs?

We are constant human developers, no matter our enterprise.

III. Leadership Is Continuous

Running is a challenge. I was challenged by Dr. Cooper's U.S. Air Force workout strategy thirty or more years ago. I needed to earn thirty points a week. Various configurations were allowed: walking, running five days, running three days. After getting by my initial quarter-mile run (my limit), I set my sights on three times per week for one and a half miles each time. Somehow, I made the goal—and continued it for thirty years! It became three to four miles, three to four times per week. How boring. How redundant. But I enjoyed the challenge, the beauty of nature in spring and winter and all year long. Running in sleet and minus-five-degree temperatures, I enjoyed every moment. It paid off in my long-term mental and physical health. Running in weekend ten-kilometer races was just a bonus. I had a whole drawer full of colorful t-shirts from the various races.

Today I keep on running. In my seventies, my doctors tell me to keep on exercising, moving and creating my own "heart healthy." I stretch, pull, lift and plant something new every day—written or organic. Better I should fall from exhaustion than to waste away on the couch.

Leadership is no different. It is continuous. One starts out in small steps, finds the pace and continues on. You just don't get to quit. Every day you rise with expectation that you can and will do it. We will study and acknowledge and nurture and guide. It is a part of our being.

We cannot be angry one day or revert to a different behavior. That will undo the best we have created. We must consistently give to all we serve. It is affirming to self and all concerned. It is about the "ABCs" suggested by radio personality Mitch Anthony, who offers that it is about our "Attitude, Behavior, and Control."

With high standards for self and organization, we will strengthen our corporate culture, enrich the lives of others we serve, and arrive at a bottom line we never would have anticipated.

We will arrive at excellence. It is our quest.

The War Comes to Goodview: German POWs of World War II

Some of us were born in the year of the bombing of Pearl Harbor. We grew up with the Victory Gardens of World War II and the necessity to get by with whatever was available in food, heat, or clothing. We were fashionable in our "coat of many colors" long before Dolly Parton sang the song. We were a patchwork of the best that parents and teachers and community could make of us. We were a part of a Mulligan stew generation.

Aside from the *Republican-Herald* daily newspaper, our exposure to the greater world was limited. We didn't travel unless it was on our bike or in the backseat of an uncle's 1940 Plymouth for an occasional Sunday ride in the country. Even after the war, shortages of sugar and gasoline and tires were with us. Rationing via government coupon books may have ceased, but limited dollars in households still severely delimited our ability to purchase.

At some time in the 1950s, my eldest brother, Frank, made a trip with friends to Florida. He brought back mesh bags of oranges and grapefruit, causing our eyes to bulge out. The only other travelers we had known were those able to return from World War II duties and those seen getting ready to be shipped off to the Korean War a few years later. We did get an annual visit from our Dad's cousin who had grown up in the area, but settled in California after the war.

Half of the men of Winona County ages eighteen to thirty-six were called to military service in World War II—3,351 men. Of those, 2,261 entered the service, as evidenced in a listing in the *Republican-Herald* of December 1944. Reading the names of that listing is to read the pages of a directory of Winona, with every ethnic group, neighborhood, and position of labor represented. One who served in the U.S. Navy of World War II said: "There was no hesitancy." The call of the nation was heeded.

Sixty-eight men of the county died in service to their country. Sixteen additional men were listed as missing. Additionally listed were prisoners of war, similar in number to the missing.

In total, German and Japanese captors held over 40,000 Americans. The permanent German camps for American enlisted men were known as *stalags* (from *stammlager*), with *lager* meaning camp. The *offizerlager* (*oflag*) was for officers and the *luftlager* for airmen. The Red Cross chapter of Winona was instrumental in locating and aiding families and camps of American prisoners of war.

Less well known were the Japanese camps for American prisoners. They were mostly undocumented and uncooperative. Extremely harsh conditions prevailed for prisoners—with starvation, slave labor, beatings, and death a standard.

The total number of opposing prisoners of war in the United States in 1945 was 358,000—including 306,000 Germans, 50,000 Italians and 2,800 Japanese. In our region, these men were housed in St. Charles (Whitewater), Galesville, Sioux Falls, Faribault, Milwaukee, Camp McCoy, Algona, and Princeton. Further north, they were placed in lumber camps and Civilian Conservation Corps camps reactivated to house the prisoners.

Minnesota's prisoners ranged from those CCC camps of the northland to the verdant fields and trout streams of Winona County. Fourteen camps with three thousand prisoners were established in Wisconsin, including at Camp McCoy and Galesville in 1944 and 1945. Nearly four hundred German prisoners were housed in the city park of Galesville in a "tent colony" and sent out to work throughout the area. From Holmen to Blair to Onalaska and West Salem, these soldiers, a part of Rommel's "Afrikan Corps," had been in the country since 1943. They were moved to Wisconsin to be used in fields and in canning plants. There were six escapees over time from Japanese work crews of McCoy, all recaptured.

The Algona, Iowa, facility of German prisoners spun off thirty-four smaller camps and ten thousand prisoners. One hundred and fifty prisoners came from Algona to a reactivated CCC camp at Whitewater State Park near Elba and St. Charles. These "aviators and paratroopers aged seventeen to twenty-five, at least one of whom was a Messerschmitt fighter pilot," worked hard. They were fed eighteen hundred to two thousand calories per day, the same as received by guards and American prisoners in German camps.

Prisoners maintained a six-day week of ten-hour days. Paid eighty cents per day by the U.S. government to work, these young men enjoyed playing soccer in the prison fields, swimming in the river-fed pool and lounging on the beach of Whitewater River in off times. Two German staff sergeants (*oberfeldwebeis*) were in charge of internal prisoner control and pay allocation. Prisoners suggested: "Their word is law!"

The prisoners were fed, clothed and housed exactly as were the American guards. If a prisoner slacked off or was difficult, that prisoner was sent back to the Algona facility. These young men felt the valleys of the Whitewater were akin to "the homeland" and frequently cried softly for the same. They admitted, "American beer was up to par with German beer."

The government rate charged for prisoners to work at outside facilities, including local farms, was fifty-five cents per hour—a fair rate of the times. The prisoners of Whitewater were available to farms of the area for planting, dairy chores or the like. Farmers were responsible for daily prisoner transportation to and from camp. A related transport of prisoners to Dakota County farms in September 1945, from Faribault, resulted in a bus crash and rollover resulting in injury to twenty-seven.

Nicholas Meyers, a Winona realtor, hired three prisoners from Whitewater on a sunny day in June 1945. They were to paint a house at West Wabasha and Hilbert Streets. They allegedly painted a swastika on the house. The local painters' union objected to the use of prisoners for painting, and the activity ceased. The prisoners were also punished, having been put on "bread and water."

A report from Whitewater of the one hundred and fifty prisoners there in June 1944 stated: "They still think Hitler will win the war and don't like to be called 'Nazis.' They are courteous and obedient, but they have a definite superior attitude." Like all young men, they liked to wear shorts in their work in the summer. Overall at Whitewater, there was "no trouble with the prisoners."

"A dozen or more German prisoners" came to our neighboring village of Goodview, according to my ninety-year-old source living only blocks away. Prisoners were responsible for a major village garden on Sixth Street in the space of the current park. They were most probably assigned from Whitewater Camp to the village to till the soil in the heart of the village, under the watchful eyes of a village supervisor and two visiting eight-year-old neighbor boys.

Wayne and Fred came by (with parent permission) to greet and observe the young soldiers at work. Wayne's father had a background in the German language. He would set up the little ones with an occasional word or two to carry to the soldiers—most in fun or jest. Fred, now older, remembers there was no guard on duty, although a fence may have separated prisoners from boys. He does remember these fearsome enemy boys "laughing like hell" over the younger boys' scrambled words and the fun of the moment.

The prisoners had their chance to be out in other fields and working the canneries in their shorts. The record-breaking pea crop of 1945 "was saved by POW labor. In southern Minnesota, 2,411 prisoners were employed in the pea harvest," a report from the time says. Others were digging potatoes in Iowa, or assisting in Sioux Falls, Milwaukee, Plainview or Princeton. The beautiful hills of Lodi, Wisconsin, in the Madison area must have been remindful for German prisoners of the Alps of their home region as they worked those fields.

The prisoner received his eighty cents per day in "canteen coupons" to purchase candy and personal items, including tobacco in bags with papers for hand rolling (probably Bull Durham). No cigarettes were available. Beer was available, although the young men were more interested in white or chocolate milk to build their bodies.

Meals at Whitewater consisted of soup and stew twice per day, with their favorite dark rye bread made at Fort Snelling, the main purveyor of food for the camp. It was reported, "meat is not plentiful enough for once a day, so it is given twice per day in soups and stews. The only whole meat served is mutton." Cabbage, lettuce, and vegetables were plentiful, with corn refused by prisoners because it was seen as "hog feed." Interesting that the Winona newspaper was reporting at the same time that the local Swift Packing Plant was having record sales and production of beef and pork.

Provost Marshal General Archer Lerch "says the War Department has abundant evidence to prove our treatment of German war prisoners has had a direct effect in securing better treatment for American prisoners in Germany."

In total, the government estimated that it "realized $102 million from [the prisoners'] work" in 1945. Interestingly, "Officers may not be compelled to work and are paid according to rank" if they choose to work.

By May of 1945, General Dwight Eisenhower and the powers in Washington decided it was time to stop receiving additional German prisoners and to return those here to their homeland. The two hundred prisoners of Whitewater were moved to Crookston in October 1945, with twenty remaining behind to take down the twelve-foot enclosures. Following suit, Camp McCoy was closed on June 15, 1946. By July 1946, few German prisoners remained in the United States." They were "being sent ahead to England and to British-occupied Germany." By August of 1947, the last three prisoners (of 430,000) had left the U.S.

It has been rumored that some of the German prisoners in this country were involved with girls of the area. In Michigan in July 1944, two German prisoners, both age twenty, left the canning plant where they worked with two young ladies, ages twenty and eighteen. Three prisoners of our area decided to attend the county fair at Owatonna in August 1945 in their POW work uniforms—but returned of their own volition to camp. It was not stated whether they had met any young ladies.

In the years to follow, we camped at Whitewater, swam at the same "pool" prisoners had visited and marched to Boy Scout Sunday services at the golf course, not knowing that these very paths and hills were accommodations to some of the world's most fearless fighters only a few years previously. Our nation, state and troop flags were held high as we marched in the sunrise.

In May 1953, a tornado struck Whitewater with a vengeance, tearing down the last vestiges of the CCC and German POW camp facilities. Virtually every building in the main campground was destroyed or irreparably damaged. Fortunately, camped-out Y-teens and Boy Scouts had returned to Winona before the whirling seventy-mile-per-hour winds struck at 6:00 p.m.

An Elba farmer in the Whitewater Valley said: "It all happened at once." All his buildings were toppled and his house "jumped the foundation." "The grave markers at the Catholic cemetery of Elba were leveled by the winds," he recounted. Two St. Charles boys sat through the middle of the storm at Whitewater in a Model A Ford. Their car was parked on the bridge near the former POW camp. When the storm passed, the car was damaged, the boys were safe—and all their tires were flat.

The Gamehaven Council of Boy Scouts held its annual camporee two weeks later. Over three hundred Winona County Scouts cleared trees in the redefined "workaree," doing a Boy Scout "good turn that drew public praise." One year later in May 1954, the Gamehaven Camporee celebrated with fifteen hundred southeastern Minnesota Boy Scouts at the refurbished Whitewater campgrounds.

As I fish for trout on the Whitewater River these days, I think of the history held by the beautiful bluffs, valleys and the hardwood forests surrounding me.

Years have passed since the days of war prison camps and personal rationing. We have moved on from Victory Gardens to backyard barbecues and to full sustenance. The CCC pavilion and stone walls of the 1930s yet stand at Whitewater as gentle reminders of earlier days.

We can be proud of the humane treatment offered by area residents to German prisoners in a time when our young men were being assaulted on the beaches of Anzio and Normandy. Former Galesville prisoner Ludwig Hilman, by then a law student in Germany, wrote in 1947 to thank the Vincent family of the township of Gale for the work, food, and hospitality provided by the Vincent family and farm.

Residing in the bombed-out shell of his German village, he and others lived with severe food and fuel shortages. In his letter, he spoke for many of the prisoners who had served their time in the Winona area. Attending classes in his overcoat due to the cold, he stated, "I would rather work for you than study here in Germany."

Kent Stever heard rumors of German POWs being in the Winona area during World War II. He needed to investigate to find the reality, the story to be remembered. He found it in the stacks of the Winona Newspaper Project at Winona State University, his alma mater. He is a frequent visitor to Whitewater.

Chapter Seven

Howie's Varsity Inn: Our Home Away from Home

Cheerleader Eugene Thrune led the charge of support for the Bowemen of Winona High in 1932. Known as Bowemen long before they were Winhawks, the first evidence of the "Winhawks" name appeared in the *Republican-Herald* of March 1941.

All-State gridiron star, tri-state shot put champion, "C Club" president and basketball team leader Loy F. Bowe came to the high school in 1923 from Carleton College. He brought his many talents as science teacher and coach to serve through twenty-three masterful years of unprecedented winning in three sports—basketball, football, and track. In all the stories of the *Republican-Heral*d from the 1920s through the early 1940s, team members were known as Bowemen.

From undefeated Big Eight football teams to national track competitors and state basketball tourney participants, the Bowemen were consistent leaders—and proud of it. Bowe eventually served as director of athletics and coach. While teaching, administering and coaching three sports, he created records yet unbroken. Not ready to rest on his laurels, he left with grand acclaim in 1946 to his hometown of Northfield and the field of business.

Some of those early 1930s Bowemen may have hung out at Paulson's Confectionary on the corner of Fourth and Johnson streets. Changing confectionary form, Jack Paulson's The Dugout—Winona's New Modern Ice Cream Shoppe opened anew in 1939. Jack featured brick ice cream, malts, sandwiches and sodas in his newly remodeled facility. The horseshoe-shaped lunch counter of 1939 stayed in style for years to come. Additionally, with "fourteen streamlined [round stools] of chrome and green leather, padded seat booths and a long candy case," the scene was set for youthful enjoyment. In the 1950s, I took my turn spinning on the stools.

It is certain that Jack Walz, Warner Buswell, and Howie Johnson of Winona's state champion basketball team of 1935 were a few of the hometown boys (and girls) who stopped by the Dugout and its predecessor. Howie was one of those who "brightened the outlook for the orange and black" in 1935. A hometown boy all the way, Johnson was basketball guard and state tournament team member.

In 1934, one thousand people saw Howie and the Bowemen team lose in district basketball finals to Rochester on their home court of the high school auditorium/gymnasium on Fifth Street. Supporters ringed the floor in the courtside balcony. Others enjoyed the main floor of auditorium seating to face Winhawk cheerleaders on the full stage. Howie had one point in the momentous loss.

Mr. and Mrs. Frank Campbell, early Winona confectioners, took over the business from Paulson to further refine their "Campbell's Butterscotch Corn," caramel apples, and peanut brittle (at sixty cents per pound). All the treats came with the sparkling furnishings when Howie Johnson took over in December 1946, to become owner and full-time operator of the "new" Howie's Varsity Inn. With his sparkling personality, ready smile, and excellent skills on the grill, he easily became the self-proclaimed "King of Hamburgers."

Howie began ownership of his newly named Varsity Inn at about age thirty, following three and a half years in World War II as an anti-aircraft gunner and a year or two working with R.D. Cone Hardware and Woolworth's. He was just old enough to run his "business based on friendliness" and also to still remember the fun-filled and celebrity roots of his beloved high school, only a block away.

As Arnold's Drive-In of *Happy Days* television fame did for youth from 1974 to 1984, Howie's made a place for all the Fonzies and Richies and Chachis and others of Winona in the 1950s. We were all welcomed at "the Vars." "The Fonz" (Fonzie Fonzerelli), Richie Cunningham, Lori Beth, Chachi, Marion, LaVerne and Shirley all would have fitted in well with the habitués of Howie's Varsity Inn and students of Winona High. It was a gathering place for evening events, a rendezvous for all manner of teenage tomfoolery. It was our home away from home—and we were all welcomed!

There were ducktails, A-line skirts, white blouses, hot rods, Triumph motorcycles, and Model A's all gathered on the corner on any given night. On brick-pathed Johnson Street, we watched teenage tire squealers, patrons of the State Theater, visitors to Buck's Candy and Corn Shop, and those filling up for twenty-five cents per gallon at the Clark and Pure gas stations across

Varsity Inn, 1955. (Photo courtesy of the Winona Newspaper Project.)

the street. Girls were there to be whistled at in summer shorts as they disgorged en masse from someone's dad's DeSoto woody convertible or 1955 Ford station wagon The public library was only a block away (a good excuse to be out)—and yet near the action of the Vars.

The only damage ever done was by some early teens who broke into the Vars in 1951 to steal candy, gum, and cigarettes from Howie. Someone clipped Howie's dark prescription glasses and billfold from his car in 1947. He offered in the newspaper a five-dollar reward (no questions asked) for their return. One night when young toughs were not on their chosen corner, a local man exposed himself to four girls outside the Vars—and then followed the girls for a couple of blocks

A booth jukebox in the 1950s. (Photo courtesy of ebay.)

The jukebox offered the best of rock and roll for a nickel a toss. Most-requested songs of the class of 1959 were: *A White Sport Coat (And A Pink Carnation), Peggy Sue, Wake Up Little Susie, Mr. Sandman* and *Love Letters in the Sand.*

Next to the jukebox, we could try a pinball machine for another nickel, when "Jukes" Briesath wasn't playing it.

We assembled over cokes, had a twenty-five-cent lunch in our allotted lunch hour and smoked a bit in the back booths, hoping that "Vic," the athletic director, wasn't lurking nearby. Football players and cheerleaders alike lost a few weeks of participation when one was caught "holding a lighted cigarette for someone else." Many assembled on game nights and on summer weekends before setting out for the school sock hop, a summer night of swimming at "the Pits" or a trip across the river to Merrick Park's unsupervised beer stand.

All in all, Howie's space was safe. All protected him and our mutual environment—save for the few rowdies who were arrested in 1958 for "egging" cars on the eve of the homecoming bonfire and snake dance. They were dealt with by the oft-noted "juvenile authorities"—one of whom we knew to be "Pus-Eye" the probation officer.

In Howie's remodeled facility and his 1955 ads, he offered his juicy burger with fried onions on a fresh Federal Bakery bun for twenty cents. Hot dogs were fifteen cents, popcorn five and ten cents, shakes nineteen cents, "extra-heavy malts" twenty-four cents—with the hot fudge sundae topping the menu at twenty-eight cents. A coke in a cup was a nickel. The Butterscotch Corn, caramel apples, and peanut brittle had vanished.

Alongside Nora Lee Kane and others of the Winhawks cheering team in the early 1950s, explorer scout, orchestra member and actor Gilbert Bergsrud was head cheerleader, following the tradition of Eugene Thrune of the 1930s. On nice football days, school pep fests were held on the front steps of the high school on Broadway. The band played the Winona fight song as principal R.J. "Rock Jaw" Williams watched over us from his office window.

All-American Paul Giel stopped by the Vars in his baseball travels from summer ball at Athletic Park to high school stardom to the hometown amateur Winona Braves and Chiefs. He moved on to the University of Minnesota and the New York Giants as pitcher, but didn't forget his shared experiences with Howie. He was unprecedented as an All-American in both football and baseball at the University of Minnesota and as a force present on my boyhood paper route, which included the Giels' small home on Dacota Street.

Howie welcomed all, superstar or not. The occasional quiet moment with him was always friendly. Like a true Winhawk (or Boweman), Howie remained a sports star in his adult years, often capturing first place in area golf tournaments. In 1957, he was the Westfield Champion golfer.

After thirteen years of 6:30 a.m. to 11:00 p.m. hours (and Sundays 8:00 a.m. to 9:00 p.m.), Howie gave in and sold the business in 1960 to another Winona native and fellow state tournament basketball player (of 1956). Bob Prudoehl was teammate to Tenold Milbrandt, Don Klagge, Chuck Wally, Mel Awes, and others who had all spent time at the Vars. As the new owner, Bob continued the traditions of long hours until the new high school opened on West Gilmore Avenue.

Bob's Vars sponsored a baseball team in the city league. He also made tickets available for community and youth events. Like Howie, he sold tickets for "rassling matches," circuses, a Conway Twitty concert at the Armory in 1960, and tickets for rides on the riverboat *Avalon*.

Howie had "no announced plans at that moment" as he left the Vars behind. He stayed with his summer drive-in at the junction of Fifth and Broadway from 1959 until 1962, when his property was auctioned off. He soon found a comfortable space on the staff of Nelson Tire Service—across the street from the Vars. He remained there for many years of successful sales of tires to former hamburger customers.

Howie was a "straight shooter" who knew how to serve a burger and make a friend. He allowed us to gather in his space and create our own culture and experiences.

We Winhawks are thankful for the memories.

"There Were Many Heroes": The Northwest Airline Crash of Fountain City

In 1948, World War II had only recently ended.

The boys were back on the farms, driving the city buses and finding new jobs in Winona's burgeoning industries. On this August day, Mercury was announcing its "all-new" 1949 model—on display at Nystrom Motors on West Third Street, nearly overlooking the Mississippi River.

The State Theater a few blocks away featured Judy Garland and Gene Kelly in *The Pirate*, with the Avon on Third Street offering a more ominous *Dark Passage* starring Humphrey Bogart. On Thursday evening coming, the Steamer *Avalon* promised to leave the city levee at 9:00 p.m. for a moonlight cruise—the "final cruise of the season." With the Duke Hampton Orchestra on board, it promised to be a fun evening on the water—for only $1.50 each (drinks not included).

Even though rain was coming, folks were enjoying another Sunday of late summer on the Mississippi near Winona. Some were traveling upstream toward Fountain City, Wisconsin. A short boat trip up the river and through the lock and dam brought one to the dockside restaurant harbor of Wally's. Folks were on their way for an early evening dinner at the famous supper club where both boaters and drivers of Highway 35 could enjoy a sumptuous dinner—and the river's beauty at sunset.

Amiable host Wally Valentine, formerly of the Oaks Supper Club, greeted patrons at dockside, while "Rusty" manned the inside bar, serving up the finest of cocktails and an after-dinner "floated B&B" for some.

A Day on the River

It had been another glorious summer on the river. With fall coming, there was the necessary change of clothing from swimsuit to sweater or jacket. Each setting was equally invigorating. Soon showy, lapped-strake, wood-sided ski boats and oversized Whitcraft houseboats would be tucked away. Fall duck hunting and fishing boats would follow. Winter's wonders would soon appear. Oak and maple and hickory trees of hardwood forests leading up and over beautiful limestone bluffs on both sides of the river brought a sunburst setting—an autumn flameout and view unequalled in the world.

All were at ease after the travesty of war. Business was happening with sales of homegrown agricultural products. Bay State Milling Flour was being shipped via barge and rail across the region. Winona's new HOPTO digger was a worldwide sensation. Commerce was engaged—with major cities of Chicago and Minneapolis handling the business of business. DC-3 plane flights to Winona by North Central Airlines were a new luxury offering, shuttling folks across the region.

For shuttle service between Minneapolis and Chicago, Northwest Airlines served its customers with a new fleet of Glenn Martin planes, the Martin 2-0-2, certified in August 1947 to replace the aging DC-3. In a matter of hours, one could be whisked from one big city to another for meetings and shopping and a move with a higher social class. Airliner trips had not yet become available—or even on the radar—for family workers who existed on their "breadwinner's" wage of $1.35 per hour at the Ford garage, as milk bottle washer, Swift Plant "hog slogger," Peerless chain maker or teller at the bank. Folks in suits and ties and Sunday finery occupied the seats of the airliners.

The Martin 2-0-2 plane leaving Chicago for Minneapolis at 3:50 p.m. on Sunday afternoon was one of twenty-five in the Northwest Airlines fleet. The normally scheduled 2:30 p.m. flight of thirty-seven, including crew, would arrive in Minneapolis by 5:30 p.m. On board were four people from New York, nine from Chicago and a half-dozen or so from the Twin Cities area. One mother securely held her two- and four-year-old children. They were assured of their safety. Northwest Airlines had two months ago received a National Safety Council Award for having flown over a billion miles without an accident.

Glenn Luther Martin (1886 to 1955) of Macksburg, Iowa, was an American aviation pioneer. He designed and built his own aircraft and was an active pilot. He founded his own aircraft company in 1912. He merged his company in 1961 to become Martin-Marietta. Today, through mergers, it has been amalgamated into the Lockheed Martin Company, a leader in missiles and space systems.

Martin flew self-built seaplanes over water to new records in the 1910s. Soon thereafter, his company designed aircraft for the military, including bombers for both world wars. An early success came during World War I, with

Former Northwest Airline 1947 Martin 2-0-2, 1973. (Photo courtesy of Wikipedia.)

production of the MB-1 bomber. The MB-2 and others were also successful. In 1932, Martin won the Collier Trophy for his involvement with the Martin B-10 bomber. His work as aircraft builder continued into World War II with the building of the B-26 bomber and Navy PBM-1 "flying boat."

On the afternoon of August 29, 1948,Northwest Airlines Flight 421, carrying thirty-four passengers and three crewmembers, took off from Chicago and headed toward an upriver rainstorm. The storm of Sunday came across the region with a vengeance, with late afternoon damage extensive in a swath from Winona to St. Charles. At LaCrosse, the pilot sought to lower his altitude to avoid the storm racing up the Hiawatha Valley. As the plane traveled over the Winona area, the Mississippi River and the beautiful bluffs of nearby Fountain City, a wing was lost.

Eyewitness Harold Rackow, living across the river on Winona's Prairie Island, stated, "There was a flash of lightning. It struck the plane. A part of the wing fell off and the ship started down." Other witnesses confirmed the sighting.

Pilots from the Winona airport immediately flew circles around the area seeking the wreckage. They located the crash at 6:30 p.m. on Sutter's Ridge, near the site of Midway Tavern (midway between Winona and Fountain City), and landed their planes at the John Sutter farm on the ridge. The Northwest plane had crashed approximately two hundred feet down a five-hundred foot bluff—with no survivors. Sheared off by the wind or buffeted so as to not stand the strain, the outcome was the same. Thirty-seven members of the flight perished on the ridge overlooking the Mississippi River between Winona and Fountain City.

Winona's First Responders

First responders were Everett Laak and Walter Haeussinger of the Winona Police Department, Executive Editor Gordon Closway of the *Republican-Herald*, and newspaper photographer Bill White. Closway received a call at 5:30 p.m. He and White were the "Newsmen in First Party to Reach Scene of Crash."

Climbing up from the Midway, they found a horrific sight as they traveled up a gully with a stream-like flow of rainwater, described as "almost a raging river." They found on the muddy hillside the first victim and another and another, documenting their feelings and photo shots as they climbed. Two of the fatalities seen on their uphill climb included a "Woman found with child in her arms."

They reported further, "As we got almost to the top of the hill, we came upon a terrible sight. There it was. Wreckage and people were wrapped around trees and rocks in an area approximately one hundred feet wide and two hundred feet deep."

Bob McQueen of Winona recently recalled to me his experiences of that fateful day:

> Bob McDougal and I were seventeen years old at the time, avid Boy Scouts, having both earned the Eagle Award. We were listening to the radio when a news flash said that this plane was missing and believed to have crashed in the bluffs across the river from Winona. The weather was horrible, but there was uncertainty if, in fact, this crash had occurred. We decided to go help in the search.
>
> When we arrived at the base of the bluff there were only a few people there, with a lot of water running in streams off the hills. We stepped on some rocks to jump over a river-let and a person following behind us let out a scream. We turned and saw an arm still attached to a headless torso lying in the mud and water. This could have been the first body found.
>
> Somehow we teamed up with Winona County Coroner Dr. Robert Tweedy, who determined we needed a way to get to the top of the bluff, as it was impossible to hike through all the mud. We aided in securing a sleigh and a pair of horses from some farmer nearby and we rode up the bluff with the coroner and maybe two other people on the sleigh. Nearing the top of the bluff and having only flashlights for light, the coroner spotted a dark hole in the ground.
>
> We jumped from the sleigh into a field of knee-high grass. The coroner commented that someone had hit here headfirst and slid down the hillside, as was evident by the tall grass bent down about shoulder width, for about 200 feet. I remember walking down there with the coroner to discover another headless body with an open torso. I held the flashlight for him as he lifted the torso onto his knee to write and tag the body.
>
> Not the kind of experience you want to witness as a young lad.

H.F. Stohr, Buffalo County coroner, took immediate action to commandeer a facility and create a morgue for victims in the Community Auditorium of Fountain City. With volunteers from Winona and the area working throughout the night, bodies were carried up the slope and to the morgue.

Ropes were used to aid "Silent litter bearers [who] fought their way up the hill, four to six to a stretcher." A team of horses and wagon awaited the first victims, with other bodies "handed up the slope to waiting trucks which brought them to the auditorium." Unidentified victims were moved to Winona funeral homes, with Winona police detectives Ev Laak and George Meiers seeking fingerprint identification through the FBI. By 1:00 p.m. on Monday, "the remains of all passengers and crew were accounted for—having been carried off in the darkness of Sunday night and Monday morning."

Armed guards were set up by police to ward off thrill-seekers and those called "ghouls" by Dr. Stohr. He reported, "looting of the crash scene was widespread, with missing rings and jewelry." Armed deputies fired shots in the air to chase off the "ghouls," who were reported to have been seen "stealing teeth with gold fillings and cash from billfolds."

Some of the regular boaters of Winona were on the river below the bluff on that fateful Sunday, including Commodore Howard Clark of the Winona Boat Harbor and his wife, well-known insurance and community leaders. The Clarks found parts of the plane's wing at the riverside.

Due to high winds, other items of the plane and victims' luggage receipts, identification cards and personal belongings from the crash were found on rooftops and driveways of Winona, and within a six-mile radius of the site. A.J. Gappa of 613 West Fourth Street found a foot-square piece of the plane's fuselage in his yard.

Winona native Jack Volkel, a pilot captain for Northwest Airlines, was spending the weekend in Winona after his usual Chicago to Minneapolis run on Friday. En route to Fountain City for dinner that afternoon, he discovered a piece of the plane's tail assembly and called NWA—the company's first notification. He later identified the found wing as that of the Martin 2-0-2.

All victims were carefully tended to by volunteers, Dr. Stohr and Winona police, who at one time numbered over twenty. Winona funeral directors helped with the proper handling of victims and their families' needs. On the day of the crash, over three hundred and fifty long distance phone calls were made to operators of the Fountain City telephone exchange. The Winona exchange needed additional operators to handle calls from across the nation.

The Flag at the Fountain City Auditorium Flew at Half-Mast

The day after the crash, Winona resident David Schmidt, age sixteen, listened on his advanced short wave radio to an evening report of the crash on a station from Leopoldville, Belgian Congo—a station to which he normally listened. He reported the reception to be "clear as a bell." At the Community Auditorium, the flag flew at half-mast.

For the Labor Day weekend and for two weeks thereafter, armed guards were at the crash site on twelve-hour shifts, being paid $1.25 per hour by the county. Farmer and landowner John Sutter reported that with guards still posted, "there must have been 8,000 to 10,000 people per day on the Labor Day weekend. It was just like a county fair!" In ensuing weeks, Sam Weisman, Winona junk dealer, gathered six thousand pounds of metal (ninety-nine percent aluminum) to be sent "to a salvage company in Illinois."

Weeks later, the Buffalo County Board offered sincere thanks, praise and acknowledgement to Chief August Bingold and the hardy police corps of Winona.

The *Republican-Herald* reported a year later; " There were many heroes. There were those who remained nameless for glory, but who undertook to labor during the disaster—police, newsmen, volunteers to handle traffic and those who struggled up the cliff with the bodies."

On the October 1948 day of Harry Truman's ten-minute whistle stop in Winona, which attracted seven thousand people at the Chicago and Northwestern Depot on Huff and Third streets, a first Civil Aeronautics Board NWA crash hearing was held at the Winona Hotel. With officials from Minneapolis and Washington following "an administrative procedure," Winona witnesses were called.

Fisherman Jack Strain had observed the storm and plane at the Winona Dam. Ralph Rydman, observer at his home in the west end, and others detailed their observations. Rydman explained; "the plane went straight down." An NWA pilot flying the same route the same day of the crash offered a competent witness. On a flight from Madison, he requested bypassing LaCrosse due to "the most vicious storm I have ever seen." He landed at Rochester, saying that even in Rochester, "there was no end to the storm."

The Aftermath

Thirty wrongful death lawsuits totaling $425,000.00 were filed against Northwest Airlines. The airline in turn filed suit against Glenn L. Martin Manufacturing, claiming "the airplane was defective" and "the wing sheared off." Northwest sought an award beyond $800,000.00.

The jury trial was held for forty-eight days in Cleveland from January through July 1953. Mr. and Mrs. Clark and six other Winonans were called to testify. After due deliberation, the reduced request of $725,000.00 was rejected by the jury. Northwest Airlines intended to appeal.

The appeal was granted in 1955 and moved forward in Baltimore courts in 1957, seeking an award of $349,095.00—to include $232,720.00 in death claims paid by Northwest. Settlement occurred in 1959, with a final award of $900,000.00.

Pilot Roscoe D. Webster, sales manager of St. Paul, often flew a circuitous flight in his small plane across the Midwest. In travels for sales and service, he found a storm in 1951 near Winona, causing him to attempt a landing on a Wisconsin bluff only hundreds of yards from the NWA site. Unfortunately, Webster struck the bluff and died. Neighboring farmers heard his engine and the resultant crash.

NWA's Martin 2-0-2 faced another weather-related challenge in March of 1950. A ferocious winter snowstorm with "visibility of zero and winds of tornadic proportions" precipitated a crash into a Minneapolis residential home—and the death of fifteen. Winona Municipal Airport assistant manager Verne Armstrong was present, following emergency vehicles to the site. He reported, "A wing of the aircraft was found several blocks from the crash scene in a residential area of South Minneapolis near Wold-Chamberlin Field.

The fatal crash in 1948 of Northwest Airlines Flight 421 revealed a serious structural problem in the wings. Structural metal fatigue was the problem in a major wing spar. Alloy 7075-T6 was used, which is susceptible to stress-corrosion cracking and low toughness. The airliner was grounded and modifications were made. The wing components were redesigned and the engines replaced.

TWA and Northwest, initial customers of the 2-0-2, eventually sold their Martin 2-0-2s to California Central and Pioneer Airline. Only one of the manufactured forty-seven planes remains—in the Aviation Hall of Fame and Museum of New Jersey.

John Sutter, interviewed on his peaceful Wisconsin land a year after the crash said; "You'd never know the place. It's changed so."

The reporting city editor of the *Republican-Herald* stated, "Nature has wiped out the scars of the disaster. Oak trees are growing normally and the ground is covered with weeds. Nature has a way of hiding scars—of trying to forget, as it were, the intrusions of man. Far below, the Mississippi flows serenely to the ocean."

Shoveling Out to Sunshine

We were still shoveling out at the end of March.

As teenagers, ever hopeful to get to the state basketball tournament in the Twin Cities in someone's 1949 Ford, we prayed for a break in southern Minnesota snowstorms to allow us to get there. Not to be. It was a given that the snow would come at March tournament time. We had outlasted below-zero days, record low temperatures and toboggan runs on soft winter snows, with only warm cocoa to sustain us. We walked to school in January and February on frozen, creaking sidewalk snow. High-banked street side paths across the top of city plow mounds allowed us to traverse the Alps. It was still winter, still fun.

March melting led us to drab days of April. But the cool rain was cleansing. Cold trickles down the back of our necks reminded us that we were yet in a combination semi-state of winter tundra and soft spring rain. It was time to take off rubber mittens and go to work reconstructing our bikes in the unheated shed. After a few cold, skinned knuckles, we rode through puddles and sprayed our backs with fenderless tires. Today we keep the shovels and snowblower handy.

This year's skies of May held blue-sky promise, but not for long. With tempestuous storms and thundercloud moments, we have been occasionally buffeted by warm south winds—and then again reminded of cooler days by a strong turn from the north. The apple trees have kept their blossoms hidden. And why not?

At the beginning of May, I put on my rubber boots and oversized rain jacket to go trout fishing in southern Minnesota—and followed the snowplow for nearly thirty miles. Staying home, I wandered the street after a rainstorm to gather nightcrawlers. What's a person to do? In Arizona, I would be out sweeping the street. No nightcrawlers there.

Today's skies of mid-May remain dismally dark. In Spokane and Seattle they settle for this as weather all winter long. In April (like us) they had one fair day, with fourteen days of rain—and ten of fog. So did we. It's been weird spring weather the past few years. I have a neverending question of whether to plant or whether to shovel. My ninety-year-old friend knew better. He kept a warm greenhouse in his heated garage.

We tell ourselves that we are hardy. Life is supposed to be a series of challenges. It's what makes us strong. How then do the Californians we see on weekend golf tournaments always look so robust? How do they do it without facing the travails of winter?

Maybe that's the problem with our feckless Minnesota Twins. The abundance of Caribbean players on the team seem not quite hardy enough to have an open-air opener at thirty-seven degrees—and win! But Toronto has adjusted. They beat up on us. The Los Angeles Dodgers won their series with ease—on our home field! Is it the weather?

This summer will bring beauty. I can see the grass inching up, nearly ready for its first mowing. I just need to keep my umbrella handy. Those miniscule petunia seeds will sprout, along with the cucumbers and mixed lettuce I risked to plant.

June will soon be busting out all over.

I think I can put my shovel away.

Planting Trees under Which We Will Never Sit

The title words of "Planting Trees" in an article of a recent issue of Texas A&M's *Spirit Magazine* jumped out at me. A new graduate reflected on his experiences at the school: "The most important lesson I learned at Texas A&M is the importance of selfless service. Serving others, putting others before yourself is critical to who we are as Aggies and as leaders. That is the most significant takeaway and something I will work to apply in leadership positions and in my everyday life."

After standing as a "Twelfth Man" at Aggie football games for four years, the young man will soon be off to Naval Air Training at Corpus Christi—and then to graduate school, where he will be a well-grounded "high flyer."

Although not a fire-eating member of the historic A&M Corps with their military uniforms, highly-polished "Aggie Boots" and "Twelfth Man" tradition, my experiences in life and at Texas A&M were similar to those of the new graduate. I was both observer and participant there for three years in the 1970s—before the A&M boom and blossoming into today's "Harvard of the South."

As a more mature graduate student with a family, I had come from the north with Winona-based values, a U-Haul trailer, four kids, some experiences and aspirations of an education leadership doctorate. I was soon to become a part of the traditions of Texas and A&M.

I had lived my own regime of personal development in Winona, a small hard-working town of the Midwest, finding my way through work and life and achievement. As a boy in grade school, my Winona neighborhood and community had expectations akin to those found at A&M. In both settings, days were filled with expectations, awareness of the value of others—and opportunity. I was fortunate to have learned the many lessons of hard work, determination and giving back to those around me through early life in Winona.

Today I write and reflect upon the many great gifts of life given to me—a wife of more than fifty years, children and grandchildren, an education, the opportunity to work and lead, and the chance to provide "for the betterment of all concerned." I'm still learning.

Life is whatever you make of it, it has been said. That is the way it is yet today. From Minnesota hometowns to the small town of Texas A&M, each of us finds his or her way in our environment. To do so, we absolutely need support, guidance, challenge and a bit of adversity to get us there. If we see the blue sky ahead, we can keep on moving and giving back as we travel toward our goal.

We each represent our heritage.

For good or bad, I represent Winona. I represent those around me. Whether home high school or expanded college setting, I was there. Place or time doesn't make the difference. The difference is what one carries inside—from place to place.

Joe Soucheray of the *Pioneer Press* recently compared great athletes Adrian Peterson, Tiger Woods, Wayne Gretzky, and Michael Jordan to conclude, "They can do whatever they imagine they can do. Well, it's even better than that. They can transfer imagination to real-time vision." They see the whole field and "go where the puck will be—not where it is," as Gretzky was wont to do.

A fellow grad of A&M (class of 1955) wrote a postscript in *Spirit* suggesting that through his giving to the school foundation, he was "Planting trees that I may never sit under." It is a beautiful phrase connoting the importance of values learned so many years ago, at the same place as I. In passing them on, he said, "I accepted the responsibility of giving back, and I endeavor to do so however I can and wherever I can."

He added, "I take the responsibility of representing Texas A&M in a positive manner every chance I get. There's a possibility every day that some person is going to look at me and think, "If this is what Texas A&M does for a person, I want to have some of it. And I may never know when it happens. No matter whom I worked for, no matter where I worked, no matter what accolades resulted from those efforts, I was representing Texas A&M. I had to be worthy of that representation and I had to be on the lookout for ways to give back. I had to be willing to plant trees that I will never sit under."

Transmutable forces are at work in Winona and at A&M. Our strengths abide—and are to be shared. We can change trace metal to gold.

We must plant trees under which we will never sit.

Chapter Eight

River Valley Ramblings and Characters Met

Walking around our small town on a summer morning in the 1950s, we would soon encounter the milkmen. They were up early, but so were we.

Old George and Carl "Shorty" Lang served on the Springdale trucks, clinking bottles across the neighborhood, with Winona Milk trucks not so far behind. Bottles of fresh milk had to be delivered daily to households on an alternating-day basis. Even on school days we saw them as they delivered the small half-pint bottles of milk to the school. There was no school lunch, but healthful milk breaks were scheduled for kids in the early grades.

Pete the iceman slowly traversed those same blocks looking for cardboard "Ice" signs in the windows of customers, signaling him to drop off a twenty-five or fifty-pound block. We were fortunate to have Pete stop by regularly to feed our oak icebox in the kitchen. We had electricity, but hadn't yet managed the purchase of a refrigerator. With a block of ice on his leather-padded shoulder, he walked right into the kitchen like a member of the family. And he was—a fellow trucker of Pa's from his time as driver at Western Coal & Ice. Pa knew his way around a set of ice tongs, as well. Pete was a friend who often stopped by for coffee.

Milkman in the 1930s. (Photo courtesy of Pieces of the Past, Winona Historical Society.)

Every day, the setting and pattern was the same—get yourself up, do household chores and be on your way. Other urchins of the neighborhood would fall in. It may have been for a gathering in the backyard shed of our house on a rainy, summer day or off for a bike trip across the bridge for the noon opening of the city's bathing beach on Latsch Island. There were morning baseball games at the West End Rec and afternoons at the playground. We were on our way from place to place, stopping only occasionally for a peanut butter sandwich.

Sam Weisman's Junk Yard driver arrived in the neighborhood proudly wearing his bib overalls with worn brass buckles. In the metal-buttoned center chest pocket of those overalls he had a long leather coin purse in which he carried necessary coin and cash for dealings of the day. From place to place, he would stop to pick up barrels of crushed metal cans, iron posts and the like, paying the homeowner based upon weight.

A bit rotund but strong in the way of truck drivers and laborers of the 1950s, he slung the pieces onto his truck with the movement of an athlete. He hauled the load to Sam's yard at the end of Grand Street, nearly on the river. The yard was backed up by railroad tracks on which the huge, sorted piles were hauled off on rail cars. This was adult business, in that the adults had a pile of pipes or barrels of cans or gunnysacks filled with old clothes or bedding to be picked by the "shenie" and his truck.

We had our own way of meeting Sam or his associate. As kids, we pulled our wagon around the neighborhood, rapping on back doors to voluntarily take away newspapers or a bag of old clothes from a basement, or occasionally some discarded metal in small lots from a garage. We pulled the wagon for blocks down Grand Street to Sam's Fairbanks-Morse scale located indoors on Second Street. There he greeted us like partners and associates. He carefully measured, adjusted the scale balances and tallied the junk value, again figured by the pound. Reaching into the long purse, he counted out the exact change for the agreed-upon rate. Fifty-two or eighty-seven cents, it didn't matter. It was more than we had before meeting our partner, Sam.

Brother Bob tells of his being raised on the farm a dozen miles from us—and his involvement in the world of junk and reclamation. He offers:

> I learned at an early age growing right out of the 1930s Depression that if you saved old pieces of copper and brass you could sell it for fifty cents a pound. I even learned how to strip the tinfoil off the inside wrapper of an empty pack of cigarettes and gum wrappers until I had a ball about the size of a softball.
>
> Then, when the junk man stopped by our farm, I'd run out to him with that ball of tinfoil in my hand and he'd grin and give me

a nickel! Yes, I said tinfoil because that's what it was. Aluminum foil had not been heard of yet.

That streak of junkie has never left me to this day.

Uncle Tom was one who found his own way, as well. Operating his single-speed bicycle with front and back metal baskets and a homemade rack attached to the bike from steering post to rear end, he cruised by soundlessly, with tobacco pipe firmly clenched in his teeth. Retired from "the shops" where he repaired all manner of trains, he was accustomed to metal and its ways. He brought discarded bike frames, motors, long pipes, and the like home on his bike a few at a time. He disassembled the parts and sold the valuable pieces for re-use, and called Sam when he had a truckload.

We didn't know his name, but one of the earliest citywide recyclers seen each day was the real "garbage man." At that time, garbage consisted of fruits and vegetables, bones, and kitchen offal. It was not today's mixture of papers, cans, and wrappers. We put the "garbage" in a newspaper-lined metal can in the back yard. The rest of the items were smashed for salvageable metal or accumulated for glass value in a barrel in the shed. That which could be burned in the wood stove or coal furnace was.

The garbage man, who actually represented the state senator of our area, drove his big truck down our street. With flopping metal covers over bins of smelly and aging foodstuff on the truck, he slung the open metal bucket with rope handles across his back to gather garbage from neighbors' galvanized backyard cans. Carrying the sloppy treasure to his truck, he dumped it into a bin and moved on down the street. His ultimate destination was the senator's hog farm in Rollingstone.

Our city passed an ordinance in 1936 to have citywide garbage pickup. Previous to pickup, the alternative had been burning it in the alleyway or wood stove—or burying it in the garden. There was a town dump over all the years where we hauled ashes and junk not recycled—if we could borrow a truck.

As early as 1904, LaCrosse, Eau Claire, and Rochester operated hog farms for their garbage. Winona was slow to come (1936), having been preceded by Mankato, Austin, St. Cloud, and others. St. Cloud chose to incinerate its garbage—charging only twenty cents per month for the residence if you delivered the garbage to their facility. Austin allowed cans of ashes to be included in their collection. From Winona, with daily loads of garbage, it was reported that they were "happy as pigs in slop" at the senator's farm up the hill of County Road 248.

We were proud to know the men on the street. In a city where strong backs and labor carried the day, there was no discrimination against those who carried the garbage or brought the ice. They were core players of our city. For each, this was full-time employment in the fashion of the mailman or telephone repairman. Each had year-long employment that brought home a weekly paycheck. After a recent world war and a national depression, full-time employment was revered.

As a teenage worker of the 1950s, I was a regular Saturday morning driver and visitor from the Ford dealership to the city dump. Backing up my load of "stuff" at the smoky, smoldering and dusty dump in the far east end of town, the "pickers" greeted me. With teenage strength, I "rassled" the Owl Motor's shiny new Ford pickup into position. The pickers often helped me unload—especially when they could sense some extra metal for the taking. Solid and heavy iron car parts of the time, a damaged fender, brake shoes, worn out mufflers or other heavy metal items were anxiously "picked" for re-sale.

Critical to production of war materials, the city and nation took recycling to heart in World War II. In October 1942, "Winona County Residents [were] Asked to Serve in Scrap Hunt." They were told to "See your neighborhood commando and book your scrap for collection."

We saw the milkmen and recyclers and the real characters of life in our everyday travels. Passing by Kindt's Grocery, Madison School, and Brozik's Meat Market on our way somewhere, we decided to "top off" our bicycle tires with the outdoor airline and dial-in hand meter at Mosiman's. Mechanic John Mosiman served the neighborhood from his small Texaco Shop on West Fifth Street.

After we finally got a car, we found him to be a bit cranky—not unlike some of the cars he worked on that needed a hand crank to start. Ever productive in his two-stall, one-man shop while serving gasoline pump customers at the same time, he was "all business." After losing a finger or two to a spinning automobile fan, he may have needed to pay even more attention to detail.

We enjoyed the scene of our town and its regulars, the Winona Wet Wash man, the ever-clean Railway Express truck and its stand-up, uniformed driver, the Schaffer's Cleaners' delivery man and van with hanging suits and folded, boxed, starched shirts for the finer households, the waving conductors and engineers of five railroads passing through town day and night. Even the hobos standing in open doors of cars of the moving trains were a part of our life's fabric. We celebrated them with Mulligan stew and a citywide Hobo Day.

There were occasional "bad guys" in our small town where the population didn't change much from 1936 to 1946, but the rate of arrest doubled.

Although we perceived the environment in which we lived as safe, there were a few who needed to be kept within bounds by Chief August Bingold, Sheriff George Fort and their city and county police forces.

The chief and sheriff were always in the news—and knew everybody. Just the arrival of a four-door Ford black-and-white in the neighborhood was enough to keep most of us in line. They were there for dredging the lake for a drowning victim, picking up the remains and pieces of another train/auto accident or leading the summer parades down Third Street.

Both leaders were early motorcycle officers of the Winona Police Department who lived with a city in the throes of Depression, Prohibition, and a "red-light district" fed by constant visitors to our city by train and auto. They were reputed to have earned their stripes with "Billy clubs" in the effective handling of ruffians. Along with Captain "Bull" Teegarden of the police department, they were local legends of toughness throughout city and county. Sheriff Fort's territory extended downriver to encompass my brother Bob's home area of Dakota and Dresbach, as well.

Boys being boys, we raided a few gardens and apple trees, scavenged boathouses on the river for a "bottle of pop," or even shoplifted a dime item at the Woolworth or Kresge store. We generally watched out "p's and q's," however.

As summer wore on and garden produce was at its peak, Mr. Nelton joined the parade of visitors to streets in our steamy, bluff-enclosed city. He lived a few miles out of town in the beautiful, verdant Gilmore Valley. We often biked past his place as we headed up the crushed-limestone valley road to challenge the major hill onto "the ridge" toward Wilson.

He was heard in the neighborhood before being seen. Driving slowly down the bus line on Howard Street, he boomed out his sales pitch with "strawberries, 'sparagus, onions" or "rutabagas, corn, watermelon, and apples," all in their season. A friendly, rotund man in suit and tie when we saw him in church on Sunday, he dressed like Casey Jones of television and railroad fame in his daily travels. Housewives were supplied with a variety of summer and fall produce as he drove his old stake truck down the street, stopping to accommodate those who met him at curbside. For kids, he always had a treat for a nickel (or sometimes free if we had no coin.) A strawberry, apple, or slice of watermelon was a kind gift he enjoyed sharing.

Along with drivers of rival Royal Cab, Shorty and Dave Krause brought their black Vets' cabs down the street, delivering folks to church, home, downtown—or to one of the sixty-five bars of town. The Winona Transit Company bus line, with Harold or Jack or Ed or another at the massive steering wheel of the bus, ran during the day for those on their way to and from shopping and work. Bus tokens were three for a quarter (each ride taking one token), compared to the usual town charge of thirty-five cents for a private cab.

With Dean and Eugene, I spent long nights on the streets of Winona in my Vets' cab—from sundown to sunup. We met the trains, did some shopping with guests hiring our car by the hour and hauled assorted individuals, couples, and small groups to constant interchanges of bars and scenes. Either Shorty or Dave chain-smoked in the small office and received coffee for hypertensive Shorty or a hot pork sandwich for rounded Dave through the door into Ruth's Restaurant, all as they directed drivers.

We stayed in our cabs and hung out at the cabstand. In a typical call, I heard Shorty holler through the speaker; "Seven!" (My designated driver number.) "Where the hell are you? Get you're a-- down to Blanche's—patron waiting." And so it would go for thirteen hours.

It was to gain a whole new perspective on my hometown. The minions moved from eight o'clock at night to the wee hours of the morning—especially on summer weekends. These were the real, nighttime, river town travelers. Dean and Eugene drove the streets and roadways with me. Eugene was a veteran, a college student, lifetime writer and poet. He constantly wrote poetry, thoughts and observations on his legal pad as we sat at the cabstand. He was my first encounter with a resident philosopher. Dean was a quiet, hardworking "townie" who smiled quietly and diligently served his customers. We had stories to tell at mid-shift—as the bar rush wound down and we awaited sunrise to end our thirteen-hour shift.

Characters of life greeted us at every turn and age. Jim was an officious usher who liked to wave his flashlight at us in the dark at the State Theater leading, of course, to even more wisecracks from pre-teen hooligans. Vi, Bill's mom, gave us a smile and an extra ounce or two of penny candy from her glass cases at Woolworth's for our thin dime. We endured the reverend's red-faced wrath at our German-Lutheran Wisconsin Synod church every Sunday morning and listened to Ernie Reck's "oompah" band on the radio from Arcadia afterward as we awaited Pa's big chicken dinner with mashed potatoes and gravy.

These people (and the mashed potatoes) were our sustenance of life.

Prodigiously Gifted: Our Daily Challenge

Radio talent Mitch Anthony with his "Daily Dose" said: "Life is what we make of it." In a recent radio spot he offered that "prodigiously gifted," yet average people are above all, resilient.

They have staying power. They are able to attack and return and attack again. They keep on keeping on. Mitch would suggest there is a strong relationship between positive emotions and resilience. Studies show that maintaining positive emotions while facing adversity promotes flexibility in thinking and problem solving. Positive emotions also serve to help an individual face stressful experiences and encounters.

It's about being hopeful that the sun will shine again after another long winter in Minnesota. We can look forward to the beauty of a mid-May, eighty-degree day followed by a gorgeous fifty-degree evening of blessed, natural sleep. That day will come. The sun will shine. We simply have to be resilient and hopeful that it will. How else can we exist on the tundra?

I have always been a believer in making a strong effort in my daily journey—in spite of cold or clouds. When I washed windows inside and out of every auto coming into Owl Motor Ford for service at age fifteen, my bony body was in the least uncomfortable when stretching toward the back window in a cramped backseat to wash another filmed-over window. I was bent to the max.

In scientific terms, resilience is the ability of a material to absorb energy when it is "deformed elastically" and release that energy upon unloading. It hurt to bend and fold and do a good job. However, I did the job in one car, stood up straight, recovered and went on to the next vehicle. I followed up after Smitty, my friend the "grease monkey," had given equal and quality oil change service and lubrication to engine and all the tie rods. We made a good team.

I moved on to the wash rack, hand-washing cars all day long with steam cleaning of autos' engines using a long, steam powered and forceful wand of steam and soap as a diversion to my steady diet of soap and suds and dampened towels on the wash rack. I stood in the sun of a hot July day in the shop's alleyway with steam in my hand—and prayed for a breeze. I could recover there, too, and move on to the next used car needing a "spiffing up," as Bill Huffman, the used car preparation manager, was wont to say. I blew off the grease. He buffed and shined.

It's no different today. For any modicum of success in writing or lawn mowing, weed pulling or personal car washing, I need to get started. I need to keep on keeping on. These same bones creak a bit more than they did some sixty years ago as I today stretch and pull—or face a computer screen. I may need to take an occasional rest period. But I persevere. I will be refreshed in the long term. Even an ancient body is resilient.

A recent major surgery took me down a new pathway. I found that the removal of a body organ is traumatic to one's body. I expected full (and quick) recovery. But I needed my body and brain to catch up to the trauma. Taking six weeks and the consultation of a physical therapist, I was able to make small steps as my body and brain caught up. It was the height of resiliency. My body wanted to recover. It just needed the guidance of a trained therapist who gave more mental therapy than physical therapy—and this willing participant to work on the physicality and self-talk necessary for achievement.

A voracious appetite for learning, perseverance, and resilience all blend together to give personal satisfaction, achievement, and the milkshake of gained knowledge. I believe that maintaining a positive emotionality aids in counteracting the physiological effects of negative emotions. Others would suggest that it also "facilitates adaptive coping, builds enduring social resources, and increases personal well-being." A garden will grow if we bend and stoop. A book will be published if we remain optimistic and hopeful.

Long before Werner distinguished and labeled three contexts for protective factors, we knew them to be true. They are the values and expectations of parents who lived through the Great Depression and World War II, inculcated in us to bring us out the other side, including personal attributes, including outgoing, bright, and positive self concepts; the family, such as having close bonds with at least one family member or an emotionally stable parent; and the community, such as receiving support or counsel from peers.

With these dated constructs we need once again to get all kids on the same page, leading toward grit, determination, perseverance, persistence, responsibility, and nurturance. These essential components of personal development are probably more critical to them than the academic. One needs to feel good as truck lift operator, fashion designer, software developer or nuclear scientist. The academics will follow.

As a young boy, I knew about *Grit.* It was a newspaper ("America's Greatest Family Newspaper") created in 1882 and sold in small towns across the nation by young boys. They approached individual homes door-to-door with a ten-cent, forty-page tabloid mix of news and comics on a weekly basis. By 1954, 500,000 copies were sold each week with a theme: "Wherever possible, suggest peace and good will toward men. Give our readers courage and strength for their daily tasks. Put happy thoughts, cheer, and contentment into their hearts."

Grit was a concept we understood. It was a natural part of our every day. It was all about demonstrating those "personal attributes." A recent U.S. Department of Education study ("Grit, Tenacity, and Perseverance," February 2013) included the interview of twenty-five national leaders from colleges and institutions (e.g. Bill and Melinda Gates Foundation, Stanford University, University of Pennsylvania). The study strongly suggested an equal focus on characteristics of personal development and resilience—heretofore absent.

The American Psychological Association, in 2014, suggested "Ten Ways to Build Resilience:"

1. Maintain good relationships with close family members, friends and others.
2. Avoid seeing crises or stressful events as unbearable problems.
3. Accept circumstances that cannot be changed.
4. Develop realistic goals and move toward them.
5. Take decisive actions in adverse situations.
6. Look for opportunities of self-discovery after a struggle with loss.
7. Develop self-confidence.
8. Keep a long-term perspective and consider the stressful event in broader context.
9. Maintain a hopeful outlook, expect good things and visualize what is wished.
10. Take care of one's mind and body, exercising regularly, paying attention to one's own needs and feelings.

Mitch Anthony and I suggest that one needs only to take a "daily dose" of positive focus. "Attitude is everything," he offers. Through positive effort we can find "the courage and strength for their daily tasks" suggested in *Grit.* Through support from others, spirituality and a sincere effort to help others, we will find our way to resilience and to long-term stamina.

We, too, may become "prodigiously gifted."

Sloppy Joe's

A sloppy joe is for me a dream come true.

My introduction to sloppy joes—with trimmings of pickles, chips, and hot chocolate—came in a childhood friend's home one evening in the 1950s after sliding down fresh snow of country club hills. I have been entranced from that point on by the oozing mixture overflowing the sides of a fresh, warm bun.

The staples of life for me seemed to have been goulash, mashed potatoes, beef roast, chicken, gravy, buckwheat pancakes and fried pork steak. I had Pa's meatloaf at home as well—with the chunks of onion I always set aside. But we didn't have the spiciness of authentic sloppy joes, spaghetti, or the really exotic and yet-to-be-introduced pizza.

Even today if there's a pot aboil on the stove with tomatoes and onions and fresh hamburger, my senses come alive. It's like a fresh pie out of the oven. I can feel the soft warm bun in hand—overloaded with a scoop or two of delicious meat sauce.

As I drove my Ford Econoline van daily down Third Street on the Vend-A-Matic vending machine route covering the city's factories and workplaces of the 1960s, I was often enticed to stop at the historic Sloppy Joe's of 526 East Third Street. But I never did—and I still haven't. I have frequented Charlie's Bar, the old Hot Fish Shop on Mankato Avenue, Tubby's Oasis on West Fifth Street, and even hung out at the Goodview "Muni," but I never graced the front door of Sloppy Joe's.

In my cab-driving days (mostly nights) I called for a patron or two (or more) at Sloppy Joe's—hauling an individual or a group to a next bar of the east end. Weekend eves were long and fun-filled. Friday payday for the hardscrabble laborers, chain-makers, hog-sluggers and machinists of our small city meant a night out for travels around the town, often in my Vets' cab.

One could start at the Eagles, cut across the river to the Midway, hit the Main Tavern (on Main Street) or Arnie's Cocktail Lounge on Third—to finally stop by Sloppy Joe's, the Cozy Corner or Blanche's. The quest was never ending in gaining another bottle of Bub's or Schmidt's or Grain Belt beer. Occasionally there was a fight or two outside the bar.

Joe's is one of Winona's oldest taverns, having now surpassed one hundred years. Founded sometime before 1900 by Frank Srnec, the bar has been a neighborhood staple and "home away from home" for thousands who have polished the stools with their backsides.

Frank applied to city fathers for an intoxicating liquor license in 1893 to sell liquor in "the front room of the brick building at 526 East Third Street." It appears that the license was continuously in force thereafter, with applications and granting of licenses evidenced in 1895 and 1900. Mr. Srnec, a member of the "Bohemian Knights of Veceslaus of his home parish," was most involved in happenings of the neighborhood.

He was elected in March 1895 as committee person of the Democratic primaries of the fourth ward at a meeting held in Kowalewski's Hall. He was very active in the Czech Radecky Society of St. John's Bohemian Church. In his home residence on the second floor of the brick building at 526 in 1896, it was discovered that his "dog had been doctored." As a consequence, someone quietly stole his cash box, which contained $49.80. The evening's proceeds from the first floor business had been taken off his bedroom bureau as he—and his dog—slept.

In an 1897 outing at Prairie Island, Frank joined his fellow "Summer of the Buckeyes" group to enjoy ball games and other festivities, including a rifle shoot. Frank won the afternoon rifle event, scoring 109 out of 125 targets. Frank stayed busy as a hunter, fisherman, ferry operator, and owner of a boat livery that he built in 1909 and sold in 1917. He was an active bowler as well (610 in 1925).

One fine day in 1909, the Winona scene was at its very best. Frank was building his Frank's Boat Livery to accommodate thirty-five boats. He had just received "a shipment of Shell Lake Cedar rowboats" and was "awaiting his runabout and excursion boat." He took a day off to be at "Camp Glory," his downriver hunting camp, with fellow Winonans.

In the column brief "Along the River Front," it was reported that many visitors "on this sun-filled day" were "making use of the new path to the top of the bluff at Bluffside Park." Also reported in the *Republican-Herald* that day was information that "F.J. Bauer has secured an excellent photograph of President Taft as he stood up in his automobile and bowed to the young lady students at the Winona seminary on his visit to Winona."

Ah, for the glories of Winona's past!

Frank passed away in 1935, at age sixty-five. He had continued his home business for some years, succeeded by William Strehlow, Clem Erpelding and Joe Loshek (1899 to 1948).

It was reported that Joe "assumed control of the business in 1916" (at age seventeen?) and yet, more likely as reported in the *Republican-Herald*, Joe announced his "Formal Opening of the Wenonah Café" at 150 High Forest on March 30, 1932, with a performance of the Burmeister Orchestra and "dancing at 8:00 p.m." He was shown in 1931 offering "soft drinks" at 526 East Third, with residence at 718 East King Street. He moved to 526 East Third in 1933, continuing on as proprietor until his sudden death in 1948 at age forty-eight, of a heart attack. In 1934, a burglar took a necklace and forty dollars from Joe's home at 563 East Fifth Street as he worked at the Wenonah Café. Mrs. Sophie Loshek became the owner and passed on the business to sons Joseph II ("Little Joe") and Edward (managers in 1955).

The Wenonah Café name was prominent (and Sloppy Joe's absent) on bowling shirts and in bowling circles at the Athletic Club on Mankato Avenue from 1931 to 1950. The first combined name "Sloppy Joe's Wenonah Café Stool Pigeons" appeared in print in 1949. In addition to liquid refreshment and lunches, Wenonah Café sold Schuler's ice cream, chocolates and tickets for community events—such as the 1951 dance with the Henry Burton Orchestra, with proceeds to the Winona Chiefs baseball team.

There promised to be a fight to the finish with the "city crown" up for grabs. The "Stool Pigeons" of the East End were to take on "EB's Corner Cuties" of the West End in an unofficial city title baseball game in August 1949 at Gabrych Park at 8:00 p.m.—in an attempt to aid the elimination of the scourge of the polio epidemic in Winona and the nation.

Pre-game guitar music, a first pitch by Henry (Hank) Kowalewski, an address by Mayor J. Roland Edde, four umpires and "no bunting" all aided the celebration. "You're welcome to attend if you can stand the sight of forty-year-olds acting like kids," promotional material warned potentail attendees.

Sloppy Joe's, not unlike many of the more than fifty bars in Winona, offered the standard fare of jars of pickled eggs and pigs feet, popcorn at the table, and an occasional shot of whiskey. Tap beer was the feature and the standard, from early morning regulars through a sedate lunch crowd and on into the late afternoon tradesmen who stopped before going home for supper at six.

The action heated up on weekend nights at Sloppy Joe's and the other fifty bars of Winona when paychecks were cashed. With weekend freedom, there was lengthened time available to sit on the stool. Tap beers flowed, discussions ensued, with many working at a steady flow on their tap beer. Bantering and shuffleboard were commonplace.

Visitors arrived, sometimes stimulating the tranquility of the locals' scene. A visiting tough guy from Arcadia, Witoka, Billings, or the West End of Winona may have been tossed or pushed out the back door of Swede's or the Main, the Oasis or even Sloppy Joe's by a bartender or a few of the locals—with a strong message not to return.

A recent story in the local newspaper confirms that the weekend trend of the past one hundred years has continued:

> Bar Fight Suspect Sprayed With Mace
>
> By Chris Rogers—*Winona Post* 8/14/2013
>
> Broken bones, mace, and assault referrals—that is how a bar fight at Sloppy Joe's bar ended in the early hours of Saturday, August 10. At 12:30 a.m., officers arrested Ryan Thomas Anderson, thirty-six, of Winona, for third-degree assault, fifth-degree assault, and third-degree burglary, and Keith Joseph Srock, thirty-one, of Winona, for third-degree assault and obstructing the legal process with force.
>
> According to witnesses, it all began when Anderson touched women inappropriately in the bar and, at one point, reportedly pulled his pants down. The bartender asked Anderson to leave at that point, and he complied, but shortly afterwards he allegedly charged back in and knocked the bartender and a patron to the ground. Anderson was forcibly escorted out again, but he rushed the door again, and knocked the bartender to the ground again, according to the report.

The second time around, Srock was reportedly holding the bartender's arms. Police said it was unclear whether Srock was trying to break up the dispute or help Anderson knock down the bartender. In any case, the results were unfortunate for the bartender, who suffered a compound fracture of his leg.

Srock and Anderson had left the scene when officers arrived but were found hiding by a nearby garage, according to the report. Anderson was arrested without incident, but Srock reportedly refused to lie down and be handcuffed. After minutes of struggling with Srock, officers sprayed him with mace, police officials said.

Still Searching

The sloppy joe of my dreams is a mixture of one's personal frying and blending of browned hamburger with assorted spices. I like the ideas provided by Rachel Ray. She's a credible source seeming to have captured all the pieces I need, even though she probably hasn't been to Winona. She uses steak seasoning blend, Worcestershire Sauce, brown sugar, onions, chopped red pepper, a tablespoon of extra-virgin olive oil, a dollop of red wine vinegar, tomato sauce and paste—all brought together with hometown ground beef over medium heat.

My joes will be served with an old ice cream scoop brimming with the delicious conglomeration. I would offer it on a fresh bun from KwikTrip or Bloedow's (both fresh and delicious), with sides of tomato slices (salt and peppered), dill pickles, deviled potato salad, and cole slaw. No need for dessert!

I tried to find a sloppy joe at Sloppy Joe's at noon on a recent weekday. As I visited the closed facility it looked tired, as if waiting for an evening rush. The large building shows the wear of the years since Frank Srnec set up soft drinks in the "front room" in 1893. It has had a long and commendable run with Joe, Joe II, and Ed at the helm.

Kent Stever has searched for best sandwiches throughout life. He made stops for twenty-five-cent burgers at Howie Johnson's Varsity Inn, for pasties in Northern Michigan, tacos in Monterrey (Mexico), mounds of unidentified (and unpronounceable) meats on a hard bun in Moscow, Mayslack's garlic-laced sandwiches in Northeast Minneapolis, and McDonald's in Missoula. He is still searching for the ultimate sloppy joe.

To Risk, Advise and Counsel: Personal Goals for Each

I wonder if I know anything.

A few years ago I was challenged to create a story of "What I Know" into a one-hundred-word descriptor for a magazine. I submitted a story about kids, but didn't get it published. I did submit another elsewhere to "Greatest Goofs"—another one-hundred-word effort, this one of a personal attack on my sprinkler system. I scored and earned my highest rate ever—one dollar per word!

After many years of personal and professional experience, I have begun to assess myself as a writer, counselor, and motivator to people of all ages. I have attempted to be a good guide to students, parents, teachers, family members, business managers, graduate school class members, Rotarians and the general community. I blend some of those experiences into writings of today, always striving to keep it light-hearted.

It has been my pleasure to assist in personal assessment and community considerations that have led many to target goals for themselves or their organizations. It's a challenge and opportunity I so enjoy. In my twilight years, I still practice my methodology in classrooms with high schoolers on a weekly basis. They seem to like simplicity, clarity and focus.

I tried in my two-thousand-member school workplaces over thirty years to offer self-reliance and create a calming effect by maintaining order and moving us ahead, in spite of apparent adversity. I attempted to be proactive with all, holding the equality of each person as a guiding theme. I liked kids in black leather jackets as much as those in letter jackets. All were treated equally.

When there were emergencies like bomb threats or seeming disasters at school—or upsets of people at school or home—I learned that patience, stability and focus were needed when there seemed to be none. It isn't something I learned in graduate school or through a book. It's a look inside.

Intuition assists me. Through empathy, others need to be allowed to share family travails or personal distresses. As a part of listening and sharing comes a great opportunity to advise and counsel, to constantly urge others to reach beyond. Each can control his or her own destiny and become more than they really believe—with a little direction.

Acts of nurturance occur today, and have occurred yesterday and the day before. These are not pre-planned actions. We succeed best when we sense the need for a cookie or a word of praise or a flower to hold. There's no magic as to the how and when. A card can be written today that may be viewed as "hokey" if we think too long about it. But the need is there to send it. Our gut tells us so. Do it.

One has to risk to write or say or do. Stand with the consequence. A card on the death of a relative, a note on a birthday, a thank you to a child, a message of support for an acquaintance whose parent (or child or grandchild) is ailing, a letter of congratulations for the smallest achievement for the quietest person. Or give a moment. A quiet moment with one is like a prayer. They know that you are with them—whether you say so or not.

I recently stood in the midst of teenagers of a large senior high school distraught by the sudden, accidental death of a classmate. I consoled by presence, by sensitivity and simply asking, "How you doing?" A smile, a touch makes a difference.

A particular area, not of greater importance than any other, is encouraging others to take a more global look at their futures and aid them in directing themselves toward their goals. In the vein of mentor, an experienced life partner can encourage young teachers or parents to strive harder—to academically and motivationally achieve. As a math teacher, I always appreciated structure and clarity. Writing things out in achievable chunks made it soluble. Teaching Dale Carnegie goals to managers, creating IEPs for selected students in special education or analyzing portfolio projects of demonstrable achievements of Ph.D. candidates are all the same. For each, one needs to write out a plan and get moving to a solution.

In the role of education lecturer, one can encourage principals and superintendents to watch other successful people in the corporate and greater world, so as not to stifle themselves and the organizations they are bound to develop. In like fashion, we can advise corporate managers with a sometimes-tight focus on finance and production to look at the soft side of the equation.

People at every level need to know that it is all right to go beyond—to risk, to act the unusual. They need to know that there is too much "usual" in the world today and that they can bring something new to the table without fear of reprisal. To do so takes counsel and quality time. Through our actions we become available for such counsel, but only if we let ourselves.

Meeting a young lady from a Kansas small town yesterday at a book signing allowed me to capture her small town strengths, foreign language skills and focus on international marketing in a few minutes. My suggestion that she introduce herself to the local IBM organization was a shock to her system. Whether she achieves a career with IBM or not, she was able to see herself in a more global position. If nothing else, she left with a smile on her face and a new friend who understood her goals.

We need to assess our priorities, our actions and our availability on an everyday basis. The priority must be to drop the paper on our desk, walk in the hallway and say "Hello." If we bury ourselves with the stuff on the desk and the seemingly essential trivia of the day, we will never be a source or guide to others.

We can guide others to a "one day at a time" mentality—allowing each to take control of his or her life one small piece at a time. These conversations and growth moments with students of any age, staff members, neighbors, and family members have been and are the most enriching moments of my life.

The role of guide is challenging. One must be what one says others can be. Guiding others requires a constant reassessment of one's own personal achievements and personal giving, of reality checks on one's own belief system, of affecting and offering a balance in life that is observable and worthy of emulation. There is no easy or right way.

It is only to begin.

Chapter Nine

The Chicago Eight: Love, Tolerance, and Understanding

Paul was nearby.

Not one of the "Chicago Seven." He may have been number eight.

Actually, the Chicago Seven was originally the Chicago Eight. Seven defendants—Abbie Hoffman, Jerry Rubin, David Dellinger, Tom Hayden, Rennie Davis, John Froines and Lee Weiner—were charged with conspiracy, inciting to riot and other charges related to protests that took place in Chicago, Illinois, on the occasion of the August 1968 Democratic National Convention. Bobby Seale, co-founder of the Black Panther Party and the eighth man charged, had his trial severed during the proceedings, lowering the number from eight to seven.

Paul was not part of the charged group, but was fully "charged up" when regaling us with his attendance at the rallies, demonstrations, marches, and attempted marches taking place on streets and in lakefront parks about five miles away from the convention site. Anti-war groups had petitioned the city of Chicago for permits to march five miles from the central business district (the Loop) to within eyeshot of the convention site. They wished to hold a number of rallies in the lakefront parks and near the convention and camp in Lincoln Park. The city denied all permits.

The activities were primarily in protest of President Lyndon B. Johnson's policies of the Vietnam War—vigorously contested during the presidential primary campaign and inside the convention. The Democratic party was split between presidential candidates Hubert Humphrey and Eugene McCarthy, both of Minnesota, Paul's home state. At a time when the "establishment" defended the Vietnam War, McCarthy appealed to many young people, especially college-age students. Paul, a Navy veteran, also took up the anti-establishment cause. The grassroots political struggle in Minnesota was indicative of a schism within the national Democratic Party.

Reported by William Lass in *Minnesota: A History*:

> Humphrey easily won the presidential nomination on the first ballot, thus becoming the first Minnesotan to run for the presidency as a major candidate. But Humphrey could not disassociate himself from [Lyndon] Johnson's Vietnam policy. When Chicago police used strong-arm tactics to contain demonstrating anti-Vietnam protesters, Humphrey refused to criticize them. The regular party lost much support. The disaffection of vociferous McCarthy supporters did not seem to be a decisive issue during most of the campaign because the polls regularly showed Humphrey to be far behind Republican candidate Richard Nixon.

Paul was there at the rallies, causing him to come a day or two late to the teachers' workshop to start the school year at our large suburban high school in Minnesota. A social studies teacher, he must have felt the urge to have "hands-on" training in making history and involving himself in modern problems—the class by the same name which he taught to twelfth graders.

It was reported that after the large rally, a few thousand protesters attempted to march to the International Amphitheatre, but were stopped in front of the Conrad Hilton Hotel, where the presidential candidates and their campaigns were headquartered. Police moves to push the protesters out of the street were accompanied by tear gas, verbal and physical confrontation, frequent use of police batons and scores of arrests. Television networks broadcast footage of these clashes, cutting away from the nominating speeches for the presidential candidates.

Over the course of five days and nights, the police used tear gas and mace, struck people with batons and made arrests. Police injured hundreds of protesters, with many officers being struck by thrown rocks Dozens of journalists covering the actions were clubbed by police or had their cameras smashed and film confiscated. In the aftermath of what was later characterized as a "police riot" by the U.S. National Commission on the Causes and Prevention of Violence, a federal grand jury indicted eight demonstrators and eight police officers.

In the trial, the seven were found not guilty of conspiracy, yet sentenced to $5,000 fines and five years in prison. Black Panther Seale led the constant attack on Judge Hoffman. Davis and Rubin told the judge that, "This court is bullshit." Upon sentencing, Abbie Hoffman recommended to the judge that he try LSD and that he would set him up with a dealer. Upon appeal, all charges were reversed and not retried. Paul resolutely followed the trials with his students.

In an age of sharkskin suits and social responsibility exemplified by "the IBM way," there were some standouts like Paul who chose to revolt in small ways and large. They mimicked behaviors of the "beatniks" of the early sixties who set themselves up as the intellectuals of the period. In their small coffee-shop environments of university "Dinkytown" settings, they smoked pipes, drank espresso and may have enjoyed a "toke" or two (for clarity and enlightenment) in their small apartments off-campus. They also went beyond the campus in traveling to Woodstock and to Haight-Ashbury, the San Francisco district noted for its role as a center of the 1960s hippie movement. Paul and others of their chosen "beat generation" (or beat movement) enjoyed their concerts and campouts in the rain.

While those of us raised in the work-a-day world of the 1950s held our noses to the grindstone, others were off to Woodstock and Chicago and Haight-Asbury in their flowered VW vans and "hippie" clothes. For the ladies, it was neat, since they could "let it all hang out"—a theme of the times. No bras, no concerns about personal hygiene—just cover it all up with one massive floor-to-neck gingham dress that flowed as they walked. Paul's loosely hanging flowered shirts over crisp white jeans were a semi-trademark of his in those days of "groovy"—and war protest. A student reported:

> I haven't known Paul all that long, yet I feel I've known him for the two years I've been here. I had feelings at first like, "What the heck's going on here?" I just walked in five minutes late on the first day (because our bus driver didn't pick me up that day) and right off, here's this "hippie" with brown hair and beard, brown-tinted sunglasses, jeans, jean jacket, and t-shirt and oh, yes, purple socks and clogs!

Our high school contained as many as 2700 students in the day and age of "flexible-scheduling" and unscheduled time to "find yourself." Students flopped in hallways in all their "independent study" time as faculty stepped over multiple bodies while traversing the terrazzo hallways. Our sister school students had more luxuriant places to flop and nap in their fully carpeted new school of the 1970s.

Protests at nearby universities drew many of our students into wanting to mimic older brothers and sisters—right down to oversize military-green coats and jackets containing an abundance of drugs and weapons. As an assistant principal responsible for wading into the midst of the many, it was not unusual for me to have a cache of accumulated weapons, drugs, and drug paraphernalia in my center desk drawer.

On one well-remembered day, I was tasked to go to a classroom where it had been reported a student was in possession of a loaded pistol. In this time preceding police liaison officers, 911, and the like, this tall, skinny twenty-seven-year-old education leader in his first days of service aimed himself toward the classroom to resolve the issue. On the way to the class, I came across Paul in the hallway. I requested him to accompany me, explaining the problem along the way. It was a normal happenstance of a friend asking a friend to join him, although only one was skilled in the ways of martial arts.

Paul had come from a successful IBM-like family of South Minneapolis. They lived on the graceful creek that meandered their backyard—and the yards of many of means. Paul grew up there with brothers and sister, developing into a risk-taker at an early age. He decided early on to defend himself against young toughs of the big city, taking lessons in the martial arts. Paul followed his path into the U.S. Navy and on to Japan, where he earned his black belt in martial arts.

He quietly tucked his black belt into the back pocket of his favored wide-wale cords. He completed his schooling in social studies at the university on the ten-year plan. He showed up in our school as a slightly aged beginning teacher in corduroys and flowered shirt—amongst structural strivers framed in suits and ties every day. When one of our colleagues went off to Vietnam, Paul stayed behind. Although single, he had earlier been called.

Our removal of the errant student from his classroom went without incident, due in part to my recognition and acceptance by students and by the support evidenced in the person of Paul—a well-recognized persona amongst senior students. Police were called to take the student (and pistol) away from this potentially violent scene repeated too often in the schools of the time. Like Paul, students were "finding their way"—albeit too often in the direction of drugs, loss and personal harm.

Paul occasionally wore beads and generally argued philosophically (and loudly) with others in the faculty lounge at lunchtime. My intersection with Paul occurred as a semi-experienced young teacher working on becoming an administrator who happened to sit at the same table of this wunderkind of wanderlust. Only a few years out of college, I was already a father a couple of times over. I wasn't able to travel the world and "find myself"—other than to know I had a full time job and a hopeful future if I kept my nose clean. To hear Paul expound was to hear from a different world.

Having recently searched out the opportunity to join IBM in the heyday of computers due to my low beginning salary as a math teacher, I nonetheless stayed firm in the school. I was soon able to increase my salary sufficiently by becoming an assistant principal of a very large high school in the exciting, nationally recognized suburban community in which we lived. Management of schools seemed to be the path to public school success—holding me closer to mainstream America and to the necessary salary to support our four kids.

As measured by my teaching colleagues, my leaving the tenured teacher ranks to become an administrator was akin to leaving the Union Army to join the Confederacy. I was a quality math teacher with good staff and student support, an eye toward personal and family improvement and a new hurdle to overcome. Paul, in spite of others' opinions, stood firmly at my side, encouraging and helpful as friend—and as challenge to some of the "wizened" veterans who were in the least a bit outspoken.

Paul seemed unafraid of the "establishment." He was undaunted in standing before the staff of one hundred or so teachers to bring challenge to the principal at staff meetings. The principal of a school of our size was seldom challenged, let alone by a new staff member in an open meeting. When Paul's wages were reduced for his absence of the first days of workshop, he screamed foul and took on the principal—only to be invited for a personal meeting with a superintendent of schools who was himself an officer and POW of World War II—a force with whom to be reckoned. Paul met his match and was uncharacteristically docile for several weeks thereafter.

The years passed as I became principal of another school in the district—soon to inherit Paul as a staff member through mutual consent. I had just the place for Paul. He was a loose cannon in part, but a strong force for kids in need—and a true friend. I could work with him and gain great strides in assisting kids with needs in our well-defined "Project Success" program for troubled youth. He assented—and was a natural fit.

We debated his principles many times in the small coffee room upstairs and over my desk in the main office. One day, in the early morning before class, he demanded I release him to the police station to rescue one of his troubled kids who was incarcerated overnight. I reminded him of his obligation to the one hundred or so kids he needed to meet that day in the classroom on the second floor. He was here to stay—or put up with the wrath of his friend and the equally volatile superintendent. Paul understood. Over the longer term, Paul became a fast friend of the superintendent, as well.

Sadly, Paul's life was shortened at his own hand on Veterans Day weekend, 1978. Without warning, Paul took his life in a small, lonely apartment a few miles away from school. As his supervisor, the police immediately called me. I would need to do my best in dealing with the tragedy on the following school day.

A fellow math teacher and I shared a strong bond with Paul and with one another. Although we didn't "hang out" with Paul, we continued to share with him as a part of our lives. He was a friend to turn to, a reasoned and intelligent voice in the forest whom we enjoyed hearing. Independently, we shared with Paul and remained his friends for life. On his passing, that teacher reminisced, saying that he felt Paul wanted us to "Be involved—Be concerned." He continued, "I believe Paul was most upset by people who put down other people, by those who thought they were better than others, by those who would impose their will upon others."

A secretary offered that Paul saw "Plastic people, not caring. So involved with their own lives—failing to see others' joys and hurts. Cool and hard, unyielding, unfeeling. Breakable. So sad."

And from a student writer, who observed, "I thought he had everything he wanted, but the only thing I overlooked was that he gave his life to helping people and no one helped him. I wish I had it all to do over again, because I would have said, 'Okay, Shanlee, you tell me what your troubles are, instead of me unloading on you.'"

No one prepared me for the wealth of sensitivity shown by staff the day following. Some of our staff members were hardened veterans of World War II and the Korean War. They sometimes didn't accept the "soft side" of Paul and his beliefs, but always held him in respect. On this tragic day of loss, their empathy was unbelievable. All knew (or sensed) that Paul's unique personality and style had reached across the ages to salve the wounds of the young.

Gathering the best of my strength, I chose to meet and stay with Paul's students for each of his five classes that sad day. With the assistance of counselors and a psychologist, we struggled through the day, including meeting individual student needs. I drafted a printed black-and-white announcement of Paul's legacy along with pertinent funeral details to post in a separate, distinguished place in the main showcase of the office hallway. It was simply not appropriate to announce such a loss over a public address system. Individual copies of the announcement were clutched in the hands of teenagers who may have been experiencing their first real loss of life.

As inspiration and lesson plan of the day and in giving a meaningful moment of recognition to Paul's life, I asked each of the students over the five hours of his classes to offer written words of remembrance. I would assemble and edit the offerings, with the promise of a copy for each in the near future. Entitled *This Is My Friend*, the booklet offered many comments from students. A few follow:

- "Paul's favorite three words—love, tolerance, and understanding."
- "When he told you something he told you the way it really happened—not the way they kinda leave . . . parts . . . out . . ."
- "He would listen to you, and he wouldn't lie to you."
- "Other people were Paul's life."
- "Even though he is dead, I know I will miss him very much. In the movie *Brian's Song*, the ending captures his life. It ended in this fashion with a few words changed to benefit him now.

  Paul B. Shanlee died one Saturday afternoon.
  He left a group of friends who think of him often.
  They don't remember how he died.
  But how he lived . . . how he did LIVE."

What I Really Know

I really know about kids. I was one, you know.

As a kid, I got to know what it was like to live an independent, free and responsible life. It wasn't about being raised in the fifties. It wasn't about our mother passing when the six of us were oh so young. And it wasn't that my father was a man of few words and high expectations of behavior and performance.

It could have been that elementary teachers and neighbors looked out for me and for all the kids of the era. They didn't care if we were rich or poor, they just taught us with strengths they had learned living through the Great Depression and World War II. They knew how to transmit the essentials—and hold us to account. Their actions showed that they loved kids—and we felt it.

I was with the kids of junior high and high school and found those with similar values and experiences. Together we ran to touch football games at the lake park, nighttime skating, and adventures at every turn. We ventured near and far—first on bikes, and then with cars bought for one hundred dollars or so. We played sports and even visited the library for study sessions on occasion—all without parental involvement or direction.

I married one of the cheerleaders, studied my math and became a teacher like my eldest brother—a self-developed scholar and leader. Although just a kid, he set standards as a teenager leading us to achievement. Now fifty years later, I still stay engaged with young people and lead them in the direction of the past—toward high expectations and personal achievement. Let me tell you—they like it!

They want to hear that they are good and that they can perform. On a recent day of my part-time teaching, I quietly directed and questioned a group of algebra students about their behavior and performance. I challenged them to meet higher personal standards. They agreed. Even though they sometimes look like they're not listening—they are.

They hear. They see. And they internalize. They even occasionally applaud.

After all, they're just kids.

Who Could Buy This Wonderful Feeling?

As teenage boys of the 1950s, we would each and often buy a personal, fifty-five cent quart of beer (or a case of twelve-ounce bottles for the group) and take a ride at night. It may have been in a parent's station wagon, a 1936 Chevrolet, a 1949 Kaiser or a friend's hot rod. Since we were all under legal age, we most often stayed hidden in secluded woods outside of town to drink our personal treasure. Other times, we ventured off to Galesville or Czechsville or another small Wisconsin town across the river to "belly up to the bar" for ten-cent tap beers—at age sixteen.

My first ride at 100 miles per hour was in a "souped-up" 1950 Ford coupe heading that way. We had the usual case of beer in the trunk, and a few bottles in the car, when the Wisconsin state trooper pulled us over outside LaCrosse. He hauled us into the courthouse. Gordy was ticketed for speeding. No mention was made of charges for the remaining carload of teenage boys and our beer.

Preparing for a nighttime venture after an out-of-town football game on Friday night, we would go to the creek out beyond Sugar Loaf the night before and place bottles of beer in the cold stream. We hoped that some trout fisherman wouldn't make a lucky find during our day in school—or before we arrived home near midnight.

While we assaulted the highways in nearby Wisconsin or dunked our Hamm's bottles in the creek, friends in another small town of the area were taking their travels and their beer in a different way—right down the railroad tracks. By letting just a bit of air out of the tires of their 1950s sedan, the grip, width and compression of tires was exactly right to fit the car to the track. This position would then allow beer-laden youth to pile on the hood, top and trunk of the car—setting sail down the tracks in the middle of the night to enjoy their "suds" in a whole new, outdoor way.

These teenage sojourners enjoyed their bottled beer in midnight travels. Nearly soundless, save for the idle of the engine and occasional teenage outbursts, they cruised (driverless) for miles through the night. Similar to earlier bike-riding exploits when the rider hollered out to observers, "Look, Ma, no hands!" these adventurers in their driverless vehicle cruised slowly and steadily past farms, across creeks and up the eight percent railroad grade without hands or driver—utilizing a brick on the accelerator to hold them steady on course. The steering wheel followed the course of the tracks. Never mind that there may have been a train headed in their direction. Captivating moments of shared teenage bravado, a full moon overhead and woods and wildlife on the move all gave a sense of freedom.

Adventures of teenage youth of the 1950s were many—some safer than others. The first time we went skinny-dipping at night in "the Pits" was exhilarating. Swinging out on a rope toward a deep hole in the lake with limited swimming skills was an undeclared fear—before Ed Spencer taught us how to swim in his "bare-assed," seventh grade boys' swimming class.

A boyhood blush I experienced in meeting a girl's parents for the first time while picking her up for the homecoming dance was embarrassing. Flashbulbs whirled and admonishments were given. All I wanted to do was bail out the door to get into the cool 1948 Mercury coupe borrowed from my big brother.

My red face must have matched the color of the backside of any wayfarer in Spencer's swimming class who got out of line. Any violator of Spencer's rules made a slow walk down the length of the pool with thirty hearty seventh-graders slapping hand to buttock—leaving marks to remember while gaining new membership in the "Red Hand Club."

A rope swing near the Winona airport, 1950s. (Photo courtesy of *Pieces of the Past*, Winona Historical Society.)

Nickel-dime poker games on somebody's back porch were games of chance and occasional bravado. Through the games, we explored card games and supposed steps toward adulthood—right down to "bluffing" our way through a poker hand with a cigarette tucked behind our ear. A pack of Pall Malls rolled in a t-shirt sleeve á la James Dean demonstrated our *Rebel without a Cause* persona.

With certain of the parents often gone on their own nighttime adventures, we had full access to dining room card games and to a living room in which to play our favorite forty-five-rpm records. When girls were present there were occasional visits by some to other rooms of the house.

We're sure the girls noticed us. We were, after all, growing "hunks" We were "cool" before the word was ever invented. First dances were expectedly smooth—or so we thought. Incidents of exploration and growth were of social activity, learning and personal growth. We grew on our own.

Parents didn't hover with wise counsel every moment. They let us find ourselves and do things they probably did when they were our age. They simply expected good behavior and continuous respect for all. The worst we could do in their eyes was to be disrespectful or immature. Rudeness and disrespect were not tolerated. We could tell the difference between good and bad. We knew enough to help clean up before leaving someone's house after a card party.

If one had an issue—settle it! The occasional fistfight out behind the "Y" tested our mettle and gave us our strength. Our sports activities allowed us to compete, to push, shove and prove ourselves. We were together on sports team bus rides to neighboring towns for an eight-hour stretch, with a restaurant dinner, ninety-mile ride, game and return all in the loop. The next day we would be back in class, hanging in the halls and being "cool" between classes—ending our day walking home together from basketball practice to supper at six.

A first real job promising a steady paycheck offered an expanded vision of who we were—and aimed us toward an adult future. There were first jobs that paid pennies on the hour. A first real job scooping nickel cones at McVey's Ice Cream Shop or washing cars at the Owl Motor Company Ford dealership gave one a first-ever paycheck to be converted into cash and coin at the massive Winona National Savings Bank, otherwise seldom visited. Cash squirreled away in an upper drawer at home paid first tuition fees to the local teacher's college. In my senior year of high school, a caring teacher offered me a personal two hundred dollar cash scholarship (enough for a year's tuition). His only condition for his gift was that I give up my "wheels," a 1953 Nash two-door. Thanks, Norm, but "not."

1954 Nash Statesman, similar to the author's car. (Photo courtesy of classiccars.com.)

As a mathematics major at the local college, I "toughed it out" for four years. With a nearly full-time job and sixteen credits per quarter, I figured out how to pay the bills, get married, have a child, get on the honor roll and gain my first teaching job in a far-off suburb—all before graduation. By August, we had a semi-new and powerful Pontiac V-8 hardtop to pull a U-Haul trailer and small family to our newly purchased three-bedroom home in suburbia.

It was a grand trip. Who could buy this wonderful feeling?

Who Will Buy?

Who will buy this wonderful morning?
Such a sky you never did see.
Who will tie it up with a ribbon?
And put it in a box for me.

Who will buy this wonderful feeling?
I'm so high I swear I could fly.
Me oh my, I don't want to lose it,
So what am I to do to keep this sky so blue?
There must be someone who will buy.

–"Who Will Buy," from the album *Nature Boy*.
© 1960, Verve. Written by Lionel Bart, sung by Aaron Neville.

What Have I Learned?

I have learned that the beauty of nature invigorates me—from a quiet moment at sunrise to a walk in the woods at dusk.

I have learned that children do grow and return to the values we attempted to instill in them in the earliest of ages.

I have learned that a loving wife is critical to life's success and that her love is to be treasured.

I have learned that family members have unique and differing perspectives on the growing-up days at home.

I have learned that keeping oneself fit is critical to personal well-being. Doing the hard and tedious steps of exercise and swinging a hammer have long-term benefits that hold body and mind together.

I have learned that there are treasured thoughts of childhood that are immutable.

I have learned that to have a friend is to be a friend.

I have learned that God is a part of our every waking moment and that His great plan will determine who we are, how long and how well we live—and that His love is internal to me.

I have learned that hurt and pain are real and that one can live through them with spousal support and the support of a loving God.

I have learned that there are a few friends who stay with you throughout your life.

I have learned that having a job is good for you. Work is meaningful.

I have learned that it is rewarding to create small things that can become other's treasures.

I have learned that students of all ages and skill levels require the same kind of reinforcement.

Lakeside photo, Lakeville, Minneosta. (Photo courtesy of the author.)

I have learned that motivational techniques are not of complex psychological rules, but instead depend upon common courtesy and individual encouragement.

I have learned that travel from home is not a cure-all for concerns in life. Problems do not have a geographic space. "Wherever you go, there you are."

I have learned that people can reverse themselves in a moment's notice, depending upon that which is convenient to their own needs.

I have learned that it is better to be a Polyanna than a cynic in life. The good will out.

I have learned that there are times when I will not be happy and that's okay. This, too, shall pass.

I have learned that it's okay to cry.

I have learned that beauty is present in all of us,

I have learned to look beyond outward appearances and look for the beauty and grace within the individual.

I have learned that behaviors are often separate from the person within. We need to listen deeply and look within for the real answers.

I have learned that I am only one and cannot do it alone.

I have learned that trout fishing is the greatest time of life in which to share God and nature—and find inner simplicity.

I have learned that my pa was a great man who held me and led me and strengthened me for the challenges of life.

I have learned that the greatest influences in my life came from a loving mother in my formative years, a father who set the standards of right and wrong, followed by a grandmother who watched over me, a wife who loves me and by teachers who cared.

I have learned that I am here only for a brief period and that I can make a difference.

I have learned that I have gifts to share.

Chapter Ten

A Hillside Scene

Squirrel hunting has been my passion.

Introduced to this special sport by Harold at the age of ten or so, the quiet, continuous searching in God's special surround became my niche. It was a niche between school, sports and friends that allowed me some time to be alone, to be free. My passion combined woods, outdoors, the hunt, and a special bond that comes between man and nature. It is where laced boots and old jeans meet up with hillside, pasture and tranquil wood.

Harold's large-hewn hands held the steering wheel of his Dodge "job-rated" truck. Carrying hundreds of empty milk cans, our shiny 1950s truck ascended the hills. On our way to pick up thousands of pounds of milk in farmers' milk houses, I watched the smoke drift upward from his cigarette. A waft of fresh air through a slightly opened window vent cleared the air and brought the smell of fresh-cut hay to us as we came from valley to ridge.

We were having our early morning conversation between farm reports and old-time country music on "Katy at 580" AM radio out of LaCrosse. Passing through Hart and Money Creek and past the Yucatan sign, we were on our way to a fresh donut at 5:30 a.m. at the Spring Grove Bakery.

I knew the squirrels were out there waiting. They would just have to wait today. Harold would take me out for a late Saturday afternoon hunt to Oche Ridge, near his home farm. It wasn't far from "Leapin' Lena's," a favorite early morning milk customer of ours.

The area surrounding the small town where I lived in the '50s was made up of small farms, two-lane crushed rock country roads, pastures and woodlands. It was the perfect setting for my autumn hobby. Whenever possible, after school, after work, early morning or late afternoon, the passion was there to drive Pa's 1936 Chevrolet off to the countryside, uncase my Remington .22

bolt-action rifle and head into the woods. Rain or shine or snow-filled day, it made no difference. Hillside outcroppings of limestone made natural shelves on which to sit to view the beauties of nature and await the "bushy-tails." In quiet moments, I could also contemplate my future.

Most often, I was still. Quietly sitting on a log or lying on a mat of fallen leaves, my foot would occasionally fall asleep. Leaning against a sturdy tree while waiting for sights or sounds of my quarry, I was mystified, as always, by my forest surroundings. I wondered about the natural hunters who had gone before me. This was the area of the Dakota, of Chief Wa-Pa-Sha, of the many who subsisted on forebears of my present harvest.

Standing in a light morning September mist, absorbed in the sunshine of an October afternoon or letting the snow fall on my gun and shoulders in November brought special moments. Nature's presentation created its own mood of the day, serving up another helping of delight and wonder.

I was in a special place, a place of remembrance and mystery. Each visit to the hills and valleys brought calm, beauty and intrigue. Standing quietly, I might hear the snap of a twig to be confronted by a deer or two—a buck with shining antlers or a doe with fawn. A red fox ran through, a woodchuck could be seen scampering toward a creek below or a grouse dropped into a tree.

An Afternoon Outing

Basking in the warmth of a late sun on the side of the hill, I reflected this September day. My eyes were closed as I lay back in tall grass deadened and straightened by the season's first frost. The mat of grass and pasture earth underneath my weathered hunting jacket and worn blue jeans was crisp and crackly. Sunshine on my face and a special girl nearby made for a perfect moment. The grass touched my face as I lay quietly with hunting rifle at my side. It was as if I were in a special place of beauty, peace and hope; a place of God's choosing.

The hike with Lacey up the hill from the wooded valley below had been exhilarating. Criss-crossing deer trails and thorny areas of hillside over the past several hours yielded a bounty of four large, gray squirrels. Jacket pockets were filled with hickory nuts gathered along the way.

A most pleasant interlude with my special partner, we observed the day, listening quietly for squirrels in the leaves and enjoying sunbeams coming through semi-barren trees holding their last large oak leaves. Seated on a large, fallen tree, Lacey was content with her newfound boy friend.

She was a young woman of the woods and pastures and hillsides who had lived her life on the farm. She had scampered after her dogs and chased the kittens in the field since the time she took first steps. Only recently had she ventured beyond the nearby fields and small country schools to try life in the bigger city. This was her second year in high school.

Lacey had invited me to stop by the home farm when I had the chance. She told me of the woods and of her joy in being out of doors. With my part-time job on the weekends driving my milk truck, I set off on my Saturday early morning, fifty-mile loop to haul about three thousand pounds of milk to the creamery.

After completing chores at home and with Lacey waiting, I grabbed my Remington and set out for her home in the hills. She was delighted with my unscheduled appearance. Showing me around the farm site, she picked some apples off the tree and introduced me to her new calves in the barn. We shared a piece of warm apple pie in the kitchen. Offered by her mother, the pie and warmth of the kitchen were enhanced by her mother's friendly presence and pleasant chatter.

Since beginning my early morning route on this special day, I had thought only about this opportunity to visit my new friend. With high school homecoming soon to be, I hoped to take Lacey to the dance.

Our time in the woods was fruitful, the afternoon fleeting. It would soon be time to head for home. By the time we returned to the farmyard, I had gained a date for homecoming, shot four fine "bushy tails" and gained a bag of apples. I felt that the apples carried the sunshine of the day, as well as the smile of the farm and its occupants. I couldn't be more delighted with my newfound treasures.

In Days to Come

I carried these remembrances and treasures of youth as I became a student, teacher and parent. Each day in the woods brought new adventure, from the joy and challenge of the hunt to the beautiful leaf carpet of red-brown majesty on which I lay. After a short dance with Lacey, I brought my own special girl of life into the woods at age sixteen—and for all the years thereafter. I met Janet for the homecoming dance the following year and never looked back. Nearly sixty years later, we tarry on a country walk to recall the beauty of it all.

Ventures with our four kids took us out hunting and camping and sharing the beautiful woods and streams and limestone hills. Camper travels all around the region took us to all of Minnesota's state parks and to nearly every state. We saw lots of squirrels and wildlife in our travels. After a day in the woods, our family would often sit up 'til midnight around the fire with coffee, hot chocolate, marshmallows and the like.

We especially loved camping in a state park near Nodine, in southeast Minnesota. It overlooks the Mississippi River from three hundred feet up. We had traveled the river below as a family in our ski boat.

We could see that setting from our precipitous, unguarded vantage point of limestone peak—as my mother had done in her youth. The view extends and overlooks the river, lock and dam, the woods of my mother's youth at Dakota, today's apple orchards of nearby La Crescent (the "Apple Capitol of Minnesota") and eastward to LaCrosse.

Snaking its way through the nearby hills and valleys of Homer south to LaCrescent is the virtually undiscovered Apple Blossom Trail. To drive it is to follow God's gift of natural beauty, and needs to be experienced at least once. As a youth, I rode through those very hills with Harold. I followed a similar route with my neighbor friend Russell on his Watkins Products route to these heavenly farms. As an eleven-year-old passenger in Russell's new 1951 fold-back Kaiser, the delightful smell of extracts and chemicals of the loaded Kaiser is as memorable and sensual as the wafts of Harold's cigarette smoke.

And Today

To fellow senior golfers at a recent golf outing near the Red Wing area's Frontenac Hills overlooking the Mississippi River I remarked, "the only thing better than going golfing in this beautiful site is to go squirrel hunting in nearby woods." We could each load a .22 rifle in our golf bag and drift off a few hundred yards into the steep bluffs of sparkling hardwoods on an autumn day to be engulfed by absolute quiet. We would enjoy a peace-filled moment and the challenge of the hunt.

Another time, raking leaves in the cool north wind at the end of an afternoon in semi-suburbia caused me to remark to a neighbor that "there is nothing more beautiful than viewing sunset in the glorious woods of southern Minnesota on a cooling day of late October." Nearing sundown in the woods of my youth, the rustle of squirrel movement in a carpet of leaves, the sight of an occasional grouse landing in an overhead tree or a greeting by an inquiring deer peeking out told me that I had met nature at its finest.

To a boyhood friend from Winona now residing in South Dakota, I offered by email: "The days keep coming—one more glorious than the next. It's my favorite time of the year. Wish I could be squirrel hunting in the woods of Winona County every day. I would stop off at LaCrescent or Dakota for a bushel of apples."

There seems to be a lifetime theme here in these thoughts and reflections. Squirrel hunting was even the first theme I wrote on in my first college English class. It earned me a B. Hunting was adventure, opportunity, achievement and total contentment all wrapped in one. To be alone, independent and dependent upon my own skills and strength, I navigated the hills and achieved a modicum of success at hunting and personal satisfaction—giving myself an A for effort.

Sitting in the woods with my girl, with a child or all alone is to be in the easy chair of life. There are no restrictions, expectations or worries. Moments under the tall oaks and maples are contemplative, restful and adventurous all at the same time. Quiet is yours, with only your breathing, the crack of a twig breaking or the landing of a leaf on the carpeted forest floor to disturb the tranquility.

A good aim with my Remington .22 wasn't necessary for survival, but it was certainly helpful in bringing home a limit of seven large "bushy tails" for supper—a "mess of squirrels." Pa cooked them to tender perfection.

Sixty years later, one of my daughters suggested to me, "You should go squirrel hunting."

That comment came in response to a picture of a beautiful fall scene at home, wherein I remarked on the beauty of the scene and suggested that I should go squirrel hunting. Permission was granted.

Where is that old .22?

A Mess of Squirrel (Pa's Recipe)

Frying squirrels is pretty simple. Three squirrels are cut up. Just lay pieces on the countertop and sprinkle with salt, pepper and garlic powder on one or both sides, flour and fry in vegetable oil (Pa used lard or Spry) until golden brown. Pa liked his big cast iron skillet. My mother-in-law, Eloise, used her pressure cooker for superb tenderness. She served with gravy.

Parmesan Squirrel—A Fancier Recipe

Three squirrels or two rabbits, cut in pieces
2 c. flour
Olive oil
1 c. white wine (Zinfandel or Liebfraumilch)
Tomatoes, chopped
1 tsp. rosemary
Dash salt & pepper
2 chicken bouillon cubes
Brown rice (4 servings)
1 c. cream or half and half
1 package onion soup mix
1 c. Parmesan cheese grated

Place flour in bag, add meat and shake until thoroughly covered. In large frying pan, heat olive oil until it's almost but not quite smoking. Place meat in pan and brown on all sides. Just before meat is completely browned, add two pats of butter to oil to finish browning. Remove meat and drain. Cook meat in wine in a shallow sauté pan, covered, on medium-low heat for about 15 minutes to tenderize. Remember to turn occasionally.

Put chopped tomatoes, rosemary, salt, pepper and bouillon cubes in water and bring to a boil. Add rice and cook according to directions on rice package. Stir and fluff to distribute rosemary and tomatoes evenly.

In a sauté pan on low heat, blend cream, onion soup mix and half of the Parmesan cheese. Stir constantly until the mixture is smooth and the cheese is melted into the sauce. Salt to taste. Use white pepper, if desired. Serve squirrel over a bed of rice, spoon sauce over top and garnish with remaining Parmesan cheese.

Other recipes and a Martha Daniels video on how to prepare the Parmesan recipe are available at the Missouri Deptartment of Conservation site where "we help people discover nature." Thanks for the inspiration.

I Found My Voice

The other day, a fine and experienced newspaper writer of the *Rochester Post-Bulletin* asked me questions heard frequently as I hold book events. How did I get started? Where did the stories come from? How did my book evolve?

People seem genuinely interested in the process. Maybe they want to take a step toward creating their own book. Or maybe they wonder how a seasoned member of the senior population can even have remembrances of so long ago.

Not being a writer, I asked friends and fellow teachers for advice and inspiration over the years. It seems that those I asked were teachers, not writers. They didn't have a fire in their belly for writing and personal risk. They could diagram sentences and speak of gerunds, but they offered little in the way of inspiration. I took an evening class from an expert who could supposedly guide me into writing. He gave a lot of addresses and copies of form letters to send to magazines, but wasn't inspiring.

I sat for many summer noon hours alone in the high school faculty lounge where I worked, enjoying my small bag of Fritos, a cup of coffee and the quiet of a summer day. I wrote my thoughts left-handed on yellow legal pads (I'm right-handed), wrote without lifting my pencil from the page and tried in the quiet of the day to "find my voice"—a real challenge. I even tried poetry. I didn't know who I was looking for.

The effort was mine to risk. My kids and wife didn't really want me to create a book of stories for them, but a few years ago I did it anyhow. They were the first to receive my hand-sewn book of a dozen or so childhood stories composed on the computer over time. I didn't want the stories to be deleted by the push of a button. They were stories of childhood fun and remembrance. Merry Christmas! The next year they and selected family and friends received the gift of another published booklet entitled "My Wagon, My Journey." Somehow my words seemed to ring true for them.

Ten years ago, one friend suggested that a friend of his would edit one of my pieces, with thought of sending it to Turtle River Press. "Finding My Voice" was my first published story soon thereafter—on the back of the Turtle River grocery store paper bags. I loved it. I was in print!

From there, more new friends came through. Folks in a loosely organized winter retirement writing class in Arizona (without an instructor) applauded and encouraged me. My story of "Sense of Order" about our very Adoba-based, Mesa community made it into *Chicken Soup for the Soul*—my first paid article.

Mike of *Minnesota Moments Magazine* published my first story, "Arms of Steel," in time for summer parades. Often with wonderful, artist-colored graphics, Mike published a half-dozen other of my essays, as he called them.

Fran, the publisher of a hometown newspaper, liked my thorough research of hometown topics and my writing style. Research done in the Winona State University computerized database of over one hundred years of Winona newspapers yielded lots of topics. I massaged the research and added personal, colorful memories into "give-back" articles to the folks of Winona who had made for my delightful childhood experience. I felt it appropriate to pay them back. Fran thought my articles "added interest" to her successful newspaper.

The *Winona Post* has since published a dozen more, with even more yet in the works. Where else can they get a free, researched history of one hundred years of bowling, motorcycles, buses, taxis, or circuses coming to town? The Pepin Pickle Company, Sloppy Joe's Bar on East Third Street, or the Northwest Airlines crash of 1948 are but a few stories yet to grace their pages, but they may one day. For now, I'm capturing these concepts and stories into my books.

There's another question that seems to appear from readers. It relates to the apparent, described values of the time. At a recent book club event I was called to in my home community, I was asked by a group of fifty-something ladies, " When did it change?" What happened that took us away from the time-honored principals we so cherished (and my stories apparently described)? We had quite a freewheeling discussion that all enjoyed.

From each one, there seemed to have been a found nugget of valued remembrance shining through in the book. In answering the question of values, it is not my role to pontificate (although I'm fully capable). I tried instead with these and other readers to ask readers comparative questions of today.

Is there a summer Hobo Day for kids in our home community where hundreds of kids appear on their bikes without parental supervision to enjoy a community-donated bowl of Mulligan stew and a tin cup of Kool-Aid? If not, why not? Who changed the rules?

Is bullying allowed and rampant in our schools? Do children seem to have escaped into a world of texting and smart phones? Should someone's granddaughter have been sent home from her middle school yesterday (as she was) for too-short shorts? Are kids out playing in the streets and camping out in neighborhood backyards as the moon comes up? Does anyone go anywhere without a parent? Is anyone accountable?

As I wandered the streets as a kid, Pogo was the title and central character of a long-running daily American comic strip. Created by cartoonist Walt Kelly, Pogo Possum was "an amiable, humble, philosophical, personable and everyman opossum." Kelly described Pogo as "the reasonable, patient, softhearted, naïve, friendly person we all think we are."

Probably the most famous Pogo quotation is, "We have met the enemy and he is us." Perhaps more than any other words written by Kelly, they "perfectly sum up his attitude towards the foibles of mankind and the nature of the human condition." The words describe choices we make and rules and expectations we do or do not choose to set in our homes and communities. We need to "take back the night." We may need Pogo to guide us.

I suggest that two things were key to our development—trust and expectation. They were certainly not explained, just learned through experience. We were trusted to be at home alone, do assigned work and go from there to be with friends and games and travels all over the county on our bikes to be home for supper at six.

We joined sports or not. We attended scheduled games through personal choice and tenacity. No one took us there or told us how to hold a bat or shoot a hook shot, save for Max or "Booby," city-assigned coordinators. We were held to expectations of behavior and positive involvement at home, in school, neighborhoods and everywhere in the community by parents and adults who didn't tell us. We understood what they were not saying.

Trust and expectations were reciprocal functions. Parents trusted kids to wander at will. Simultaneously, we were held to expectations we carried like a fitted backpack. Adults reinforced unwritten standards at every turn. We weren't mental giants, but we knew what was expected—and how to "be good." We also learned that production, achievement and accomplishment were individual responsibilities or opportunities. Nobody did our math for us. Responsibility, personal respect, and respect toward others were clearly understood.

Unlike Linus of the more recent *Peanuts* comic strip, we didn't have a theme of "I want my blanket back." The "no whining" sign was not needed in our life. It was unsaid and inculcated. We simply stepped over setbacks and moved on. Many of us were miniature adults. Those who didn't learn the lessons or have the guidance found one another, formed meaningless gangs and found themselves outside looking in.

What lies within us? Do we have what it takes to make it in life?

It is within us to discover, to change our attitude and create our future course. It is not about the absence or prevalence of cell phones and the Internet. It's about knowing what is right to do—and following through.

To achieve the standard is to learn guidelines at the earliest stage. Little ones can't hit the puppy, refuse their food or speak inappropriately to their grandmother. Adults must constantly (read: all life long) enforce standards through consistent behavior, expectations and love of their children. They need to treat their thirty-six-year-old the same as they did at his or her age three.

Trust them, expect them, nurture them and love them. They will follow.

As with this story, my books and life have evolved. I am thankful for those who have asked the questions and cause me to explain.

It seems I have found my voice.

Small Town Travels

Childhood walks on the sidewalks of my hometown were moments of familiarity, necessity and adventure. As with all the days, our walks were natural and filled with ease, safety and comfort. These were times of moving from place to place without "rides"—a time of being on our own. It was a time of feeling okay—a natural part of being.

We could scoot off the few blocks to see a friend, go to the playground for afternoon games in summer or travel the blocks to school and back two times a day in all the seasons with total comfort. One might head to the local grocery store, to Grandma's house, or across town for skating at the lake rink.

Events ahead or on our return to home brought thoughts of joy. Passing Norman Rockwell-like sites of home and hearth gave comfort. To achieve the comfort of the destination ahead was always the goal, daylight or eve. Grandma's house was just ahead, the warmth of the YMCA beckoned. The worn spot on the oak floor upon entering the neighborhood grocery store or stepping on the granite steps at school was like getting to home plate—another run scored, another mission accomplished, a journey safely completed.

With wonder, occasional trepidation and fear we scurried past darkened places to avoid less-than-reputable denizens. Imagined creatures of the night or a shift in the wind sometimes caused a quickstep and a heart flutter. Beads of perspiration formed on pre-adolescent brow in moments like these.

On any of these journeys, moves were made under trees of historic girth languishing beside homes with moss-covered walls, stucco sides or tarpaper brick façades. Created by turn-of-the-century immigrant workers or successful business owners in the fashion of their class traditions of small town, European heritage, these classic abodes were representative of individual and personal achievement.

Walks across the cement slab sidewalks with imprinted dates and masons' names were walks akin to following a trail of history. The 1880s brick sidewalks in older parts of town were especially unique and delightful with their patina and patterns.

As quick as the breeze in soft summertime, as frozen as the ground in a mid-winter Midwest, one's steps were hastened as the school bell was about to sound or due to the household curfew ahead—or as slow as the length of the free day ahead.

All were familiar homes and sites of comfort. A light in the window of a friendly neighbor, the yelp of a familiar dog or the meeting of a friend or stranger on the sidewalk added familiarity, security, speed or adventure—dependent upon circumstances of time, comfort or fear caused by whom you met and the time of day you were traveling.

There was purpose to the step. Whether fast or slow, there was a need to get to the other end of the journey. Once achieved, that destination became central to the next outbound mission. Evening moves across the turf of the small town were most exciting—bringing mystery, mystique, and sideways moves from shadow to shadow. Little time was taken to unwind along the way.

A venture out may have been as brief as a five-minute walk to Thorn's Grocery for the necessary pick-up and charge to our account of a two-pound butter roll or a can of beans for supper. Upon arrival, the multi-coated green screen door of the corner grocery greeted us.

One knew that the grocer cared for us as much as any uncle, iceman or older neighbor. Our extended family was a reality. Positive expectation for our future was the norm by all. Visiting place to place in the community, one was included as part of a larger family.

We heard from teachers that it was okay to dream, to hope, to expect a future of support and performance from our community. As we were to move ahead in our natural way to assume positions of leadership, social contribution and caring for our larger world, we would find a caring world of brothers and sisters across the town and across the world. We knew we were the upcoming Paul Reveres and Amelia Earhardts—with the intellect and expectation to carry on.

The practice of using government ration coupons for sugar, groceries and other commodities in days directly after World War II taught us that sacrifice for others was part of the greater plan. From parents who lived through the Great Depression of the 1930s, we learned the value of ecology and conservation—long before the popular approach to recycling.

Our tin can barrel in the shed was the place for crushed cans that went off to help the United States rebuild after World War II. CARE kits assembled in our elementary classrooms were sent overseas to aid war survivors. With them we sent a message of hope from one small grade school in America to another in England, Germany or Italy, destined for those who needed to believe in goodness, hope and real concern. Halfway around the world someone received a package of our personal expression. These small kits of toothbrush, hand soap and assorted sundries, along with a personal note from our second grade class, must have brought a ray of sunshine to an otherwise bleak day. We were proud to reach out to others less fortunate.

The receipt by some of us of new warm clothes and buckle boots at Christmas time from "The Goodfellows"—a local citizens group—caused us to understand that we could be receivers, as well as givers. We were part of a world much larger than the limited one we saw in our schoolroom, home or church.

The messages of the grocer as he or she handed us a piece of penny candy that we might not be able to buy, of the teacher who paid our dental bill, of the barber who provided a sucker and sage advice while spinning us around in the leather-and-porcelain barber chair facing the street were remarkably similar, unspoken yet understood gifts of kindness.

We, the young, were the treasured ones of the society. People had fought long and hard through their own enterprise, through the challenges of economic shortfalls, through the planting of Victory Gardens and through the gift of their own sons on foreign fields to guarantee our freedom. Sacrifice and loss was a part of our neighborhood. On every block of our neighborhood and on our paper route, Gold Star mothers displayed in their windows the stars as evidence of their personal loss and sacrifice—and yet they gave.

Anger was not a part of the byline of the everyday message of people with whom we grew. Scuffles between kids were just that—scuffles. They occurred and then they passed. People didn't seem to harbor envy or anger toward others. It just wasn't there.

It was expected that the child would give the gift of personal strength and agility in assisting older residents and neighbors. It would have been unheard of to strike out at an older person or steal a purse or harm their home. People were secure within their homes. If they needed help with cutting a lawn or painting a wall or shoveling a sidewalk, someone was there to assist, without a hand out in expectation.

If you were offered payment, it was most likely that one would attempt to refuse—only to accept when the giver was understood to be able to dispense their hard-earned quarter or half-dollar. It was also likely that one shared the bounty of his garden or the "extra" sunfish you caught with those in need or not. It was just the thing to do.

There were boundaries and problems created by adults between themselves in their world, but most of those attitudes hadn't trickled down to our streets and our classrooms. We lived in a child-adult world that was based upon mutual respect and shared views.

Cars that appeared at or near our house on Grand Street belonged to neighbors and to visiting relatives. We didn't own one. Uncle Carl and Aunt Elinor from Wilson Street had what must have been a 1937 Plymouth four-door.

One beautiful Sunday morning in summertime, we piled in the car and ventured off to the Arches County Park—with a beautiful trout stream running through it—for an inspiring, outdoor Lutheran church service. Another time, we were off on a trip in fall to view the leaf colors along the Mississippi River to the north when we learned about the vulnerability of tire tubes, overloaded cars and the combination thereof.

I know not my age, but do recall my first experience with a flat at roadside. Soon fixed, we headed off toward the south and west of Winona to

The author is on the left, with assorted family in the 1940s. (Photo courtesy of the author.)

enjoy the varied and often challenging hills and valleys that surrounded our hometown. Memorable on this trip was the stop for the lightest, softest sugar sand at roadside that had washed down from the limestone hillsides. So white, so pure—and there yet today.

Across the street, "Old Man Engel," a single gentleman most often dressed in a suit and tie, often piled an assortment of kids into his 1934 Plymouth sedan to take us to the Sky-Vu Drive-In movie on the edge of town. A nice man with an ever-present lit cigar, we were fortunate to have his friendship and his gifts. I assume that he piled us in on "Buck Night," which was Tuesday, since it allowed all the car's passengers in for one dollar.

As we faced Mr. Engel's house from our front porch in late afternoon, we could expect to see Mr. Neumann drive by in his Model T stake-bed truck, which must have been a ton or ton and a half. It was meticulous and seemingly always empty. Mr. Neumann was a large man with glasses, bib overalls and a red bandana. He spent his days seated in a railroad tower in the west end of town, where he controlled the switching of the rails to accommodate some of the multiple trains that visited our town every day in the 1940s and '50s. Mr. Neumann kept a goldfish pond in his backyard that we visited with regularity and wonder. The pond was as clean as his dark-green, immaculate truck on a summer afternoon.

Next door to us was Mr. Adrian Kesler, who served as a mechanic for the local Packard dealer. We never called him Adrian. We probably never knew his first name. Everyone was Mr. Kesler or Mr. Engel or Mr. Neumann or Mrs. Vater or Mrs. Brumberg. People didn't have first names at that time, did they?

Nevertheless, Mr. Kesler had a classic, well-tuned Jeep station wagon with simulated wood sides. With Mr. and Mrs. Kesler and their son (my friend) David, my brother George and I ventured off on Sunday afternoons to their cabin near Homer. I guess we always went on Sunday afternoons to maintain our perfect attendance record in St. Matthew's Lutheran Sunday School, and to uphold the Keslers' strict, Catholic responsibility of attending Mass each Sunday. At the cabin that overlooked the Mississippi River, we usually caught some slab-sized sunfish to fix for dinner.

Downstream from the cabin just a few miles was the childhood home of our recently deceased mother, Erika. We all thought of her often as we headed off to Homer or LaMoille or Dresbach or Dakota. Her parents' family farm of eighty acres was located just up the valley from Dakota. There my brothers and I occasionally visited to pick raspberries, feed the geese and ducks and chickens and otherwise wander around the idyllic Southern Minnesota farm hills and dales of Grandpa and Grandma Voigt.

Across from David's house, Woody lived in the upstairs apartment on the corner. Being raised alone by his mom, a slight wisp of a lady with an ever-ready smile and gracious nature, Woody enjoyed a clean and comfortable life. Heading up the stairs for a visit to Woody on Christmas morning or en masse as part of a neighborhood gang that bobbed for apples in a washtub at Halloween, all were certain to be warmly greeted.

The small apartment was tidy and filled with the books and inventory of an elementary school teacher and the tidily kept toys of her single child. On my visits, it was a world of exploration—with flip viewers of Disney characters, stereoscopic world scenes sliding in and out on the holder, science kits, Erector sets and comic books—all special delights not present in our household.

Woody was a special friend who camped out with us in backyards in the summer and played in the barn/fort in our backyard all year long. Different in behavior from the rest of our rag-tag collection, Bobby (as his mother called him) had to go upstairs in the middle of the night when camping out with us to get permission from his mother when we "raided" apples or pears from neighborhood trees.

Our other side neighbor, the Donnellys, had several cars around their house. Their father Fred, the railroad engineer, had a car that seemed to get around the community and find its drunken way back into the garage in the afternoon under the liquor-induced guidance of Mrs. Donnelly when Fred was off on a railroad trip.

I can't remember the model, but do remember her as the driver when, upon return from one of her afternoon forays, she strung a string line along the side of her dirt driveway next to our house to indicate where we were expected to stay. The challenge was whether she could stay within her own boundary as she drove the car up the drive and into the garage. We were there to cheer her on, of course.

Her son, Pat, is remembered for having had a Model T (or A?) with a rumble seat that we were allowed to sit in as it sat on the street in front of the house. We did not get a ride from him, though. Pat was later a cook in the Army—on his way to a place called Korea.

The Brunbergs across the street had a 1939 Nash or Plymouth four-door sedan that sat outside their house in the street in all seasons, since they didn't have a garage. Except for Mr. Brunberg driving to work and to church on Sunday, we don't remember the car moving very much. Mr. Brunberg was a quiet accountant at the local Bub's Brewery, and mostly stayed indoors and smoked his pipe.

Mrs. Brunberg was a very large and exceptionally nice lady who seemed to care about each of us. The Brunbergs were one of the first in the neighborhood to have a television set. I remember seeing a very small seven-inch screen in a rather large cabinet that sat on a table next to Mr. Brunberg's chair and pipe stand. We never had occasion to be in the Brunbergs' car.

One of the local car dealers, Mr. Seifert of Seifert-Baldwin Motors, lived around the corner. We did not get to know him or be a part of his cars, but it was still a nice place to walk by. He always seemed to bring home the new models. It's amazing that we were able to restrain ourselves so well. On our way to school, we would walk the opposite side of the street to see a new DeSoto convertible, a Chrysler wood-grained sedan or the new Dodge or Plymouth in the Seifert driveway. On one occasion, I remember seeing one of the first Crosleys (a true mini-car) parked in front of their house.

Just a couple of blocks up the street from the Seiferts we were introduced one Saturday afternoon to the Duck. This combination boat and vehicle was designed for the military in World War II—but one ended up right in the Yakish's backyard. The driver was one of the older Yakish brothers.

He must have spent some of his time in the military and returned with this unique vehicle that thrilled us all. He took us for a ride around the neighborhood and past our beloved Madison School. The only place I ever saw a Duck again was at the Wisconsin Dells to the north of Madison, Wisconsin, where a collection of Ducks were (and are) used to transport tourists for rides on the local river to view the majestic bluffs.

The usual mode of transportation for the common person in Winona was the very efficient and economical bus line that served the whole community. A half-block down the street from our house was the Lake Line bus route, where buses ran every fifteen minutes or so year-long. Kids walked or ran their way around town, but many adults used the busses.

Grandma didn't have a car and took the bus downtown each week for shopping or for an occasional visit to our house, having started on the Main Line in the east end of town, transferring to the Lake Line in front of Choate's Department Store in the heart of downtown with a paper transfer issued by the first driver, and finally dropped off just a half-block from us.

Pa was a regular walker about town, but used the bus on Saturday morning to bring home the fresh meats and sausages from Turner's Market and the fresh Vienna bread from the Boston Café and Bakery next to Turner's. We met him and the bus at high noon (or seven minutes after the hour, as the bus schedule predicted) to help with the heavy armful of treats for our family of seven.

Aunt Olga, who lived with Grandma, didn't have a car until later—a 1950 Ford. We never rode (or sat) in that car. Interesting that some people had cars, but seemingly few had garages. Interesting, too, that some people's cars were places of invitation, whereas others were personal property that we knew to be theirs and definitely off limits.

Unless they invited us to be a part of their car, it was a private property that was their right. It was theirs alone to possess. The expectation was that someday we, too, would have such a fine personal possession.

I don't know if teachers had cars or not. We did not dwell on their lives. The school didn't have a parking lot, so how were we to know? We never noticed them leave. Maybe they had a private exit from the school and a "souped-up" car waiting that took them to elegant homes miles away. Where did they live? Except for the Miss Carrolls (elderly spinsters in our neighborhood—one a teacher and one a nurse) and Woody's mom, we didn't have any teachers in the area.

Most of the people seemed to walk to and fro. The grocery store was on the corner, the meat market nearby. The butcher, the barber, the judge and the railroad worker all walked by—since their jobs and businesses were in the neighborhood. Thus, a five or ten-minute walk to work took precedence over a drive. I do remember George Kratz, an elderly mechanic I worked with at the Owl Motor Company.

George lived in the East End of town and rode his bike to work every day—summer and winter. He must have been nearing seventy when he retired in the late 1950s. One day as he visited with us at Owl, I discovered that George owned an absolutely beautiful and mint 1937 Ford coupe. He had treasured and kept the beauty showroom-new for more than twenty years. Where is it today?

The years go fast. The memories are vast. As we walked these sidewalks, we didn't know that a view of neighborhood was imprinting as treasures on our souls for all the years to come. Sounds of springtime rains and summer thunder, sloshes through puddles, winter's creaky steps on frozen snow, giant steps over new-fallen piles of leaves, summer's lightness and opulent smells, night calls of southern-bound geese in autumn all created a natural harmony of youth.

Oh, joy!—to have traveled with the grand people of our youth across Wapasha Prairie's living room of nature.